Miriam

OTHER BIBLICAL NOVELS BY
LOIS T. HENDERSON

Abigail

Hagar

Lydia

Ruth

Miriam

A NOVEL

Lois T. Henderson

1817

Harper & Row, Publishers, San Francisco

New York, Grand Rapids, Philadelphia, St. Louis
London, Singapore, Sydney, Tokyo, Toronto

Dedicated to my brother

THE REV. J. RAY THOMPSON

with my love

FIRST HARPER & ROW PAPERBACK EDITION

Designer: Jim Mennick

Library of Congress Cataloging in Publication Data

Henderson, Lois T.
  MIRIAM

  1. Miriam (Biblical figure)—Fiction   I. Title.
PS3558.E486M5 1983   813'.54   84-48257
ISBN 0-06-063869-9

91 92 93 94 95 MPC 10 9 8 7 6 5

Acknowledgments

Like all books, *Miriam* owes
its existence to a number of people. Gladys Donaldson
continues to read and to make suggestions, and I continue
to be grateful. Grete Carlson also read the early parts of the
manuscript and provided emotional support when I needed
it badly. Margaret Wilson, librarian of the Coraopolis Memorial Library, and Dikran Hadidian, librarian of the Barbour Memorial Library of Pittsburgh Theological Seminary, both continue to provide material and guidance to
assist me in my research. I am indebted to Blanche Ewing
for the typing and retyping that has been necessary. And,
finally, I am grateful to Roy M. Carlisle, of Harper & Row
San Francisco, who has reinforced my conviction that a
caring editor is as essential to the writing of a book as an
author.

Prologue

Night still hung over the city of Raamses. Not even a hint of dawn showed in the sky as the pharaoh's soldiers left their barracks and began their silent, sullen march toward the sprawl of huts where the Hebrews lived. The soldiers, helmeted, shod in sandals, their bare torsos gleaming in the torchlight, moved swiftly through the streets. Irritated at being forced to get up while it was still night, they fingered the whips they carried and looked forward to the moment when they could take out their anger on the slaves they had been sent to recruit.

The sound of marching feet filled the Hebrew huts, and women woke with a fear, like nausea, crowding into their throats, while men turned heavily in their sleep, groaning in sick anticipation of the lash. Children whimpered, flinching from the dark dread that flickered in their dreams, even though they did not understand what it was that frightened them.

Woven and skin curtains were ripped from doorways, and the soldiers shone their torches into dazed, terrified faces. Cursing, the soldiers grabbed those boys and men who looked most able and thrust them out into the street. Whenever they met hesitation, the soldiers used their whips, grinning malevolently as the leather thongs cut into shuddering backs and shoulders.

A few men cried out, but in a remarkably short time, the slaves had formed quiet ranks, complying almost eagerly to the snarled commands of the soldiers. Those whose backs bore scars knew better than to rebel, and those who were still whole had seen and heard the consequences of resistance. Compliance was less dangerous than protest.

The wailing of women, the cries of sleepy children rose and then died away as the men were marched off. By the time the soldiers and their prisoners were gone, the only sound in the Hebrew settlement was the muttering of prayers from a few men who still hoped that someday their God, Yahweh the Most High, might remember them and free them from their bondage.

Now a new king arose over Egypt, who did not know Joseph. So they appointed taskmasters over them to afflict them with hard labor. And they built for pharaoh storage cities, Pithom and Raamses. . . . Now a man from the house of Levi . . . married . . . and the woman bore a son. . . . She got him a wicker basket . . . and set it among the reeds. . . . And his sister stood at a distance to find out what would happen to him. . . . So God heard their groaning; and God remembered his covenant.

Exodus 1:8; 11:1a, 2a, 3b, 4

ᵗ1ᵗ

Although the rising sun sent a
level apricot glow across the sky, the small dressing room
in the women's quarters of the palace in the city of Raamses
remained nearly dark. Guided more by touch than by sight,
Miriam moved around the room, performing the first steps
of her morning ritual. In contrast with the rest of the princess' suite, this plain room contained only a few pieces of
furniture: a simple couch with wooden boxes in front of it.
Miriam lifted a sheer white linen dress from one of the
boxes and spread it across the couch, then moved quickly
to the table that held the cosmetics. She removed the top
from a small jar made of polished obsidian and placed beside the jar the slender ebony stick with which she would
apply the contents to the eyelids of her mistress. She cen-
tered the silver mirror on the low table, knowing that Princess Hapithet would want it to be where her hand would
fall directly on it so that she need not fumble. She liked
everything to be precise.

Miriam took a bottle of oil-of-lily from a shelf on the wall
and placed it carefully at the back of the table. She would
not unstopper the bottle until the moment came to apply
the costly, fragrant perfume. Her fingers lingered briefly on
each item that she handled. In a life that was often monotonous and occasionally terrifying, she found a curious comfort in the carved loveliness of the alabaster and obsidian
jars and in the carnelians and lapis lazulis that studded the
silver mirror.

In the dim light, she stole a glimpse of herself from the burnished metallic surface of the mirror. Fashioned for royalty, the mirror was not intended to reflect the face of a slave. But Miriam's pride had tempted her to look many times at her widely spaced dark eyes, her strong nose, and her full mouth that made her look so much like her brothers. She was no longer young, and yet, she reflected with satisfaction, her skin was lighter and softer than that of most Hebrew women, and her hair was still dark and glossy. Being a palace slave instead of a field hand had its advantages.

Guiltily, she turned the mirror over and laid it face down on the table, admiring, as she always did, the image of Hathor that formed its handle. She knew a sense of uneasiness over the admiration she felt for the golden delicacy of the goddess Hathor, but she told herself that when one lived in a foreign country, it was natural, and sometimes expedient, to like some things about it. And Egypt was still a foreign place, Miriam thought, even though her fathers and her fathers' fathers had been born along the Nile.

The light grew steadily in the room as Miriam continued her tasks, and she began to hurry. It would never do for the princess to arrive before the preparations were complete. And the princess was always prompt.

But Miriam's hands were practiced and sure. She had been laying out these cosmetics and perfumes, attending the morning toilet of the Princess Hapithet for how many years now? More years than she wanted to think about, Miriam reflected. Or, in fact, more years than she could remember. Who could be sure of the number of years? The passing of time was lost in the monotony and the weariness of life. With nothing to work toward, nothing to look forward to, the days became lost in a blur of months, and the months passed into years.

It had been different, Miriam thought, when she and the princess were young, when she had helped care for the royal children, when in spite of being a slave, each day had held the promise of growth or excitement or change. It had been different when Moses was here.

Miriam's hands grew still. No matter how many years he had been gone, no matter how great the disgrace and danger that had driven him away, no matter how minute the possibility of ever seeing him again, Miriam could not forget her younger brother. Her other brother, Aaron, and his wife, Elisheba, were good to her, and they had provided a home for her since her husband, Jehu, had died under the lash of the Egyptian overseer's whip—but no one could take the place of Moses. Was it only because she had saved his life, had helped to draw his woven cradle from the waters of the Nile? In saving him, had she assumed responsibility for his life? But it was more than that. It was—.

A cool greeting startled her out of her reverie. She turned to see Princess Hapithet entering the room.

"My lady," Miriam murmured. She bent from the waist, extending her hands in a gesture of obeisance, then lifted her face to smile into the narrow, lined, brown face opposite her own. "Good morning, my lady. Did someone bathe you or have you waited for me to do it?"

Hapithet glanced down at her thin, naked body. There was no shame in these Egyptians, Miriam thought. Even clothed, their bodies were clearly visible through the sheer linen, and they seemed to think that only right and proper. How strange, her thoughts ran swiftly on, that even though the Hebrews have been residents of this land for more years than anyone can remember, still we are different. She fingered the coarse white cloth of the straight shift that covered her from beneath her arms to her knees. Even during the years before we became slaves, she mused, we never really adopted Egyptian ways. There was nearly as much satisfaction in that thought as there had been in the idea that she was a palace slave.

"I'm bathed," Hapithet replied. "That girl did it—the daughter of your brother Aaron. She's learning well. But of course no one can take your place with me." She seated herself on the backless bench before the low table, "I'm ready," she said.

"It is only because you're used to me, my lady," Miriam murmured. The words were formula words, smooth with a pretended humility. They served as a shield to hide the pride that warmed her when the princess praised her. She may have stumbled into this position through the accident of being Moses' sister, but she had earned the princess' affection and trust through her own ability. Not everyone, Miriam thought complacently, could successfully serve royalty. Her fingers started to apply the cosmetics to the slender brown face. "And you taught me well. You were always patient, even though I was an awkward child when I first came to you."

Hapithet laughed. "I was young and could afford to be patient. Besides, I was grateful to you for helping me find my first son. It was you, after all, who helped me lift the basket out of the bullrushes. Such a small girl you were to be so devoted to a baby brother."

"Yes, my lady," Miriam murmured, aware that this sort of talk was leading to another time of reminiscing. The older the princess grew, the more she turned to memory.

Hapithet smiled. "I knew even that first day that it would be his real mother you would fetch to be his nurse. But I didn't mind. I wanted only the best for Moses."

She was holding the hand mirror in front of her face, and as she spoke, she tilted it a little so that Miriam's face, too, was reflected. Their eyes met.

"I was thinking of him only this morning," Miriam admitted.

"Moses," Hapithet murmured. "The most beautiful, the most intelligent of all the royal children." When Miriam started to protest, the princess raised a slender hand to silence her slave. "No, it's true. He filled my heart as none of my own children ever did."

"Perhaps because you were still childless when you found him, my lady, and he helped to ease your grief."

"I thought I was barren. My father believed I was barren. My husband, too. But it was as though having Moses to love and care for healed me of all my emptiness. Within months, I was with child."

Miriam dipped the ebony stick into the malachite that filled the obsidian jar. Deftly, she painted the green ointment across Hapithet's eyelids.

"But even after your own children came, you never neglected Moses," Miriam murmured, continuing to play the game of remembering. They had talked of this many times, but the princess never seemed to tire of it. "I was only a girl, but even then I realized that he was never pushed aside, never treated as though he were different from the others."

"Why would I push him aside? He was superior in every way." The old voice grew suddenly intense. "I loved him very much. Have you heard anything from him?"

"Not for months and months. He sends a message with a traveling caravan when he can."

"But never to his mother." Hapithet's tone was bitter.

"He's probably afraid, my lady. The messenger might be sidetracked by your brother. It—it wouldn't be safe."

Hapithet shrugged her shoulders. "Oh, my brother," she said shortly, dismissing him.

Miriam gasped. "My lady, Rameses is pharaoh of the land —the most powerful man in all the world. Even his sister had best be careful how she speaks of him. He could have you killed."

Hapithet turned the mirror from one side to the other, frowning at what she saw. "I'm an old woman," she said. "In spite of all your skill, there's no beauty in me anymore. My husband is dead. It's only natural that I should long to enter the House of Death."

Miriam's voice was suddenly sharp. "My husband is dead, too, my lady—killed by the whips of your brother's overseer. That doesn't mean I have the right to long for death."

Hapithet's face softened. She put out her hand to touch Miriam. "Do you imagine that I've forgotten about your husband? Rameses and I came closer to having a quarrel the night Jehu died than we ever have before or since. It was only his lack of interest and my own grief that prevented the quarrel from being worse. He was too indifferent to discuss it. I was too close to tears."

"Because of me, my lady?"

"Because of you, my dear. Haven't you been almost a daughter to me for all these years?"

Miriam knelt suddenly and kissed Hapithet's hand. "If all Egyptians were like you, my lady, how easy our life would be."

"Then why don't you live here in the palace with me? Why do you insist on going back to your brother's at night? It needn't be that way, you know. You could live here with me all the time. You could eat at my table."

"My lady does me honor," Miriam said with prescribed humility. But when she sat back on her heels and looked up into the princess' face, there was no humility in her. "But I'm a Hebrew, and although our God has forgotten us, I can't forget my people."

Hapithet put her mirror aside. "So you've said over and

over. I suppose you said the same things to Moses as he was growing up?"

"You've always known that, my lady."

"Yes, of course. I couldn't see any harm in his knowing that he was a Hebrew. I never tried to pass him off as my own. How could I when he looked so different from my own sons? And he had to know why he was different."

"Yes, my lady. And so I—I told him."

"And about your God, I suspect?"

"Yes, my lady. And about our ancestors."

"The legendary Joseph?" Hapithet's tone was amused. "A friend of the pharaoh, wasn't he?"

"Yes, my lady." Miriam's voice was as sturdy as the princess' had been light. "It's true, my lady. Joseph came from our own land, and the pharaoh loved him and gave him great power. But then there came pharaohs who had not heard of Joseph."

"Or maybe they had heard of him, all right, but didn't like what they heard. Your people have a way of multiplying, my girl."

"It is perhaps the only sign of our God's caring for us," Miriam replied bitterly.

Hapithet laughed. "You speak always of one god. Poor people who do not have a goddess of joy and love, like Hathor, or a god of light and sunlight or—."

"Our God is the God of all things," Miriam said stubbornly, then realized that she had interrupted her mistress. "I'm sorry, my lady." She made her voice contrite. "I didn't mean to speak up so rudely."

Hapithet stared intently into Miriam's face. "And did you instill your conviction into the child Moses? I mean, I've always known that you told him things. Did you insist that he accept your god?"

Miriam's eyes met the narrow, dark eyes of the princess. "Yes, my lady," she said simply.

Hapithet shrugged her bare brown shoulders again. "Oh, well, he's been gone a long time. He has probably adopted the god of whatever desert tribe shelters him. Men change their gods to suit their conditions."

"Yes, my lady," Miriam responded, but wished she had dared to protest.

Hapithet spoke again, this time in a tone of discovery. "But not always, you're thinking? The Hebrews are still faithful, aren't they? After years of persecution and neglect, they remain faithful."

Miriam tried to smile. "Some of us remain so, my lady. But it's not easy to worship a God who has forgotten you. No matter how great that God might be."

Hapithet stood up. "Heavy talk for an old woman and her faithful slave," she said. "How did we come to this subject anyhow?"

Miriam brought the sheer linen dress from the couch and slipped it over the princess' head. Through its gauzy filminess, the princess' brown body was discernible, and Miriam thought it fortunate that the fall of pleats in the skirt blurred the lines of the too-thin hips and legs.

"We were talking about Moses, my lady," Miriam reminded her mistress. She lifted a heavy blue wig from its stand and slipped it over Hapithet's shaved skull.

"Oh, yes. Moses." She glanced at Miriam. "If you had been Egyptian, you could have been his wife. Brothers marry sisters."

"He's my full brother," Miriam said stiffly. "Such marriages don't take place among the children of Yahweh."

"Nevertheless—" Hapithet began.

But Miriam interrupted for the second time that morning. "I'm a slave, my lady, and Moses was your son. Even in Egyptian eyes, it could not have been seemly."

"I suppose not," the princess conceded. "But still. . . ." Her voiced trailed away, then suddenly sharpened. "I would like to see him before I die," she declared. "But I don't suppose he will ever come home, will he?"

Miriam spoke slowly. "No, I don't think he'll come home. Your father's decree that Moses should die because he killed the Egyptian overseer might be remembered."

Hapithet was silent as Miriam unstoppered the flask of oil-of-lily and smoothed drops of it on the princess' throat and wrists. The sweet scent drifted between the two women.

"You needn't worry," Hapithet said. "Rameses doesn't remember. He thinks only of his cities, his battles, his sons." Her face changed. "Moses has children, too. You told me that you had heard he has sons."

Miriam studied the princess in the morning light that now came slanting through the open door and was suddenly aware how old she looked. "Yes, my lady," she said gently. "At least two sons. Or so we think. News crosses the desert slowly, you know, and we can never be sure if it is accurate."

"They are my grandsons," Hapithet said, "and yet I have never held them or stroked their faces. I don't even know what they look like."

"I know, my lady. They are my nephews."

Hapithet nodded, and when she spoke again, a faint tremor betrayed her emotion. "We are only two women who have been forgotten. His mother and his sister. He won't remember that I rocked him in my arms, that you held his hand as he learned to walk." She hesitated, then spoke with intensity, "Did he still think of me as his mother after he learned that Jochabed had borne him?"

"I've told you that he did, my lady. He always loved you. As I do." The words were daring, but it seemed to Miriam that she could not bear the slump of Hapithet's shoulders, the agitation of the thin brown hands that once had been so supple and strong.

Hapithet did not smile. "Then," she said, "if you love me, you must promise that if Moses ever comes home, you will tell me. In spite of my brother or palace intrigue. In spite of long memories. You must tell me if he ever comes home."

"I promise, my lady," Miriam said.

Hapithet nodded with satisfaction. "Then pray to your god—as I will pray to mine—that before I die, Moses will come back to Egypt."

"Yes, my lady," Miriam said. But she knew she would not pray for Moses' return. In the first place, she was not at all sure that Yahweh heard any of the prayers of the Hebrew people. If He did, wouldn't their burden of bondage be eased? And even if He did hear, would she ask that Moses return to a land where he had once been sentenced to death? Oh, no, better by far that both she and Hapithet go lonely into their graves.

Hapithet spoke clearly. "Straighten up this room and then come to me after I've eaten. I want to take a walk in the garden, and I feel easier when I can lean on your arm."

"Yes, my lady." Miriam bowed in respect, waited until the princess had left, and then turned to the task of putting the cosmetics in their proper places. But as she worked, her mind retraced their conversation. She was remembering her acquiescence when Hapithet had said that men change their gods to suit the changing conditions of their lives.

Oh, surely that wouldn't be true of Moses, she thought. Hadn't the caravanner told her father, all those years ago, that Moses had married into a Midianite family? And everyone knew that the ancestors of the Midianites could also be traced back to Abraham, who had been the father of all men who worshipped Yahweh?

Moses won't forget, Miriam told herself. He won't forget that he's a follower of Yahweh, a child of the Hebrew people who are oppressed in a foreign land.

But deep in her heart, she knew that she had no guarantee that the years hadn't obliterated Moses' memory of all she had taught him, just as surely as the blowing sands obliterated landmarks in the desert.

= 2 =

Night fell with the suddenness of a curtain dropping and caught Miriam halfway between the palace and the poor section of town where many of the Hebrew people lived. She felt a constriction in her chest. It wasn't fear exactly, but apprehension. Most of the Egyptian guards were aware of the identity of the palace slaves and allowed them to travel in peace. But there were always a few who liked to exercise their power.

It wasn't for herself that Miriam was afraid. She was no longer young enough to tempt the soldiers, and she had learned to speak with a voice of authority, backed up by the ring she wore that marked her as Princess Hapithet's slave. But this evening she was not walking alone. Aaron's daughter, Isha, was beside her. And Isha was young, slender, dark-eyed—beautiful enough to excite any man.

"It's blacker than usual," Isha said in a thin voice.

"We were kept at the palace longer than usual," Miriam replied, apprehension straining her voice. "The princess is not strong, and when she begins to feel breathless or unusually tired, she begs me to stay. I can't ask her to release me from my duty."

"She's only an Egyptian." Isha's tone was sullen.

"Of course. And so you believe that I should hate her. But how can I hate her when she has been so good to me for most of my life?"

"She's an Egyptian," the girl insisted.

"So she is," Miriam agreed. "It doesn't change anything."

"Where do you two think you're going?" The man's voice was so unexpected that Miriam and Isha both jumped.

Miriam peered through the faint light and saw that he was not alone. With him were several men wearing the helmets and carrying the shields that marked them as soldiers.

"To our homes, my lord," Miriam said meekly. It was always best to try meekness first. "We're palace slaves who are free to go to our own homes at night."

The man made a sound of derision. "Palace slaves! A likely tale!"

"I think this starlight gives enough light," Miriam said, keeping her voice steady, "to see the ring my mistress has given me to identify my position. See?" She extended her hand and the men came forward to examine the ring.

"It's the seal of the Princess Hapithet," one of the men murmured.

But the first soldier was not satisfied. "What of the girl?" he demanded. "I doubt that she has a ring." He caught Isha's hands and drew her closer. "See," he said to his companions, "her fingers are bare. I don't feel any rings."

"She's my niece, my lord," Miriam said. "She, too, serves the princess. But she is too new in the palace to have been given a ring. The princess has assumed that I would be able to protect her."

"It's possible the princess assumes too much," the soldier said as his arms closed around the girl and Miriam saw the glint of terror in Isha's widened eyes.

Miriam forced herself to be calm, but she allowed authority to replace meekness. "No, my lord, you mustn't touch her. She is the personal slave of the princess. You may take us back to the palace to prove it, if you like. The princess will be angry if you harm the girl."

"I have no intention of harming her. I only want to enjoy her."

Miriam saw the man's head lower to the girl's, and she

had to clench her hands to keep from striking out in defense
of her niece. It would be madness to attack a soldier who
was bored and restless and probably drunk.

"My lord," Miriam said in the tone of voice she would
have used with a misbehaving child, "you must let her go."

"The princess has influence with the pharaoh," one of the
men said. "Maybe what the woman says is true. Why can't
you take one of the wenches who works in the fields?"

The man's head came up, and his teeth showed in a
derisive grin. "One who smells of sweat and hard work?
Not likely. This one here is as fragrant as a flower."

"Small wonder, my lord. We have just come from the
princess' chamber where we have used oils and perfumes to
massage her tired body." Miriam's voice was still strong,
but she felt her courage starting to fray. "Surely that should
prove to you that we are what we claim to be."

If this soldier raped her, the girl would never make a
decent marriage, Miriam thought in anger and despair. She
would be an outcast from the decent families of the tribe.
She would be scarred until the day she went to her grave.

"Please, my lord," Miriam began, knowing that in spite
of her desire to sound authoritative, she would grovel for
Isha's sake.

At that moment, another group of men came through the
darkness.

"What's going on?" The words were shot out in a voice
of command.

"Just a bit of fun, captain. The night watches are boring."
The soldier who held Isha spoke easily, as though he were
confident that the captain would approve.

"Who's the girl?"

As the officer spoke the second time, Miriam recognized
his voice.

"My lord Peraton!" she cried, bending low and extending her hands to the newcomer. "Don't you recognize me? I'm Miriam, slave of Princess Hapithet. The girl is my niece, also a personal slave of the princess. I beg of you—."

The officer's voice grew sharp. "Miriam? Is it you? Here, come closer so I can see."

Obediently, Miriam moved toward him, turning up her face so that he might be better able to see her in the faint starlight.

"Leave the girl alone," Peraton barked. "It's true what the woman says. She's belonged to the princess for years. Since I was a child. The princess would be angry if you took the girl, and the pharaoh doesn't like to have his sister bothered."

The young soldier spit out a short expletive as he pushed Isha from him so roughly that she stumbled and fell. "Get on, then," he growled. "Get out of my sight."

"Oh, come on," Peraton assured his subordinate. "There are dozens of available girls." He turned to Miriam. "As for you, you shouldn't travel alone after dark. Hurry up, you've got only a short way to go. I'll wait here. If you need help, call out."

"Thank you, my lord. May prosperity and fortune and blessings heap themselves upon your head." She reached out a shaking hand and helped Isha to her feet. "We'll hurry, my lord."

With the girl beside her, Miriam broke into an awkward run toward the flickering light of the oil lamps that shone through the inadequately curtained doors of the Hebrew settlement.

She heard Peraton's irritated voice behind her. "You've got to be a little careful, even of these Hebrew dogs. Go find your fun somewhere else."

Miriam and Isha fled in silence to the hut that belonged

to Aaron, and as Miriam pushed her niece through the door, she felt a vast sense of relief, knowing that the Hebrews were rarely troubled once they were within their own walls. The dreaded call for forced labor might invade their security, but usually a Hebrew's own house was inviolate.

Elisheba, who was pouring wine into clay cups, looked around at their breathless entrance. Her eyes widened. "What's the matter?" she cried. "Isha, you're all right?"

The girl, pale and silent, seemed unable to shape her terror into words.

"The soldiers," Miriam explained briefly. "If Peraton hadn't come along, who knows what would have happened?"

Elisheba's face was as pale as her daughter's. She took one of the cups and pressed it to Isha's lips. "Rape?" she breathed.

Miriam nodded. "But why talk about it?" she snapped. "It didn't happen."

"Next time Peraton might not come along," Elisheba wailed. "Next time she might be ruined forever. Or killed."

"There won't be a next time," Miriam replied. "She won't travel back and forth with me anymore. She'll stay at the palace with the princess' slaves. She'll be safe there."

"Not come home?" Elisheba's wail grew shriller. "But she's the joy of her father's life. She's the only laughter or happiness we have in this house with both of our sons gone, and Aaron—."

Miriam sighed wearily, remembering that both of Aaron's sons were away in the labor force and that Aaron's back was still raw from the last time he had been whipped. She moved over to the rude stool on which Isha slumped and began chafing the girl's wrists.

"What's more important, my sister?" Miriam argued,

sure that, as usual, Elisheba would accept her sister-in-law's decision. "Your lord's joy or your daughter's chastity?"

Elisheba burst into tears and sank to the floor, sobbing hopelessly. "There's nothing but grief in our lives!" she cried. "There's nothing but sorrow and hard work and grief!"

Isha spoke up at last, pulling away restlessly from her aunt's ministrations. "I was telling Dodah just that when we first started home," she said, the intimate term for *aunt* slipping out even in this time of tension. "The Egyptians are cruel and evil and—."

Miriam clapped her hand firmly over the girl's mouth. "And the walls listen to what slaves say," she whispered fiercely. "How can you be so foolish?"

Isha twisted her head away. "I'm tired of being afraid," she said, but in a lower tone of voice. "I'm tired of just submitting to the kind of life we have. I *hate* being a slave!"

"No one likes it," Miriam agreed. "But if you fight it, what then? You are beaten or tortured or even killed. You think I don't know?" The bleak memory of Jehu's beaten body must have shown in her face, because Isha spoke up again.

"You should be proud that Uncle Jehu was man enough to stand up to the men who whipped him!" she cried. "Didn't father say that Uncle Jehu kept insisting that our God would hear the cries of the Hebrew children?"

Miriam felt the familiar stab of pain and anger. "Oh, yes," she agreed. "As a matter of fact, he died shouting his defiance. Do you think that's any comfort to me?"

"It ought to be," Isha insisted.

Miriam sighed and went to where Elisheba sat with her head on her arms weeping. "Well, it's not. Defiance doesn't warm me on a cold night or dry my tears. If he had bowed his head, he might still be alive."

"All the Hebrews feel like that," Isha said scornfully.

"There's no one among us who dares even to hope for a release from the Egyptian cruelty. No one."

"If Yahweh ever remembers us," Miriam said, but without much hope, "he might make a leader to rouse the people."

"Yahweh!" Isha's voice was angry. "It gets harder and harder to believe in a God who pays no attention to us."

"Shame!" Miriam snapped. "We belong to the tribe of Levites, and if the sons of Levi forget Yahweh's power and might, who will remember?"

"Maybe no one," Isha said in a sullen voice. "And it might be better that way."

The goatskin curtain at the door was suddenly pushed aside and Aaron stood there, blinking at the flickering light of the small wick burning in its saucer of oil. "I had a dream," he said without seeming to notice that the women were upset. "I fell asleep out under the tree and I had a dream."

"You'll be stung by a scorpion," Miriam said, "if you insist on sleeping out on the ground like that."

Elisheba looked up. "A dream, my lord?"

"A dream," Aaron repeated. "A dream in which Yahweh spoke to me." He ducked his head to enter the room and then stood there, apparently dazed by his dream.

Miriam, seeing the scorn and irritation that came and went in Isha's face, felt a moment of understanding for her niece. It was true that Aaron spoke often of dreams and of Yahweh's words, but too many times there was nothing to show for it.

"He told me that Moses was coming home," Aaron announced in a quiet voice, but there was none of the of the ecstasy he sometimes displayed. "He said that Moses had already left Midian and was on his way to Egypt. I'm to go out and meet him. I'm to take a two-day journey into the wilderness to meet him."

Miriam, Elisheba, and Isha all stared at Aaron, and then Elisheba spoke. "You can't go out into the wilderness alone, my lord," she protested. "Your back is still swollen and raw. Besides, you'd get lost. It was only a dream."

"You're always having dreams, father," Isha said. "Don't worry about it."

"Worry about it!" Aaron's voice was irritated. "I'm not worried. I must leave in the morning. And I won't get lost. I know exactly where to go. Yahweh showed me."

Miriam continued to stare at her brother. For once, she had nothing to say.

"Fix a bag of bread for me," Aaron said to Elisheba. "And a skin of water. Don't tell anyone—anyone—what I plan to do or where I'm going."

"They'll catch you," Elisheba moaned. "The soldiers will catch you just as they almost got Isha tonight."

"Isha?" Aaron swung toward his daughter. "What happened?"

"Nothing," Isha said. "Dodah took care of everything."

Aaron looked at his sister. "What?" he repeated.

Miriam shrugged. "A threat. Nothing more. The girl will have to stay in the palace at night for awhile. Until we can work out a safe way of traveling back and forth. It's nothing."

It had seemed like the end of the world when it was happening, but in the face of Aaron's proposed journey, it was nothing. Miriam felt a strange mixture of hope and doubt churning in her mind. Could it possibly have been a true vision that had come to her brother or was this just another of his ideas doomed to disappointment?

"Did Yahweh truly speak to you, my brother?" Miriam asked, the doubt surfacing in her voice. "Do you really believe that Moses is coming home?"

Aaron glanced at her. "Of course. I'll leave before daylight. We'll be home—Moses and I—in four days."

"Was it different, then?" Miriam asked cautiously, anxious to avoid offending Aaron. "The voice of Yahweh? Was it different this time?"

Aaron nodded. "Different," he agreed. "I can't explain how. I only know that Moses is coming." He went to a corner of the hut, wrapped himself in his robe, and lay down on a mat that he unrolled on the floor. "I'll sleep," he announced, "and rest myself for the journey. Get the food and water ready as I said."

He turned his face to the wall, and the three women looked at each other.

Isha shrugged. "The poison in his back has affected his thinking," she whispered.

"He'll be killed," Elisheba moaned.

But in spite of herself, Miriam was remembering the confidence that shone in her brother's eyes. Confidence and something else. Something too bright for her to name.

"Do as he told you," she commanded. "If Yahweh has chosen to speak to my brother, then we must obey."

The dream might be true, she thought, allowing hope to bloom in her heart. Moses might really be coming home.

≈ 3 ≈

Each morning for the next four days, Miriam was in her place in the rooms of Princess Hapithet when the sun rose. And each morning as her fingers stroked and smoothed and anointed the old, dry flesh of her mistress, she struggled with the temptation to tell of Aaron's dream and his trip into the wilderness.

Yet each time temptation encouraged her tongue, she would remember that Aaron had had dreams before and not all of them had been accurate. True, many of them had. And her brother had gained a certain standing among the Hebrew people as a prophet. He was a man who saw visions and who spoke of them in words that caught and held the attention of anyone who listened. But he was not infallible, and it would be foolish to raise the hopes of the princess if this particular dream were not to come true. And common sense told Miriam that it probably would not. Why, after all these years, would Moses leave the land of Midian and come back to Egypt? He had relinquished his royal heritage when he had killed the Egyptian overseer. He would never be welcome in the palace again, except by the princess, and even if she greeted him with love and joy, theirs would have to be a clandestine meeting.

Nor would he be welcome among the Hebrews. What reason had they to trust a man who had grown up in the pharaoh's palace and who had ridden the pharaoh's chariots down streets paved by Hebrew labor? Oh, no, Moses would not come back. It had been foolish of her to trust in Aaron's dream, foolish of them to allow Aaron to go out into the wilderness for a rendezvous that could never possibly occur. And yet Miriam knew she had not imagined the peculiar light that had shone in Aaron's eyes, a light she had never seen before.

On the fourth day after Aaron's departure, Miriam worked in silence on the princess' morning toilet. It seemed that she could keep her hopes to herself only if she kept silent.

But the princess was restless and inclined to chat.

"Have you nothing to say?" Hapithet asked at last, biting the words off with a snap.

"I'm sorry, my lady. My mind was wandering. Forgive me."

"What are you thinking about?" The old eyes were greedy as though Hapithet were hoping for a morsel of gossip.

"I was thinking of my brother," Miriam said before she could hold back the words.

"Moses?"

"No—oh, no. Aaron. The one I live with, my lady."

"And what about Aaron?"

"He's . . . well, he's not well," Miriam replied quickly. "He was among the men called for forced labor several months ago, and because he moves slowly—he's a dreamer, my lady—he was beaten badly. The cuts festered, and a poison set in. He was feverish for days, so I can't help worrying about him."

All of that was true, Miriam told herself in a effort to justify the fact that it hadn't been Aaron about whom she had been thinking.

"You never told me," Hapithet said.

"Why worry you, my lady? It's not your fault that the men are taken and beaten."

Hapithet drummed her fingers on the table. "But I feel the blame," she confessed. "I understand why my brother uses the Hebrew people for his labor force. There are so many of them, and they are superior workers to slaves captured in battle. The Hebrews *expect* to work. You know that. They rear their children to believe that labor is honorable. So they are perfect for slave labor. But I feel a sense of guilt, nevertheless."

"Because of Moses, my lady. You loved him and so you feel a kind of—well, almost an affection for his people as well."

"I suppose that's it." Hapithet cocked her head and looked up at Miriam. "Do you have medicine for your brother's back? We have marvelous salves here in the palace. I could get one of the physicians to give me some."

"Oh, would you, my lady? That would be wonderful."

"I'll see to it."

Silence fell again between the two women while Miriam slipped a fresh white dress over the princess' head and finally smoothed on the drops of perfume.

At last Princess Hapithet said abruptly, "Is your brother Aaron like Moses?"

Miriam hesitated. "It has been a long time since I've seen Moses," she hedged.

Hapithet was impatient. "Don't be silly. I know that. But you remember what Moses was like. Is Aaron like that?"

"They're alike in some ways," Miriam replied, choosing her words with care. "They're both more intelligent than most men. They both have—at least, Moses *had,* so I suppose he still does—a great sense of duty. But Aaron has a gift for words that I don't think Moses has."

"He stuttered sometimes," Hapithet remembered. "When Moses got very excited, he stuttered."

"Yes, my lady. And Aaron speaks with grace. Yet Moses

is—or was, at least—far better with people. Naturally he would be, my lady. For he was taught in the palace to be a ruler of men. He was taught the military secrets of how to command companies of hundreds, of thousands. Moses was more practical. But I have no idea what he's like now."

"He won't have forgotten," Hapithet murmured. "He never forgot anything he was taught. But he will surely have changed. You've said he's a shepherd for his father-in-law. Surely a shepherd would not think like a prince."

"No, my lady."

"Well, he won't have become stupid," Hapithet announced with finality. "Somehow he will have found a way to grow, to learn." She was silent a moment, then whispered, "I wish he would come home." And she spoke so wistfully that it was all Miriam could do not to cry out that perhaps he was coming home. Perhaps even before this day was over. . . .

Instead she spoke with caution. "If he ever came, my lady," she said, "how could we arrange a meeting that would be safe?"

Hapithet looked at her hands folded in her lap. "He wouldn't be in as much danger as you seem to think. Don't forget, Rameses was—is—Moses' uncle. He was fond of the boy once. But, of course, first you would bring him to my room. No one pays any attention to your coming, and there have been days when you said that Peraton or some other soldier accompanied you for safety's sake. Moses could appear to be only another soldier."

Once more, the old woman looked up at Miriam. "We make plans almost as though he were really coming," she said. "I don't know why, after so many years. . . ." Her voice trailed off.

"I don't know either, my lady." Miriam made her voice brisk. "We're being foolish. Now, come, let me take you into breakfast, and then I'll come back to tidy up this room."

Hapithet nodded and rose to take Miriam's arm. "He might come," she confided. "He just might."

"Yes, my lady," Miriam said in the docile tone of a slave. But there was nothing docile about the hope that sprang up in her at Hapithet's words.

Miriam's work at the palace was finished before dark that evening, and she hurried to the house of Aaron with an eagerness she had not known for years. She tried to tell herself that she was being foolish, that neither she nor the princess had any reason to hope for Moses' return. But none of her admonishments to herself could quench the excitement that carried her to her brother's door in such a rush.

She heard voices as she reached the doorway of her brother's house: Aaron's voice, vibrant and excited . . . Elisheba's voice, sounding more frightened than anything else . . . and another voice—one she had never been able to forget. Miriam's heart leaped in astonishment and joy.

"Moses," she whispered and put out a shaking hand to push aside the hanging curtain.

"Drop the curtain," Elisheba hissed even before Miriam got inside. "We don't want anyone to know."

But Miriam wasn't listening. Her eyes were darting around the room, seeking the source of the remembered voice. For a second, she saw only Aaron, his face blazing— and then beyond him, so tall that his head brushed the ceiling of the hut, a man who wore the robes of a desert nomad. Was this really Moses? He had been clean shaven when she saw him last, lean and eager in his royal Egyptian clothing, bare-legged, shod in fine leather.

Now here was this bearded stranger, wearing coarse

homespun that covered him almost to his ankles, his skin darkened by the sun. Then he smiled at her, and the years dropped away. No one but the child Moses had ever had such a brilliant smile. No one else had ever had eyes that warmed with such affection.

"My brother," Miriam breathed and would have knelt before him, but in two strides, Moses crossed the small room and caught her in his arms.

"Miriam," he cried, and to her astonishment she felt tears on his beard as he kissed her cheeks and then embraced her so tightly that she felt as though she could not breathe. But her arms, of their own accord, had gone around his neck, and for a few seconds, she held him as closely as he held her.

Finally he released her and stepped back. "You look just the same," he said. "I should have known the years would change you less than anyone else."

While he had held her, the overwhelming fact of his physical nearness had blunted her perception. But at arm's length, she suddenly realized that Aaron's dream had been true prophecy, that Moses' arrival was a miracle.

"Did Yahweh really tell Aaron you were coming?" she said in a tight, breathless voice. "Did you just meet in the wilderness without plan? Or had you sent messages to prepare Aaron, and is your coming a thing which our brother kept from me until now as a surprise?"

Moses shook his head gently, and she caught another glimpse of the tears drying on his cheeks. "No, my sister, I didn't send any messages to Aaron or to anyone else. We met in the wilderness as though we had both been walking down familiar streets in a busy town. Yahweh led us!"

His words ignited a fire within her. So Moses had not forgotten Yahweh! Even in a foreign land, he had not forgotten the God of his people nor the things his sister had taught him.

She felt a wave of dizziness, and Moses, sensing that she was overcome, helped her to a stool.

"It's a shock for you," he said simply. He turned to Aaron. "You told me that you warned her, that you thought she believed you."

"I did tell her, and she acted as though she understood. I expected her to be waiting—."

"I did believe," Miriam interrupted. "Or I tried to believe. It's not easy to believe in miracles."

Moses smiled. "There's so much to tell you. Most of it miracles."

The curtain at the door was pulled aside again, and a woman and two small boys entered the room. They were all as dark as Moses, and it was obvious they had been sent out for bundles that must have been left some distance away. The woman was lovely, tall and slender, with large dark eyes, a wide mouth, and unexpected dimples that appeared briefly when she smiled. The boys were enough alike to be twins, and Miriam looked with delight at their dark eyes, tousled curls, and strong white teeth.

"This is my wife," Moses was saying. "Zipporah, this is my sister. The one I've told you so much about. This is Miriam."

The woman nodded shyly. "Greetings, Miriam."

Miriam also bent her head politely, but her attention was focused on the little boys. "Welcome, my sister. And these are your sons?"

"Yes," Moses answered. "Gershom and Eliezer. The bigger one is Gershom."

Miriam went quickly to the boys and ran the palms of her hands softly down their cheeks. They did not draw away, but she saw the apprehension in their eyes. Poor little boys, she thought, to be so far from home.

"Come, all of you," Elisheba said. "Put your bundles in

the corner. There's food here for everyone. My lord, if you and your brother will sit here, I will serve you, then the children and my . . . my sisters and I will eat."

Though the room was small and they were crowded together, there was very little talking while the men were served. Even after they began their meal, there was no real conversation. A hundred questions were clamoring inside of Miriam, but she restrained her curiosity and contented herself with fixing bowls of lentils and chunks of bread for the little boys.

"They're surely hungry," she murmured as an excuse for feeding them while their father and uncle still sat eating.

Gershom nodded. "We haven't eaten since last night, except for a few dried dates."

"Let them eat," Moses said carelessly over his shoulder. "They're weary from traveling and frightened besides. They'll sleep when their bellies are full, and then we'll talk, we three."

Elisheba and Zipporah both looked at Miriam, but there was no resentment on their faces. It was as though they accepted as normal and right that the brothers would talk to their sister in a way they did not talk to their wives.

And why not? Miriam thought. I'm older and I work at the palace, so I know things other women don't know. But there was more than that, and she knew it. A close bond had always joined the three children of Amran and Jochebed. Not even the fact that Moses had been reared as an Egyptian prince had lessened the love and loyalty these three had felt for one another.

Miriam had a sudden memory of the day she had brought Aaron with her to the palace. He had been small, but the princess had not objected to his presence.

"Let him play with Moses while you and I care for the baby," she had said to Miriam. Her voice had been merry.

"Let them go out into the garden to play."

"Yes, my lady." Miriam had put out her hands to the two boys. She was the eldest, but the child Moses was growing so rapidly that she knew it would be only a few years until he was taller than she.

"You will be good, won't you?" Her eyes had gone from the chubby Aaron in his rough loin cloth to the slender Moses, whose hands and wrists glittered with gold.

"We'll be good," they promised.

"You're brothers, you know," she whispered, sure that neither of them would comprehend. "So love each other."

Aaron laughed, but Moses looked at her solemnly. "If he's my brother, I'll love him. The same way that I love you."

Her heart lurched. In telling him the stories of his people, she had mentioned that she was his sister, but she had never emphasized it. She did not think she had the right. Even so, Moses had remembered and responded.

"And I love you," she replied quickly, before she lost her courage. "Now, play in the garden while I help the princess."

The memory of the two boys, walking side by side, was as clear in her mind today as the sight of them had been on that sunny day. Now, seeing them together again with joy on their faces, she knew that their love for each other had not changed. And their love still reached out to encompass her as well, even though she was a woman. She might not have a husband or sons, but she was someone to be reckoned with in spite of that.

= 4 =

"A bush that burned but was not consumed?" Miriam asked at last, her voice more awed than skeptical, although she knew there was a kernel of skepticism in her. "And a staff that turns into a serpent?"

Moses and Aaron both nodded. The three of them were sitting in one corner of the room while the rest of the family, already asleep, sprawled on mats.

"I saw it," Aaron said eagerly. "Not the burning bush, of course, but the staff writhing on the ground and flicking its tongue at me."

Miriam drew a deep breath. "I don't know what to say," she confessed. "It is beyond anything I have ever heard of in all my life."

"Yahweh has remembered us," Moses explained. "He called me to bring his people out of bondage."

She heard his tongue trip on several words. He had not overcome his old malady, then. And yet he had been called by Yahweh?

"And are you willing?" she asked as though she believed every word. "Are you willing to be the leader Yahweh wants?"

Moses grinned and shook his head. "I? A shepherd who was once a fugitive? A man who sometimes stutters? You think I would be willing?"

"Well then?" she asked and waited.

"The Lord was angry," Moses remembered, his eyes losing the mirth that had briefly sparkled there. "He said there was my brother Aaron who could speak like a poet or a statesman."

Miriam glanced from one man to the other. She had heard what lay under Moses' simple words about Aaron. The Lord had been angry, he said. So the naming of Aaron was not a comfort to Moses but a reprimand. Because he had doubted, because he had been afraid, Yahweh had named two leaders instead of one.

"And Yahweh told you to go to the pharaoh? Just go to him and ask that all the Hebrews be released from their labor? Doesn't this seem ridiculous to you?" Miriam glanced at Zipporah, Elisheba, and the two boys sound asleep on the floor. Never had she felt less like sleeping.

Moses leaned his back against the wall and stretched his feet out in front of him. "Of course, it seems ridiculous. I would never have thought of it myself. Only Yahweh could propose something so far from practicality. It's one of the reasons I believe," he ended simply.

"There's more than the staff that becomes a serpent," Aaron said as though he, too, felt the need to convince her. "Moses can afflict his hand with leprosy and then heal it again just by thrusting it into his robe. Do you think you would dare use the spell to show her, my brother?"

Miriam, suddenly cold, spoke hastily. "No, don't show me. Don't waste your power on me. Besides, I hate leprosy, even the thought of it, more than anything in the world. I couldn't bear to see leprosy in this house."

"Well, no matter," Moses said. "I know it will happen. There is nothing, nothing that frightens me any more."

"How did you manage still to believe in Yahweh after so long a time?" Miriam asked. "Surely, in a foreign country, that must have been difficult."

"My father-in-law, Jethro, is also a believer," Moses explained. "As a matter of fact, his faith is greater than that of most Hebrews—at least, the Hebrews I remember. He talked to me time and again about the God of Abraham and Isaac and Jacob."

"Perhaps it was Yahweh's plan that you should leave the royal court," Miriam suggested. "Perhaps it was necessary for you to get away from the Egyptians and their religion, to meet someone like Jethro."

"Perhaps." Moses agreed. "Do you think she could be right, Aaron?"

Aaron spoke softly. "The ways of Yahweh are mysterious and wonderful. His word comes sometimes in dreams or visions."

"Not to me," Moses said. "To me, he speaks as though we were face to face. His words are clearer, sharper in my mind than the words of any man."

Miriam's lips felt dry. It was one thing to think about Yahweh, to pray to him, but it was another thing to be with someone who claimed, who believed that he had proof that Yahweh had spoken to him as to a friend. "When did you first begin to hear him?" she whispered.

"Never before the burning bush," Moses admitted. "And yet, there were a hundred, a thousand times when something stirred me, something moved me. In the wild and still stretches of the desert, I used to watch the stars and the moon and the sun that swung across the sky. I watched how the plants grew, even when there was no rain to water them, no earth to nourish them—only the bare rock of the mountains. And more and more, in the silence of the wilderness, I became aware of Yahweh's presence."

Aaron was nodding with understanding. "How blessed you are, my brother, to have had those years of solitude and silence. A man cannot hear his God speaking when he is constantly with people. Or when he must work with desperation or feel the lash on his back."

"So I've come to believe," Moses agreed. "At first, I thought I was cursed to have to flee to the desert. I missed the riches and the splendors of the palace. I longed for my Egyptian family." He stopped suddenly and turned to Miriam. "The Princess Hapithet? Is she still alive?"

"Alive and well, though she's growing old. She speaks of you all the time. Only this morning, in fact. Nothing has changed the way she feels about you."

"Nor the way I feel about her," Moses replied. "I hope to see her soon. It would have been a greater grief to hear that she was dead than it was to learn from Aaron that our own parents have died. Does that seem wicked?"

Miriam shook her head. "How could it? She raised you from infancy and loved you dearly."

"Even our parents understood that," Aaron added.

"Yes, well, at first when I left Egypt, I missed her and the palace and my friends and both of you. I knew a time of bitterness. But then I met Zipporah at the well, and she was lovely and good. We lost several children before Gershom was born, but still I was contented in the tribe of Jethro. And lately I've come to believe that only in such a place could I have come face to face with Yahweh."

"You know the people won't believe you." Miriam had spoken more abruptly than she had intended, but she knew it was the truth.

"Of course they will. When they've seen the signs, they will believe."

Aaron shook his head. "She may be right. They have not always believed my dreams."

"But they are slaves who will welcome the idea of freedom," Moses protested. "They have been abused and mistreated. The babies have been killed." His face grew dark. "Do they still kill the babies?"

"Rameses is not as cruel as his father," Miriam answered.

"He works the men harder and uses bigger labor forces. Maybe he thinks he will only need to work the men to death and the babies will be taken care of." Her voice was bitter.

Moses shifted restlessly, but there were too many people sleeping on the floor to allow him to pace around as he obviously longed to do. "So the cruelty goes on, and the people of Yahweh are broken over the rack. Even my own brother has the mark of whips on his back."

"But they won't understand," Miriam insisted. "The people will be afraid to rise up against the Egyptians."

"We won't rise up against them," Moses said sharply. "We will disappear. We will go out into the desert—a three-day journey—and make sacrifice to our God."

"And never come back?" Miriam guessed.

Moses only shrugged and spread his hands.

Aaron yawned widely. "I'm very tired," he said apologetically. "My back is not wholly healed, and the long walking was hard on me."

"Lie down," Moses said quickly. "I'm sorry. You and I have talked without stopping for two days and two nights. I will speak a little longer to our sister, but you must rest. Lie down."

Aaron grunted thankfully, kicked off his sandals, and lay down on a mat near the wall. He was asleep almost at once.

Moses and Miriam sat for a minute in silence.

"What will you do first?" she asked, feeling that she had a right to know. Hadn't she been the one to teach him about Yahweh?

"We will call a meeting of the leaders of each tribe," he answered readily, as though he, too, felt she had a right to know. "We'll get their approval first, and then I'll find some way to meet with the pharaoh face to face. With my Uncle Rameses," he added with a wry smile.

"There's a way," Miriam said, eager to display her skill at planning. "The princess and I have already discussed it.

We were . . . pretending that you might come back. Or dreaming of what it would be like. We figured out a way that I could get you to her room. Once there, she will be able to think of some way to get an audience for you with her brother. She still has some influence, even though she's old. You'll be shocked, I think, to see how old she is."

"Dear Miriam. You've always been able to help me when I needed it most."

She smiled and looked modestly at the floor. She was remembering that she had not been able to help when Moses had been forced to flee from Egypt, but she prudently kept such memories to herself. Let Moses think all the good things about her that he wanted to think.

"You really must rest," she said, looking up again. "Tomorrow I'll tell the princess you've come home. And then we will see what can be done."

Moses reached over and laid his hand briefly along her cheek. "Aaron will speak for me," he said, "and Yahweh will guide and protect me, but you will be the one who listens and shares."

Involuntarily, Miriam glanced at Zipporah who lay snoring on the floor.

"She's a good woman, and I love her," Moses said softly. "But she doesn't understand what I think or feel. She prepares my food and gives me sons and comforts me when I'm tired. But—."

Miriam's heart swelled with joy. This, *this* was what she wanted: to be important to Moses, perhaps more important than anyone else. This was *better* than being a wife.

But she did not allow the elation she felt to show. "I understand," she replied quietly, "and I will serve you in any way I can."

"I count on that," Moses said, and they each sought out a place on the crowded floor where they could find enough room to sleep.

"Now that you're dressed and ready," Miriam said to the princess next morning, "I have something to tell you."

She had made plans and discarded them a dozen times, trying to think of a way to break the news to Hapithet without giving her too great a shock. She had finally decided that she would wait until the last minute of the morning ritual and then be as casual as possible.

Hapithet had started to rise from her stool, but she sat down again at Miriam's words. "Something to tell me?" she asked.

Miriam knelt and looked up into Hapithet's face.

"Yes, my lady. Something that will astonish and delight you. Something that . . ."

"Moses has come home." The old woman's voice was low, and Miriam saw how the brown hands knotted together in her lap.

"Yes, my lady. I never dreamed it would happen. I never—."

"Never mind that. How is he? When will I see him?"

"He wants to come as soon as possible, my lady."

Hapithet's face lit up. "You mean—he talked about me? He thought about me?"

"He said, my lady, that to hear of your death would have been a greater grief to him than it was to hear that our own parents are dead."

"He said that?" The long dark eyes filled with tears, and Miriam hurried to blot them before they could smear the newly applied cosmetics.

"Yes, my lady, he did."

Hapithet picked up her mirror. "He will find me very ugly."

"No, my lady. He will find you as dear as ever."

"But if he comes with you," Hapithet said, her voice shaking, "then he will see me before I'm dressed, before you've had time to put on my cosmetics."

"I've thought of that, my lady. He's been living with nomads, you know, who cover their bodies from the sun. It's possible that he has become very modest. I could put him in the slave's pantry until you're ready."

"What if someone finds him?"

"No one will. No one else comes to these rooms so early. Then, when you're ready, I could call him through that door there, and you would be able to talk to him."

"I can't think of a better plan," Hapithet said after a few moments of silence. "All right, then. It will have to do. Is he here to stay?"

"I will let him tell you, my lady. I will let him explain what has happened to him and what he wants to do."

A look of immense satisfaction washed over the dark face of the princess. "I should have known," she said with pleasure. "He wouldn't come without a mission or a plan. He was always one to have a plan."

"Yes, my lady," Miriam said very softly, lifting the old woman from her stool. "You might say that. He has a plan."

When Miriam arrived home that evening, she found only the women in the house. She greeted them, then looked around the room.

"My brothers?" she said. "And my nephews? Where are they?"

"The boys are playing out behind the house," Zipporah said. "In the way of children, they've found playmates already. As for my lord and his brother, they've gathered together all the leaders of the tribes—or all of them who are not with the labor forces of the pharaoh." She turned to Elisheba. "That's what you said, isn't it? The labor forces of the pharaoh?"

Elisheba nodded mildly, but Miriam spoke up sharply.

"You do know what it means, don't you?" she said. "My brother has explained to you what the forced labor is like?"

Zipporah looked embarrassed. "It's hard for me to understand," she confessed. "We were always free in Midian. We lived in the desert and we owned nothing except our flocks, but neither were we owned by anyone. It's hard for me to understand."

Miriam's irritation subsided. "It's even hard for *us* to understand," she said slowly. "We were free for so long, and we had power—even here in Egypt. Our ancestor, Joseph, had much power. No one seems to understand how it happened—how we lost that power and became slaves."

"But why should Moses care about it?" Zipporah cried out. "He had cattle and a good tent. He had sons and food to eat. Why should we have to come trekking across the desert to a foreign land where, if he is caught—." Her voice broke, and she covered her face with her hands.

Miriam refused to let herself think about how Zipporah felt, how any woman would feel who had been forced to follow a dream she did not understand.

"Our God spoke to him," Miriam explained impatiently. "Surely he told you of what Yahweh commanded him to do?"

"He speaks constantly of Yahweh," Zipporah replied, her voice muffled by her hands. "But how can Yahweh speak to an ordinary man?"

He would seem like an ordinary man to her, Miriam thought with a resurgence of irritation, because she fed his physical hungers. Because she prepared his food and bore his sons, she was acquainted only with his physical appetites. She had never tried to follow his thoughts. It was the way with husbands and wives. Unless a woman stretched her heart. . . .

"Don't think about it." Miriam forced herself to speak

soothingly. "Think only that you have come to your husband's family, as all wives should do. Try to be content, my sister."

"But if they kill him?" Zipporah asked. She looked up and her eyes were frightened. "What if the leaders of the tribe kill him? You yourself said they would never believe him."

So she hadn't been asleep all that time last night, Miriam thought. Maybe she hears more than Moses gives her credit for hearing.

"Would Yahweh send him if his own people were going to kill him? They may not believe at first. They may laugh or mock him. But they won't hurt him. I assure you of that."

At that moment, the curtain at the door was pushed aside. The women turned their heads to see Moses and Aaron striding in, their faces bright with satisfaction.

"We're home," Moses announced. "And hungry."

The women acknowledged their presence with a quick nod and then hurried to carry food to the men who sat down on the floor.

"Your words were like a river of gold," Moses told Aaron. His tone was that of admiration, but, Miriam thought, held a trace of envy. "You'd have persuaded me, even if I hadn't already believed," he said.

"In time you will come to talk to them as well as I," Aaron said. "And it wasn't only my words that caught them. It was your staff squirming and hissing on the ground. It was the sight of your hand when you pulled it from your robe."

"The important thing is that they were persuaded," Moses said, picking up the bowl Miriam set before him. He drank briefly and then looked up to meet her eyes. "So it's arranged, my sister. The leaders have agreed that I should see the pharaoh. Tomorrow you will take me to the princess and we will begin to lay our plans."

⸗ 5 ⸗

Half hidden in the shadows, Miriam watched the reunion between Moses and the Princess Hapithet. At first, there had been no words, only tears. But gradually, as Hapithet regained control of herself and Moses was able to steady his voice, they began to talk. Miriam didn't even try to listen. This was a moment that belonged only to the old woman who had once bent lithely to lift an infant from his floating bed and to the man who had been her son.

Most of the Hebrews would never be able to understand the feeling between these two people, Miriam reflected, because they see the cruelty of the overseers and the power of Rameses in every Egyptian. Moses would have to be made to understand that his affection for the princess must be hidden. I'll explain it to him, Miriam thought easily. She had explained many things to her brother when he was young.

As the conversation between Moses and Hapithet grew more relaxed, Miriam slowly moved toward them. They must not stay here too long or someone would come searching for the princess. Her meticulous keeping to schedules was well known throughout the palace.

"Don't you think you ought to go in for your morning meal, my lady?" Miriam finally suggested. "Someone will come looking for you soon."

Hapithet looked up, her face shining. "Yes, of course. You're right." She turned to Moses. "And you just want me to ask my brother to grant an audience? For whom?

Shall I tell him who wants to see him?"

Moses shook his head slightly. "I've given this a great deal of thought," he said. "If he is told that Moses is asking for an audience, it will be too easy for him to refuse. Better, I think, that I come unannounced. But if you ask him to see your son, he will simply think that one of the princes wants to ask a favor and he may be more genial."

Hapithet nodded decidedly. "As a matter of fact, Rameses is fond of my other two boys and is willing to grant nearly everything they want. I'll just say that my son wishes to ask if the mighty pharaoh will grant him a favor."

"Exactly," Moses agreed. "Could you suggest that the meeting take place this afternoon? I am eager to see him as soon as possible, but I shall need time to get Aaron and my staff."

"Your staff?" The princess looked puzzled.

"My God has given me a sacred staff to persuade people to believe me. I didn't bring it this morning because I knew I wouldn't need it to persuade you."

Hapithet reached out to pat his arm. "But you haven't made it clear what you're going to ask for. Are you simply going to ask that you be allowed to live in Egypt again? Will you come back to the palace or will you stay with your Hebrew brothers? If you stay with the Hebrews, you'll be forced to work, you know. You'll be forced to make bricks in the hot sun like the others."

"I don't plan to come back to the palace *or* to make bricks," he said. "But it's best that you don't know what I plan to ask the pharaoh. Then if he questions you, you can say in all honesty that you know nothing."

A shadow passed over the princess' face. "You won't do anything foolish?" she begged.

"Carrying out the commands of my God can hardly be considered foolish."

But the princess shook her head. "Gods have demanded

terrible things of their followers," she insisted.

Moses touched her cheek. "Don't worry, my little mother. There is nothing that can hurt me. Nothing."

Hapithet sat for a moment longer looking at the large bearded man in front of her. At last she submitted to Miriam's hands that had been urging her to rise.

"I'm coming, I'm coming," she said sharply. "I'll ask for an audience with my brother directly after I've eaten. You will come with me," she added to Miriam, "but you, my son, must go back to Aaron's house and stay hidden there until we're sure the pharaoh will see you."

Moses stood obediently. "A wise suggestion," he said. He pulled his head-covering down over his forehead, so that nothing showed of his face but his mouth.

"And don't smile," Hapithet begged suddenly. "If you don't smile, no one in the whole country of Egypt will recognize you."

Moses glanced at Miriam. "You both worry too much," he said mildly. "My sister told me the same thing, so I'll have to accept the fact that my smile must give me away. Well, before this day is over, there may not be much to smile about."

He bowed slightly to the princess, nodded at Miriam, and then seemed to melt from the room.

"He moves like a shadow," Hapithet marveled.

"He learned that in the wilderness of Midian," Miriam explained. "How to move without sound, I mean. Because of the animals. But he won't move noiselessly in Egypt, my lady. I am afraid that before long everyone will know he is here."

A long-handled fan covered with brilliant feathers, denoting both nobility and servitude, trembled in Miriam's hands. The very fact that she was allowed to wave the fan over the princess' head indicated to all who saw them that she was Hapithet's chosen attendant. The waving fan not only stirred the hot air a little, so that the person who walked beneath it was cooled by its movement—it also kept the persistent flies and other insects away. The Egyptian royalty loved comfort as much as they loved beauty. A fan in the hands of a slave provided both.

But there had been many times, Miriam thought, when she had carried the fan with greater joy than she carried it now. Now as they approached the throne room of Rameses II, she realized that there was more at stake than Hapithet could ever dream. If she knew, Miriam's thoughts went on, just what Moses had in mind, Rameses' sister would not be approaching the throne with so much confidence.

Miriam entered the royal room behind the princess. No matter how many times Miriam had seen the throne room, she always found the first sight of it breathtaking. Sunlight, shining through the high clerestory windows, touched the painted walls and elaborate palm columns with a brilliance that enhanced the colors of the paintings and the decorative touches of gold. A sleek leopard, collared and chained with gold, lounged in front of the carved throne.

After a quick look around the room, Miriam forced her thoughts to stop fluttering in her head as the fan fluttered above her. She needed to be alert, to observe the mood of the man who ruled their world. And she needed to hear what Hapithet would say, so that she could report her discretion or lack of it to Moses.

Rameses was elegant, lean, and clean shaven, except for a small goatee. He looked up with indolence, noted that his older sister was coming toward him, and carelessly beckoned her to approach the golden chair in which he sat. The heavy metallic collar that rested on his shoulders glittered with the same jade and turquoise that shone in the heavy gold headpiece that rested on his naked skull. And the bored droop of his heavy, sensuous lips seemed an odd contrast to the malicious glint that shone in his dark, narrow eyes.

"I request your ear, my lord," Hapithet said in a voice that failed to be completely humble.

"You have it, my sister. What now? Surely no more problems about the living conditions of your children? Haven't I already given orders that each should have a house as splendid as the other?"

Hapithet risked a small smile. "Indeed, my lord, you have been wonderfully generous. But my son seeks an audience with you, and I have promised I will ask for it. Will you grant it, my lord?"

Miriam, who dared not look directly at the pharaoh, felt tension build up in her. If he asked which son, what would the princess say?

But the pharaoh was evidently not to be troubled with trifles. "Why not?" he replied carelessly. "I'm busy with a dozen critical things and haven't much time for petty requests. But if he wishes to come before me this afternoon, immediately after the noon meal, I'll see him, for your sake. But remind him the audience must be short."

Hapithet started to back away, and Miriam concentrated on keeping the proper distance from her so that the moving fan would stay above Hapithet's head.

"I'll remind him, my lord. Accept my gratitude for your unfailing courtesy, your . . ."

But the pharaoh had already turned to the next person who sought audience, and Hapithet's voice dwindled to silence. Miriam noticed, however, that the princess' eyes were darting swiftly around the room, taking notice of every man who stood within hearing distance of the pharaoh. The narrow eyes were shrewd, calculating, speculative. She might be getting old and even frail, Miriam thought, but she hasn't lost any of her skill with people. She'll know who might be Moses' enemies even before he will.

Moses and Aaron, brought by a young servant to the princess' rooms, stood waiting for the call of the pharaoh. Aaron wore his best robe that showed he was a priest of the tribe of Levi, and Moses, still dressed as a Midianite shepherd, held a slender black staff in his hand. The staff was as smooth as silk, and if it had not retained the shape of a branch, one might have believed it to be carved of some rare stone. Moses held it as though it were a scepter, Miriam noticed, and his body was straight with the bearing of a king.

"And he'll see me now?" Moses asked.

"He'll send a messenger. A soon as he's finished with his noon meal. It should be any minute." Hapithet reached over and twitched a fold of Moses' robe into place. It was a gesture of intimacy that denied the many years of silence between these two.

Moses smiled at the princess, but before he could say anything, a young boy came running up to the door.

"His royal majesty will see your son now, my lady," he said. His eyes swept the room, skimming over Aaron and Moses as though they had not been there. "Isn't your son ready, my lady? You know how the pharaoh hates to be kept waiting."

"Just lead the way and announce me," Hapithet said in a haughty tone. "The pharaoh will not be kept waiting."

With her thin brown arm, Hapithet made a gesture that brought Miriam, Moses, and Aaron into line behind her. In silence, they walked down the long halls with the carved walls and mosaic floors, and Miriam wondered if it were the hurried pulsing of her own heart or only the swish of the princess' sandals on the floor that she heard.

They entered the royal presence, and Hapithet spoke clearly from the edge of the room. "My lord, I present to you for your generosity and compassion, my firstborn son."

She stepped aside. Rameses glanced up with a bored expression, then looked startled. He narrowed his eyes and motioned imperiously with his hand to bring Moses and Aaron closer to his golden chair. "Your firstborn son, my sister?" he asked.

"My firstborn. Moses."

Her voice was thin but steady, and at the sound of Moses' name, both brothers bent at the waist, extending their hands toward the pharaoh.

For a long time, it seemed, Miriam felt the silence pounding through her head with short, painful strokes.

Rameses spoke at last. "Moses? I don't believe it."

At this, Moses raised his head, and Miriam saw the glint of his teeth as he smiled. "Ah, but it's true, my lord, my uncle. I've come back, and I beg you to grant me a hearing."

Incredibly, Rameses got up from his chair and moved toward Moses, while Moses watched and stood erect.

"Welcome home, nephew. Your long absence and silence had persuaded most of us that you were dead. Except for my sister, of course. She has always hoped for your return." He put forth a hand and placed it on Moses' shoulder. It was not an embrace, but it was a warmer greeting than he would have offered most men.

Moses did not presume to imitate the touch. He lowered his head respectfully, then looked to Aaron. "This is my brother, my lord. My birth brother."

Rameses glanced at Aaron, greeted him in a disinterested fashion, and then turned back to Moses. "Well, tell me, what are you doing in this dreadful outfit and with a beard on your face that makes you look like a foreign peasant?" As he asked his question, he went back to his chair, and Moses followed to stand easily before him.

"I've been a Midianite shepherd, my lord," Moses explained. "I could hardly dress as an Egyptian prince in the wilderness of Midian."

"Especially when you were hoping that no one would know you were an Egyptian prince. Or had been," Rameses added with a sharp emphasis. "Don't think for a minute that I've forgotten why you fled from my father."

Moses replied smoothly. "I wouldn't think that my lord would forget anything. I have too strong a recollection of his mental and physical powers. I would as soon think that the sun would forget how to shine."

Rameses smiled. "I see that although you still stutter, you haven't lost your way with words."

"I hope I haven't forgotten anything I learned in this place, my lord."

"I'm a busy man. I haven't time for flattery. Tell me: why did you want to see me here in my audience chamber?"

"My lord." Moses hesitated, then spoke with sudden vigor. "My lord, I ask you to let my people go."

Rameses looked puzzled. "What on earth are you talking about? What people? I have no control over the Midianites."

"Not the Midianites, my lord." But his tongue tripped so badly over the words that Moses turned to Aaron. "If my lord will allow my brother to speak?" he asked.

"Quickly, then."

And so Aaron's voice, smooth and rich, flowed between the two men. "My lord, my brother speaks of the Hebrew people. Those who live in Goshen and serve my lord as laborers to build his magnificent cities. My brother asks only that his people, the children of Yahweh, the descendants of Joseph who was once loved by a pharaoh, be allowed to go three days' journey into the wilderness that they might make proper sacrifice to their God."

For a few seconds, Rameses stared incredulously at the two men. Then he said coldly, "Are you serious?"

"Yes, my lord." Aaron's voice was soft but stubborn. "Our God, Yahweh has commanded us to come out to sacrifice to him, and we ask your permission to leave."

Rameses ignored Aaron and spoke to Moses instead. His voice was shrill with anger. "I think the Midianite sun has addled your thinking. What sane man would ask such a thing? You think I'm a fool? You think I don't know that if you ever got 'your people,' as you call them, away from my taskmasters, they would ever come back? I was willing to welcome you, thinking you had returned to Egypt as an Egyptian. I would have forgotten my father's anger. But I won't deal with a fool."

"Our God, Yahweh—" Aaron began, but Rameses cut him short.

"What do I know of Yahweh? Yahweh is nothing to me and you are less than nothing. Take your foolish request and leave me."

Aaron drew a breath as though to speak again, but Moses shook his head. "We'll leave, my lord," Moses replied. "We can only pray that our God will move you so that you will grant us mercy."

Rameses laughed, a short, bitter sound. "Don't look to me for mercy. If you had come with an intelligent request —that you might enter the court again or fight in my army —I might have listened. But this. This is insane. It's insulting."

He motioned to his attendant. "Next," he said and did not look at Moses again.

Moses and Aaron backed away from the pharaoh and left the room with Hapithet following. Miriam was the last to depart, and it was she who heard Rameses snap the order to his scribe.

"Make a note of this," he said, "to remind me to make a judgment on the Hebrew slaves. Help me think of a way to increase their burden. I don't want this crazy Moses to think he can get away with anything with me."

= 6 =

"He did *what?*" Moses cried out in anguish.

Two men had entered Aaron's hut a few minutes earlier with the angry bravado of fighting cocks. Now their fury paled at the sight of Moses' pain.

"You heard us." The shorter man's voice was sullen. "We dared to go to the pharaoh ourselves—just Jacob and I. We thought it must be the fault of the Egyptian overseers that we didn't have any straw. They kept yelling for the same number of bricks, but they wouldn't give us any straw. So we went to the pharaoh and told him—asked him to get his men to find straw for us."

"And then? Go on, man, go on!"

The little man straightened his shoulders. "I'm a foreman, and my name is Pagael."

Impatience flared in Moses' eyes, but he kept his voice civil. "All right then. Pagael. Tell me, Pagael, what happened."

"The pharaoh said it was because of you. Because you asked that the Hebrew people be allowed to go off into the wilderness, our work has been doubled. Now we have to find our own straw and still make the same number of bricks that we made before. It's cruel."

Moses stood staring at the little man, his jaw hanging down, as though all comprehension had been knocked out of him. In the silence that filled the hut, Miriam crouched near the door, pretending to grind grain. And now she found herself thinking: I tried to warn you. I told you what I'd heard the pharaoh say to his scribe, but you wouldn't listen. I tried to tell you.

Of course, she would not say this. Not now, when other people were around. And quite possibly not even when she and Moses were alone. She had learned already, in the few days since Moses had come back, that the man was different from the boy who had once listened to his older sister. He was a man who kept his own counsel. He did not tell her to stop babbling, as some men might have done. He merely looked through her with eyes that did not see her. So she was learning to hold her tongue, not out of humility, but for the sake of expedience.

Moses took an abrupt turn around the little hut and then faced Pagael again. "Does the new rule apply only for this day?" he asked.

Pagael was bitter. "As far as I can tell, it applies for as long as the Hebrews have to make bricks for the Egyptians. You've had it soft out there in Midian. Shepherding your father-in-law's flocks, I'm told. What do you know of how it is here? Why did you come meddling in what was none of your business?"

The hut became utterly silent. For long seconds, Moses stared at the little man, then turned away from him with a weary droop of his shoulders. "You're right," he muttered. "I must go to Yahweh and ask him why he has allowed this terrible thing to happen."

Pagael's eyes narrowed. "What do you mean, 'go to Yahweh'? You talk as if you could speak to the Lord—same as you'd speak to me. That's—that's crazy."

Jacob muttered something, and Pagael answered tartly, "What if he *is* of the tribe of Levi? They might be priests, but they're still just people, same as us."

Moses was agitated, and when he replied, some of his

words tripped and stumbled. "I speak to Yahweh and he speaks to me. That's why I came here—because he commanded me to come, to free the people from the burden of slavery."

"You came to free the people?" Pagael snorted. "How free are we now that we have to gather our own straw? There's no way in the world a man can gather straw and still make the same number of bricks. We'll have to get our women and our children out to gather up the straw. Is that your idea of freedom? To turn the children and women into slaves, too?"

Before Moses could answer, Aaron's voice slid smoothly between his brother and the small, angry foreman. "Now, Pagael, be easy. My brother had no notion that this would happen. And he will have to find a way to mend it. But you must believe that Yahweh does speak to him and give him power. As a foreman of the men, you especially must believe." He turned to Moses and said simply, "Get the staff, my brother."

Moses walked to the corner where the staff leaned against the wall. Taking it in his hand, he returned to stand in front of Pagael. For a few seconds, his eyes met those of the little foreman. Then Moses looked up and called out in a strong, steady voice, "Yahweh, my Lord, give me the power you promised!"

Swiftly Moses threw the staff to the floor, and instantly the black wood softened and smoothed itself into the sleek, glistening body of a serpent writhing sinuously through the dust. The women screamed, the men gasped, and a moment later, Moses stood alone in the hut. Even Miriam found herself outside, peering with horror around the edge of the door opening.

Moses spoke sternly. "Pagael, come back so you can see."

Reluctantly, the foreman edged closer to the door and looked cautiously into the room. The serpent had wound itself into a malevolent coil, its head swaying slowly from one side to the other. Pagael inched away, but Moses spoke again.

"No, don't move. Just look. Don't take your eyes from the serpent."

Miriam, on the other side of the doorway, could smell the sweat of fear. Pagael, she saw, was a man for whom the snake carried more than normal terror.

Moses reached down into the silky coils and grasped the serpent's slender tail. Pagael's breath rasped in his throat. With a sharp upward movement, Moses pulled his hand to his chest, and the black thing in his fist was once more a polished stick with the normal knobs and whorls of wood.

"Touch it," Moses said.

But at first, Pagael would not. His face was white and slick with sweat, and he only shook his head, refusing to move.

When Moses spoke again, his words were a command. "Touch the staff and see what Yahweh has done."

Slowly, hesitantly, Pagael moved toward Moses and put out a shaking hand. When his fingers encountered the staff, he gasped with disbelief.

"It's only wood," Pagael said stupidly.

"Shall I show you again?" Moses asked.

For a minute, Miriam thought the little man might throw himself on his knees, and she felt almost inclined to join him. The terror of that writhing thing on the floor still coiled coldly around her chest.

"Oh, no!" Pagael cried, almost babbling. "Oh, no! Don't show me again! I believe you have power. I believe."

"It's not I who have this power," Moses corrected. "This

power comes from Yahweh and flows through me. This is what you have to know."

"Yahweh hasn't paid much attention to us lately," Pagael replied, sullen again in spite of his fear.

"But now he has remembered," Moses said. "And he will show me—he will tell me what we must do about this added burden on the Hebrew children. Maybe I've done something wrong, but you must still have faith in Yahweh. You must believe that he will bring you out of this place."

Pagael looked from the staff to Moses' face and then back to the staff again. "It wasn't just a magic trick?" he asked fearfully.

Aaron now spoke persuasively. "I've seen magic as much as you, my friend. I've seen magicians with oiled ropes that looked like serpents. But have you ever seen an oiled rope that could flick its tongue at you or shape itself into coils?"

Memory darkened Pagael's eyes. He licked his lips. "No," he said, "of course not."

"Then," said Aaron, "when people ask you, you must tell them that Moses carries the power of Yahweh within him, that Yahweh will give us a way to solve the problem of the straw. You must be one of the believers, Pagael. You must tell the people how it is."

By this time, Jacob had also crept back into the room and was nodding in a fervor of agreement. "I saw it, too!" he cried. "Pagael wasn't the only one to see the miracle. I'll tell everyone who works under me. And my family and friends. I'll tell them that Yahweh will surely find a way."

The men had been gone only a few minutes when Moses turned to Aaron. "You're suddenly more certain than I," he said. "I feel only fear and horror. What have I done to these innocent people?"

"Only what our God told you to do," Aaron replied.

"Aaron's right," Miriam snapped, feeling something close to contempt for Moses' humility. "Could you have done otherwise?"

"No, of course not," Moses admitted. "But I trusted him. I believed that he would lift his people up, not cast them down and grind them into the dirt."

"If he weren't true, if he weren't faithful," Miriam argued, "wouldn't you have lost the power? Would the staff have turned into a serpent?"

There was a silence, and she could see that both Moses and Aaron were weighing her words, balancing them against their own feelings, their doubts and uncertainties.

It was Moses who finally answered. "No, of course not. There is no question about the truth or the faithfulness of our God. The question is with me. Did I misunderstand? Have I done something wrong?"

"It seems to me—" Miriam began, but Moses raised a hand to stop her.

"It doesn't matter what *you* think or feel. It only matters what Yahweh wants. I'll find a quiet place somewhere— though where, I can't imagine—and perhaps he will speak to me again."

Hearing the reprimand in Moses' voice, Miriam felt the same pain and resentment she had felt when she was first married and Jehu had told her that she was foolish and young and could not possibly know what a man might be thinking. Hot, hasty words formed in her mind, but before her tongue could shape them, Moses plunged out the door.

"I'll go with him," Aaron said hastily. "He needs someone who knows this part of the city to help him find a private place."

Let them find their private place, Miriam thought. They obviously don't need any help from me.

"You see," Zipporah said quietly. "He has moved away to where no one can reach him."

How short a time ago, Miriam thought ruefully, she would have felt only scorn for Zipporah. But not tonight. Tonight she knew exactly how Zipporah felt.

"Do you realize that your brother is beginning to anger and frustrate the pharaoh? No matter how often Rameses dismisses him, he—your brother, that is—manages to find some way to approach the pharaoh and repeat his ridiculous request. Are you aware of that?"

Miriam looked down at the princess and her hands became still on the small naked skull. A little of the scented oil dropped from her fingers onto the princess' neck, and Hapithet dabbed at it angrily as though it were a fly.

Always the princess had called Moses by name or spoken of him as "my son," Miriam thought. Now, all at once, he was relegated to the humbler position of brother to a slave. Did this mean that the princess herself was angered and irritated?

Seeing the princess' small jerky movement in response to the sliding bit of oil, Miriam willed her hands to move again. Deftly, she caught up the drop and massaged it gently but firmly into the gleaming bare head. There had been times when the nakedness of the skull had seemed pathetically vulnerable to Miriam, when she had pitied—if a slave dare feel pity for her mistress—these rich Egyptian women who did not want the long, thick hair that fell over Hebrew women's shoulders at night. But today, frightened and uneasy, she was aware only that new hair on Hapithet's head made a faint stubble under her fingers. She must put out the razor tomorrow.

"I don't know anything except that the pharaoh has not kept any of the promises he has made to my brother," Miriam said cautiously.

"Nor will he!" Hapithet's voice was sharp. "Moses is insane to think he might."

Hapithet moved under Miriam's hands, but her face, when she looked up, was twisted with worry, not anger. "I'm afraid for him," Hapithet confessed. "I would never have arranged for a meeting if I'd had any idea what Moses had in mind."

Breathing was suddenly easier for Miriam. "He can't help it, my lady. Our God has spoken to him, and Moses has to obey."

"Oh, nonsense! Do you really believe that foolishness?"

"I have to believe some of it, my lady. When Moses casts his staff on the floor and it becomes a serpent, I have to believe that he has some special power."

The princess made a sound of protest. "Mirak was telling me about that. About Moses turning a stick into a snake to persuade the pharaoh. The court magicians did the same, Mirak told me."

"But theirs were not real serpents, my lady. Merely trick ones. And the serpent of Moses swallowed all of the others. Did Mirak tell you that?"

The princess stood so that Miriam could slip her embroidered linen dress over her head, then sat again for the buckling on of the jeweled collar and the adjustment of the heavy wig.

"Are you sure?" Hapithet demanded. "Mirak didn't say so."

"Ask him. Ask your brother. It happened."

The thin, brown face was severe. "Careful, lest you, too, become insolent."

Nothing would be gained by angering the princess, who was, Miriam reflected hastily, the only door into the palace that was open to Moses.

"I don't mean to be insolent, my lady. I'm frightened,

too. And Moses doesn't tell me all that happens—or all that he plans to do."

"My brother has tolerated Moses' insolence only for my sake. If he were anyone else, the pharaoh might have issued a death sentence—or at least banished him from Egypt. Surely you know that."

Miriam had said almost the same words to Moses, and his answer had been that the pharaoh had been more intimidated by the black, silky serpent that destroyed the products of the Egyptian priests' magic than he would ever be by thoughts of his sister's anger. But she could never say that to the princess.

So she only murmured a low sound of acquiescence and stood with lowered head.

"He threatened the pharaoh. Did you hear?" The princess' voice had grown less sharp and there was a tremulous note in it.

"No, my lady, I hadn't heard. Threatened to hurt him, you mean?"

Oh, surely, Moses would not be so foolish, so headstrong, so—so childishly trusting in the promise that his God would protect him. Every man knew that he should not tempt his God too far.

"He threatened our whole country. He said the wrath of his God would pour out over us and soften the heart of the pharaoh."

Miriam stared helplessly into the old, lined face. She knew the fear in her own face must match that which she saw in the princess' eyes.

"I don't know what to say, my lady," she replied at last.

Hapithet stood up and spoke in a hard, clear voice, "You must go home tonight and tell Moses to stop. You must tell him that I, his mother, have commanded it. He must stop this stupid attempt to free the Hebrews from slavery.

Rameses believes, as well he should, that the Hebrews belong to him, and he won't give them up. If Moses angers the pharaoh too far, even my love won't help him."

"But that won't do any good, my lady," Miriam cried in despair. "Moses no longer listens to me—or to the people —or to your brother—or to anyone. He hears only the voice of our God. And his mind is set, my lady. He believes that somehow, some way, the people must be free. Free," she added quickly, "to go into the desert a three days' journey to make sacrifice to our God."

Hapithet shook her head. "Don't insult me with such talk. I know what Moses is after. So do you. And if I made as many wagers as my sons do, I would bet that Moses will die before any slaves get beyond the borders of Egypt." She stopped, breathless. "And I can't stand it!" she cried, clenching her fists. "All he has to do is forget this crazy thing, and I would see that he could live in a house with a carpeted floor and a small grove of trees to shade him."

The two women stared at each other, and when the princess finally turned to leave the room, Miriam saw how shrunken she looked, as though she had suddenly grown very old.

Now the Lord said to Moses . . . "present yourself before pharaoh . . . and say to him, 'Let my people go. . . . For if you will not let my people go, behold, I will send swarms of flies on you . . . and the houses of the Egyptians shall be full of swarms of flies. . . . But . . . I will set apart the land . . . where my people are living.' " . . . Then [the pharaoh] called Moses and Aaron at night and said, "Rise up . . . and go." . . . [So] all the hosts of the Lord went out from the land of Egypt . . . [and] the sons of Israel walked on dry land through the midst of the [Red] sea. And Miriam, the prophetess . . . took the timbrel in her hand, and all the women went out after her with timbrels and with dancing.

Exodus 8:20, 21b, 22a; 12:30a, 41b; 14:29; 15:20

⸗ 7 ⸗

Although Miriam and Isha both worked for the princess and spent most of their time in the same part of the palace, it seemed to Miriam during the days after Moses' return that there were times when Isha tried to avoid her aunt. Sometimes Miriam saw the girl at a distance giggling with the assistants of the court sorcerers or chatting with slaves whose company Miriam had never believed quite suitable. But when Isha saw Miriam watching her, she usually hurried in the opposite direction.

So one afternoon after Miriam had settled the princess for her midday rest, she went seeking Isha. She found her in the anteroom of the smaller harem, huddled together with several slaves, talking busily.

"Isha!" Miriam's tone was cold. "I want you."

The girl looked up in surprise, shrugged with an apologetic look at her friends, and came over to her aunt.

"What do you want?" Miriam noted that although the girl was not exactly insolent, she was certainly not respectful either.

"I want to talk to you. Come with me."

Miriam stalked along the corridor, her mind seething. Wasn't it enough that she had to worry about the princess, agonize over Moses, and make plans to keep everyone as safe as possible? Was it also necessary that she had to concern herself with this saucy girl?

They came to a small, walled garden where the princess took her walks, and there, being careful not to use the paths reserved for royalty, they came to a bench. After looking around to make sure they were alone, Miriam sank down on the bench and pulled the girl down beside her.

"I'm worried about you," Miriam hissed. "I've seen you several times talking to the sorcerers' assistants—and to the slaves of some of the harem women. Do you think this is fitting company for my niece? I have some position of respect, you know."

Isha's face had been blazing with excitement, but at her aunt's reprimand, she turned surly. "Do you think I've only been trying to cultivate new friends, Dodah? Are you so unaware of my uncle's needs that you would think that?"

"What are you talking about? What's it to you what Moses does—or Aaron, for that matter? And what do you know about what's going on, anyhow?"

Isha slid a little closer to Miriam. "I talk to my uncle every time I'm allowed to go home for a few hours. I know that he's trying to take us away from Egypt. I know that, at least."

"And so you make friends with his enemies?" Miriam asked bitterly.

Isha looked more astonished than angry. "Of course not. You should know me better than that. But I have to learn things for him. Already I've learned a great deal about what the sorcerers can do and cannot do. Didn't you hear how Moses and the magicians turned their staves into snakes?"

"Well, of course. But what did you have to do with that?"

"I told my uncle that the sorcerers' snakes were only a sort of magic, not true serpents, and that a real snake could destroy them. I'm sure the information helped him make his plans. That's all."

Miriam stared at her niece in amazement. "But what if someone suspects you of being—a sort of spy?"

"Then they'll tear out my tongue or cut off my hands,"

Isha declared with the quick passion of youth. "Or they'll kill me. But I would risk anything to be free."

Why did Isha feel this way, Miriam wondered, when most of the Hebrews were so stifled and terrorized and sodden in their slavery that the idea of freedom never even crossed their minds? Certainly, until recently, it had not crossed hers. And if she, with her superior position, could be content, what right did Isha have to be rebellious?

"Most of our people will not agree with you," Miriam said coldly. "All of them have drunk the waters of the Nile since their birth, and they have no desire to leave this fertile valley, even though they are slaves."

"Most of our people are fools then," Isha said. "But they're capable of learning. The miracles that Yahweh has promised to my uncle will influence the Hebrews even more than the pharaoh."

"You seem to know a great deal," Miriam snapped, fully aware that what she was feeling was jealousy. "Has your uncle confided so much in you?"

Isha grinned. "He has told me practically nothing. But I've heard him talking to you, to my father, to Pagael when he comes to our house. And I've been using my head. It only follows that the more my uncle knows about the Egyptian court, the better off he'll be."

"And does he agree with you?"

Isha looked rueful. "Not him," she replied." He doesn't seek information, and he refuses to make plots with anyone. He listens, but that's all. He claims his God can do everything."

"You speak of 'his God' as though Yahweh were a stranger to you. Your father is a priest of Yahweh. You've been brought up to believe—."

Isha interrupted rudely. "I don't believe anything. When I put the ointment that the princess gave me on my father's back and saw the terrible marks there, I found it hard to feel any respect for a God who would allow something like that to happen to one of his priests."

"There has never been a god," Miriam declared in a tone that did not permit contradiction, "who saved his followers from pain or trouble. You talk like a child."

Isha turned away, then glanced back again. "If anything could make me believe," she admitted breathlessly, "it would be the faith of my uncle. I've never met anyone who believes the way he does."

Their privacy was suddenly invaded by a weeping slave who ran into the garden. "I saw it with my own eyes," the girl babbled, looking about wildly. "Where is the princess? Someone will have to tell her."

Miriam stood up and spoke sternly. "Tell her what? Stop that bawling or you'll wake her up. What's the matter with you?"

"The Nile!" the girl gasped. "The waters of the Nile have been turned into blood."

"You're mad." Miriam's sharp tone and the resounding slap she gave the girl should have jerked the slave out of her hysteria, but she only wept louder. And between sobs, the girl found words that seemed to transport them all to the bank of the River Nile.

Moses stood on the edge of the wide river, holding his staff above the surface of the water. Aaron, beside him, stared calmly at the surging crowd of Egyptians that surrounded them. Merchants, sailors, tradesmen pushed closer and closer to the two men.

"What do you mean his staff can do miraculous things?" shouted one man. "Is he a magician then?"

"He doesn't look like a magician," shouted another.

Aaron's voice, strong and smooth, rode over the babble

of sound. "No, not a magician! A servant of the Most High God. But he has power you've never seen before."

A priest, his head clean-shaven, pushed close. "What power?" he sneered.

"The power to turn the Nile into a river of blood," Aaron announced.

A gasp of horror and protest came from the crowd.

"It will be a sign of our God's displeasure," Aaron went on. "When the pharaoh hears of our God's anger and power, he will be forced to let our people go out into the wilderness to make a proper sacrifice."

An angry, threatening mutter came from the crowd, and the priest raised his arm as though to strike Aaron.

At that moment, Moses lowered his staff until the tip of it touched the water. Instantly, a spot of red formed around the staff.

"Fakery!" shrieked the priest. "It's only dye flowing from a hollow rod."

"You give away your secrets," Aaron jeered. "Could a bit of dye change a whole river?"

The crowd on the river bank gazed in horror at the crimson spot that spread into streaks, reaching out like tentacles. In a matter of seconds, the muddy water had taken on a reddish hue.

"Taste it!" Aaron commanded, but the priest turned to run.

"Somebody has to tell the pharaoh!" he cried and disappeared into the crowd.

A brash young fellow stepped forward with a show of bravado. "It will only taste of mud and dye," he insisted, stooping to touch the ruddy liquid. But when he lifted his finger to his mouth, a look of terror crossed his face. "Blood!" he gasped. "It's blood."

The dreadful verdict ran through the crowd, spreading

like pestilence. At first, the people shrank back in fear, but suddenly someone shouted, "Kill them! Kill the foreign dogs who dare to destroy our river!"

Fear flashed in Aaron's eyes, but Moses merely lifted his staff and said in a loud voice, "Our God will not permit harm to fall on his chosen one!"

Incredibly, the crowd became silent and motionless while Moses and Aaron turned and walked away. Not until the two brothers had disappeared did the crowd resume voicing its panic over the bloody water that moved so sluggishly along the river bed.

"It was as though the air had swallowed them up," the young slave babbled hysterically to Isha.

"Is every slave in the kingdom huddled in my garden and howling under *my* window?" The words were clear and biting, and the princess stood, naked and angry, in the door of her apartment.

"My lady," Miriam cried. "Let me dress you. Let me get your wig."

"Make her tell you," the slave girl screamed. "Make her tell you that the foreign god of the Hebrew people has turned the Nile into blood and even the pharaoh is helpless!"

Hapithet swayed where she stood, and Miriam ran to her. "Call Isha, too," Hapithet whispered when Miriam caught her. "Take me to my room. You must leave here. The palace isn't safe for you anymore. What can I do to protect a man whose god can destroy the Nile?"

Not until the princess had called for her sedan chair and insisted that Isha and Miriam be carried to their home by four strong men and two armed guards did Miriam begin to grasp the seriousness of the situation. Neither she nor

Isha said anything to each other during the ride to their house. True, they could have spoken in Hebrew so that the carriers and guards, if they were Egyptian, might not have understood.

But how do I know who can be trusted? Miriam thought with a feeling of despair. She had always known that men betrayed other men for money or power or sport. But the circumstances of her own life had sheltered her, even though she was only a slave. From the moment she had helped Hapithet draw the infant Moses out of the waters of the Nile, she had been surrounded by a kind of protective shield. Not that the shield was wide enough to protect her family, as Jehu's death and Aaron's festered back showed all too plainly. But she had rarely, if ever, been afraid for herself. Now she was afraid, so she and Isha rode in silence.

At the door of their house, the carriers stopped, and the guards assisted Miriam and Isha from the chair, averting their eyes and wiping their hands surreptitiously on their skirts.

"Thank you," Miriam said, yet even the guard who knew her looked away and failed to answer. She and Isha hurried into the house, but before she dropped the curtain, Miriam saw how rapidly the men scuttled down the street, as though they, too, were afraid.

The hut seemed terribly crowded. Rarely were there ever so many people in it during the day, standing up, moving around. For the first time, Miriam realized that her banishment from the palace was probably permanent, and she knew with shame that she would miss the spaciousness, the elegance, the richness of the royal chambers. I'll miss Hapithet most of all, she thought, glancing at Zipporah and Elisheba and seeing only a passivity in their faces. The princess, in spite of her age, sparkled with wit, and her comments were often profound. How can I ever look upon her as my enemy? Miriam thought with grief.

Without waiting for permission, Isha pushed herself as close to the knot of men in one corner as she could get. But even by the doorway, where Miriam stood in a sort of stupid weariness, the words of the men could be heard distinctly.

"Why did you do it? The pharaoh will have us all killed." It was Pagael who spoke, rocking back on his heels, squinting up at Moses with an expression of fear and curiosity.

"No, the pharaoh will not have us all killed," Moses said. "He needs the work force, and although he went back on his word about freeing us, he's afraid of the power of our God. He won't kill any of us."

"How do you know?"

"I just know," Moses insisted.

"Why doesn't your—our God soften the pharaoh's heart?"

Moses shook his head, honest bewilderment in his eyes. "I don't know. I only know that Yahweh has said that he will harden the pharaoh's heart and that many disasters will plague the Egyptians before the pharaoh will let my people go."

"What kind of disasters?" The voice was Isha's, and her eyes were sparkling as though this were a game.

Moses frowned. "I don't know all. Not yet. I know some. There will be death and pestilence and the smell of corruption throughout the royal city before the pharaoh finally submits to my demands."

"And will our swords taste Egyptian blood?" Isha's voice was bold and brash, and Miriam glanced at Aaron, hoping he would reprimand the girl.

But before Aaron could open his mouth, Moses spoke sharply. "Hold your tongue, girl. First, this is a matter for men. Second, you know perfectly well that we have no swords. Not yet. And, finally, only Yahweh will administer death. We are to do nothing." He turned to the others in the room. "Do you all hear me? It's not for us to do anything but to believe."

The light went out of Isha's face, and Miriam felt relieved that the girl had been properly chastised.

But Moses spoke to his niece again. "Nevertheless, Isha, you have a task to do. You and all the young people, the strong young people among us."

If the girl had felt any resentment at Moses' first words of admonishment, none of it showed in her face now. She waited, lips parted in eagerness.

"It is for you," Moses said slowly, "to convince our own people that we will be doing the will of Yahweh when we leave this place. Some of us," he said, glancing at Miriam, "have grown to love our Egyptian masters. We have bowed so long that we've forgotten what it's like to look at the skies. I need men and women, boys and girls, to go among our people, to tell them of the sacred staff, of the river of blood, of the promises of Yahweh. While the Egyptians are suffering from disaster after disaster, the Hebrews must be organizing for flight."

Once more Isha's eyes were blazing. "I'll persuade them to hate every Egyptian, to spit on them in the street."

"Foolish child!" Moses declared. "The Egyptians must never know that a rebellion is growing among us. They must think of us as helpless and foolish, as dirt under their feet. They must never, for one minute, believe that we have the courage or the intelligence to leave." He gave a short, bitter laugh. "They must never suspect that we are capable of plundering—in the most innocent way, of course—so that we will leave this country with gold and jewels among our belongings. For so our God has promised us."

He stopped and took a deep breath. "Your job, my child,

is a subtle and dangerous one. With utmost secrecy, you must persuade the Hebrews that they are human beings, not slaves. You must convince them that we can and will escape. You must teach them that Yahweh has chosen me to lead us out."

"Into the desert?" someone asked.

"No," Moses said, and his voice dropped to a whisper that shivered itself into the heart of every listener. "Into the land which Yahweh promised to our father, Abraham. Into the land of milk and honey, where we will be free and where the name of our God will be lifted up in every home."

Miriam looked around, dazed and confused. Something was happening before her eyes. The apathy, the weariness, the lethargy had disappeared from the faces of the people who crowded about Moses and Aaron. Their faces shone instead with conviction, hope, and commitment. The people were being changed!

And for this moment, Miriam, too, was filled with the same passion that motivated her brothers and her niece, and she knew that she as well had been changed into a creature of faith and courage. She felt sure that the change was as great a miracle as the transformation of the Nile into a river of blood. What she was not sure of was whether or not this faith and courage would last.

⸗ 8 ⸗

The days that followed were filled with prescribed activity, but the conviction that had filled the people that night in Aaron's hut wavered frequently into doubt. Surely, the Hebrews said, this is only Moses—reared as royalty, it's true, but only a normal man for all that. Had he really gained some magic power from Yahweh, the God of Joseph and of Jacob? Or was it all some monstrous joke?

Gradually, the crimson color of the Nile faded, but the air was foul with the stench of decay. The fish of the river died and floated, belly up, in the polluted waters, and the Egyptians wept and suffered from thirst and from a fear that was greater than thirst, especially when they discovered that the Hebrews were able to find fresh water.

But the pharaoh was adamant in his decision that the Hebrew people could not leave. The work of building the royal city went on with bricks that had to be smoothed and shaped with bloody water.

Then Moses raised his staff, and the land was covered with a horde of frogs. The infant frogs, which ordinarily would have been eaten by fish, floated unharmed among the corpses of their predators, and in a short time crawled out of the river and invaded the land. Women shuddered and cursed when they found the ugly creatures under their bedmats and floating in their cooking oil. Farmers plowed over the swollen green bodies, and the stink of decay grew.

Yet a small but brisk breeze kept the foul smell away

from the Hebrew settlement, and none of the frogs found their way into Hebrew houses. So the Hebrews began to tell each other that the God who had forgotten them, the God they had forgotten, was still able to do marvelous things. Once again, awe and reverence and hope filled the hearts of the children of Yahweh.

But the Egyptians knew only anger and despair.

"Cursed be the day you Hebrews first set foot in our land!" Muta, an Egyptian who lived close to Aaron's house, shrieked at Miriam one morning.

Miriam nodded solemnly, remembering the whispered words of instruction that had been passed from Hebrew to Hebrew. "I know how you feel, neighbor. I shudder for you, knowing what miseries you must be suffering. But it's not our fault. Surely you know that. If the pharaoh would let us go out into the wilderness to make sacrifice to our God, none of this would happen."

Muta scowled. "What nonsense is that?"

"It's true," Miriam said, her voice quiet and respectful. "Our leader, Moses, has asked only that the pharaoh let us go out, but the pharaoh will not. So the plagues come."

"The pharaoh is a god, too. He knows what's best."

"There are no frogs in our houses," Miriam said softly.

"I don't believe you."

"Come and see."

Throughout the poor section of the city, Hebrew women were taking Egyptian women in to show off their clean floors, their dry meal, their unpolluted bedding. And an odd friendship was growing among them, because the Egyptian women were afraid, and the Hebrew women pretended to be generous by sharing a little decent bread.

But when Aaron and Moses and Miriam talked about the situation, Moses refused to listen to all of the plans Isha and her friends had worked out.

"The less I know, the better off I am," Moses said. "I must put my faith completely in Yahweh, and if I start to think about what the people might accomplish, it will poison my mind."

"I'll tell you only, then, that the girl is clever," Miriam said, reluctant admiration in her voice. "By the time you're ready to move, my brother, the people will be ready to go with you."

"So be it," Moses said and seemed to dismiss the idea from his mind at once. "The pharaoh is as hard-hearted—hard-headed, I might say—as the Lord promised he would be. I can't understand why the frogs haven't forced him to listen to us. They've made a horror on the land."

"But not for the pharaoh," Miriam argued. "I know how his slaves will protect him. They'll keep him in his rooms, and there will be someone scrabbling over the floor every minute to make sure no frogs come near him." She paused and then added, "I wonder if the princess is being as well cared for? She abhors anything that crawls or hops."

"Well," Moses said in a heavy voice. "The next plague will be worse. And the slaves won't be able to protect the pharaoh. He'll suffer from the bites of lice as much as anyone."

Lice! Miriam shuddered with disgust. Loathesome little creatures, almost too small to see, and nothing to fight them with. At least there was no hair on the princess' head or body to harbor the tiny torturers, but would the servants keep her clothes clean enough, would they sprinkle the fragrant powders on her so that the insects might stay away?

"It hurts me that the princess might suffer so!" Miriam blurted out.

But Moses gave her a look that was level and uncompromising. "She'll suffer greater difficulties than the bites of insects," was all he said.

It was not the plague of lice, however, that finally gave Miriam the courage to go back to the palace. It was the plague of flies that followed. All her life, she had seen flies crawling stickily on the eyes and mouths of the ill, the helpless, the neglected young. But never had it been like this. Never had there been clouds of the insects hovering in the air, buzzing with an incessant whine that made people run screaming into the street, beating ineffectually at the swarms around their heads.

Incredibly, only the usual number of flies flew and crawled around the Hebrew houses, and careful mothers kept even those from the faces of their children or the faces of the ill.

One day on her way to the market, Miriam passed an old Egyptian man lying in the street, his face almost hidden under a black crawling mass of insects. The part of his face that was still visible was thin and brown, and Miriam was suddenly filled with horror. Was it like that with the princess? She ran back to Aaron's house to get an Egyptian shawl that had been given to her long before. She pulled it out of the basket in which it had been stored and wound it around her head and face, draping the ends over her shoulders as she had seen some Egyptian women do to protect themselves against the flies.

"What are you doing?" Zipporah asked as she stood staring at her sister-in-law.

"I'm going back to the market to see if any oil has come in. We're running low."

"But why dress yourself up as an Egyptian?"

"Why risk having someone attack me because they think I'm responsible for the flies? Better they think I'm a fellow sufferer."

Out on the street, Miriam wondered why she had not told Zipporah the truth. Why hadn't she admitted she was going to the palace? Because Moses would probably be displeased, she realized, and so it seemed better that she go secretly. If all went well, she could return to their house before the evening meal, and no one need even know what she had done.

The closer she got to the palace and the farther she walked from the Hebrew houses, the thicker grew the clouds of flies. Children ran howling from the torment, but there was no escape. Old people lay helplessly by the roadside, too weak even to brush away the loathsome pests.

Because of the flies, no one even looked at Miriam. Each person's attention was given to fanning away the suffocating hordes. And although the flies could not get to Miriam's face, they buzzed around her until it seemed as though the sound had worked itself into her head, behind her eyes, inside her ears. Her feet moved faster and faster as her concern for the princess grew.

There was no guard at the entrance of the garden, and Miriam made her way, unmolested, to Hapithet's apartment. She slipped through a door that was known only to the personal slaves of the princess and came at last to the royal bedchamber. A feeble moan drifted toward her.

The princess was alone. Miriam had expected a dozen slaves wielding fans, but instead the princess lay unattended on her couch, her narrow face almost black with flies. Her eyes and mouth were pinched tight in an effort to prevent the flies from blinding and choking her, but even so, Miriam saw several flies crawling up Hapithet's nostrils.

Miriam ran to the couch. With vigorous motions, she wiped the flies from the princess' face, then caught up a shawl that lay on the floor and deftly wound it around Hapithet's head, leaving it loose around her mouth and nose to permit breathing.

"My lady," Miriam gasped, undone by the pity she felt.

"Why are you here alone like this? Why isn't someone caring for you?"

Hapithet's hands came up like those of a blind person, groping for Miriam's face. "Miriam, my child, my dear one. You've come."

"But where are your other slaves?"

"Their minds are addled from the torment of the flies. Even the pharaoh must use his whip to control the slaves. I—I'm not strong enough."

Impulsively, urgently, Miriam spoke again, shutting her mind to the possible consequences of the action she was suggesting. "Come with me," she said. "To my brother's house. It's rude, my lady, with only a dirt floor. But there are no flies."

"No flies?" Hapithet's voice was weak and laced with doubt.

"No flies, my lady. Will you come? It's unseemly, I know, for a royal lady to go into the house of a slave. But, oh, if I could only take you to where the air is pure and there is no buzzing."

"No buzzing?" A faint hope colored her words.

"No buzzing, my lady. But the going might be dangerous."

"Better to die on the way than stay here and go mad with this horror," Hapithet said. She put forth her hands so that Miriam could help her up. "I'll go."

Miriam took only enough time to find a coarse, plain robe to throw over Hapithet's sheer linen dress. Then she led the princess through the garden gate and down the dusty road toward the poor section of town.

Hapithet, shrunken and hesitant, continued to walk as though she were blind, and Miriam realized that she must still be holding her eyes closed, afraid to risk opening them.

"Be glad you can't see, my lady," Miriam whispered in

the princess' ear. "The ugliness is too awful to be endured."

They walked through the frantic city as unnoticed as Miriam had been on her way to the palace. Each person fought his or her own helpless, hysterical fight against the droning pestilence, and so no one paid any attention to the two women who hurried toward the house of Aaron.

They were nearly there when the princess asked, "Am I going deaf? The buzzing is not so loud."

"You hear well enough, my lady. We're in the Hebrew quarter of the city, and there are only the usual number of flies here."

Cautiously, Hapithet opened one eye and then the other. But she did not relax her clawlike grip on Miriam's arm. She stared about her as though totally bewildered.

"I don't believe it," she whispered and was silent.

It was not until she led the princess into Aaron's house that Miriam realized the enormity of what she had done. She had brought an Egyptian, a royal Egyptian, into her brother's house. She had acted out of pity, prompted by an old love, but now she realized that Moses might be very, very angry.

As they entered the house, she was aware of the way the normal sounds of conversation subsided into silence. Averting her eyes from all her family, Miriam led Hapithet to a stool near the back wall and helped her to sit down. Gently, quietly, she unwound the scarf, forced several times to loosen the frantic old fingers that clutched at the cloth in fear.

"It's all right," Miriam soothed. "It's all right."

Still she was afraid to look toward the corner where her first glimpse of the room had shown her Moses was standing. Finally, when she had removed the scarf from Hapithet's head and loosened the coarse robe at her throat,

Miriam dared to stand and look at her brother.

"She was all alone," she explained defensively. "The flies would have driven her mad."

Moses looked beyond Miriam to where the princess sat, his eyes filled with pity and compassion.

But before he could say anything, Isha spoke up. "She's an Egyptian," she snapped. "If you waste your pity on Egyptians, you'll only be weakening our cause."

Hapithet straightened on her stool. "Cause?" she asked coldly. "It was my understanding that you were only seeking a few days of freedom to go and make sacrifice to your god."

Moses stepped smoothly into the exchange. "And wouldn't that be a cause, my mother? If any people strive toward their God, surely that's a cause." His eyes met Isha's and the girl's face flushed.

Moses moved over to the princess and knelt before her, taking her hands in his. "My heart breaks for you, my mother. I would do anything in the world if I could spare you added suffering."

"Anything?" Hapithet asked in a skeptical voice.

Moses looked at her squarely. "Anything short of displeasing my God."

For long minutes, Hapithet stared at Moses. Her whole body was shivering from the terror she had so recently endured and the strain of walking so far. But her eyes were as lucid and aware as they had ever been.

"And to show pity to even one Egyptian would displease your god?" she asked at last.

"No, not if the Egyptian were to throw in her lot with us and believe in Yahweh."

The words were spoken to the princess, but Miriam felt they were also directed at her. There was no place, Moses was saying, for an individual with divided loyalties. Even if the denial of one loyalty were to break that person's heart.

Hapithet smiled slightly. "And could the daughter of a pharaoh—one with divine blood in her veins—throw in her lot, as you say, with a foreign god?"

"Yahweh is a great and mighty God," Moses replied. "He has given a promise to me that the pharaoh's power over us will be broken. But it will be broken by suffering, and I cannot shelter you from that."

"She could stay here!" Miriam cried.

It was Hapithet who answered. "And what would you do with an old, sick woman who's accustomed to the care of slaves? No, my dear, I'm grateful for a few minutes away from the flies, but—."

"By tomorrow," Moses said quickly, "the flies will be gone, and the next plague will afflict the cattle, not men. It will hurt the pharaoh's purse, but not his skin. Please, little mother, feel free to stay in this house until tomorrow."

But Hapithet shook her head. "If Miriam can come back with me and stay with me until the flies are gone—" she began, seeming to accept, as all of them did, that Moses could predict the end of one plague and the beginning of another.

"Would she be safe?" Aaron asked, speaking for the first time.

The princess tried to shrug her shivering shoulders. "How do I know?" she whispered.

"I'll go," Miriam announced. "No one even looked at me when I went to get her."

"But when the flies are gone?" Aaron said doubtfully.

"Then I'll come home again," Miriam replied quietly, certain that Moses would approve of what she proposed to do. Someone had to take care of the princess.

Once more, she wrapped the princess in the shawl and the coarse robe, then helped her to her feet. Hapithet took a few faltering steps toward the door before she turned back to Moses.

"I'm very old and tired," she said. "If things were different, but—things are as they are. I may never see you again. The buzzing of flies cannot be heard if one has entered the House of Death."

"Mother!"

"No, my son, it's all right. I asked only that I might see you again before I die. And that has been granted me."

Moses embraced the small, trembling body and then stepped away from her.

"Come, my dear," Hapithet said to Miriam, holding her head high. "Come with me."

With no further word of farewell, Miriam and the princess walked out into the street and made their way back to the repugnance of the flies and the unreality of a palace where no slaves were in attendance.

As Moses had promised, the flies were gone by the following afternoon, their buzzing silenced, their dead bodies lying eveywhere in powdery heaps. Miriam, exhausted from the night-long battle to keep the insects off the princess, slept in a sodden heap on the floor next to Hapithet's couch. She did not hear the princess get up and take a small bottle out of the innermost section of a wooden chest. She did not even feel the final touch of the old fingers on her hair.

When she woke, the small vial had fallen from Hapithet's hand and rolled a few inches away from the trailing fingers. The princess, Miriam realized with grief and horror, had walked, of her own volition, into the House of Death.

Miriam stifled the sobs that crowded into her throat. There was no time now for grief. If she stayed here any longer, she might be accused of murdering the princess. She had to get out before anyone knew that she had even come.

~ 9 ~

Miriam looked for one last time at the quiet face of the woman who had been as dear to her as her own mother had been. Then, noiselessly, she slipped out of the room through the private door and into the garden. At each corner, she stopped and held her breath, certain that she heard voices or the shuffle of feet. But she met only empty halls and corridors. She was not yet outside when a shrill wailing from Hapithet's rooms told her that either guilt or the pharaoh's commands had finally sent a slave in to the Princess. Her death had been discovered.

Now, Miriam thought with relief, Hapithet will be wrapped and sent to the House of Death, given the dignity of preservation that her belief demanded. And though Miriam neither understood nor approved the elaborate embalming customs of the Egyptians, she knew how much it had meant to Hapithet and how much it would mean to her children that her body would not lie neglected.

Nevertheless, that shrill cry brought fear as well as relief to Miriam. She could only hope that the initial shock of finding the princess' body and the empty vial of poison would create so much confusion in the palace that no one would notice, or even think of, the Hebrew slave who had served Hapithet.

The distressed cries of the slave receded, and Miriam realized at once that the slave had run toward the main part of the palace. "Yahweh be praised!" Miriam breathed. "Blessed be the name of Yahweh!"

Trying to walk in a perfectly normal way, when every

fiber of her body longed to run, Miriam slipped out through the garden gate and headed down the streets toward the Hebrew settlement. She was only vaguely aware of the piles of dead flies and of the people sweeping them away from their houses. No one looked at her, and she kept her eyes straight ahead, pulling the Egyptian shawl closer about her face, even though she felt as though she might smother from the heat.

Suddenly she saw Peraton, the captain who had saved Isha, coming toward her. He can't miss seeing me, she thought, and if he is questioned, he will remember that he saw me walking away from the palace at about the same time that the princess' body was discovered. Panic churned her stomach and sent a thick flood of nausea into her throat. Unable to control herself, she turned aside and pulled the scarf away from her mouth so that she could vomit in the gutter.

Incredibly, Peraton crossed the street and passed by on the other side. It was as though her sickness had frightened him, as though he were trying to avoid some kind of pestilence. He looked away from her and so never saw who it was that lifted a shaking hand to wipe her lips.

She walked the rest of the way to Aaron's house in a daze. Not until she was safely inside and with Moses, who took her hands in his, did she begin to emerge from the cold terror that held her.

"You're sure it wasn't a natural death—brought on, perhaps, by the exertion of her walking here?" Moses asked.

"The bottle was lying on the floor," Miriam insisted. "Where it had rolled from her hand. There's no question about that."

"What about the stopper for the bottle?"

She shot a startled glance at him, puzzled by his question.

"The stopper?" she repeated. "What about it?"

"Was it in her other hand? Do you remember?"

Miriam tried to collect her thoughts, but they scattered in a dozen directions.

"Think," Moses begged.

She stared at her brother, and slowly she understood the significance of his question. She closed her eyes, willing her memories to shape themselves into a recognizable form. Against the darkness of her shut lids, she saw again the still body on the couch, one hand trailing on the floor, the other clenched against the quiet breast. There was a glitter between the thin, cold fingers. The bottle cap, of course.

"She held it in her left hand," Miriam reported. "I didn't notice it at the time—at least, I didn't think I did—but I'm sure I saw a golden stopper. Held in her hand."

Miriam and Moses continued to stare at each other, tears in their eyes.

"She must have made an effort to hold onto it," Moses whispered, "knowing it would persuade anyone that she had taken her own life." Then he asked, "Did anyone see you leave?"

Miriam shook her head. "I passed Peraton on the street, but he never even glanced at me. It was—."

"It was the act of Yahweh," Moses declared.

Miriam felt her head nodding in assent. "I suppose so," she said, "Since Peraton always seems to notice everything. But his eyes were blind to me this day."

Moses spoke slowly. "I don't understand it. I can't even begin to understand it. Not yet. But everything—even the death of my little mother—." His voice broke and he paused to steady himself. "Even her death is a blessing," he continued." Yahweh must have guided her hand. How else could I become a true enemy of the Egyptians if my mother were one of them? Her death releases me to be what I have to be."

"Do you think she knew that?" Miriam whispered.

Moses shook his head. "No, of course not. She only knew that I've been given a strange power and that I've told the pharaoh he will be defeated by it in the end. She was old and tired and frightened. Death was the easy way out for her."

"I'm glad," Isha declared. "I'm glad she's dead."

Miriam grabbed the girl by one wrist and forced her to the floor in the same fashion that she had pressed the hysterical slave to her knees in the royal garden. "Don't say that!" she hissed. "Hapithet was good and kind, and she loved us. All of us. Even you, though you did nothing to deserve her love. Until you know what you're talking about, be quiet."

Isha winced in pain, but did not cry out. Her face was stiff with pride.

"Besides, Isha," Moses said, reaching out to loosen Miriam's fingers from around the girl's wrist, "I thought you were learning to be discreet. Yet you announce in a loud, arrogant voice that you're happy for a death we aren't even supposed to know about."

Isha bit her lip while color climbed into her face. "I'm sorry," she said humbly to Moses, then turned to Miriam. "Forgive me, Dod, forgive me, Dodah."

Moses touched the girl's hair with an absent gesture and went out of the hut.

Miriam saw the embarrassment in Isha's face. She felt an unexpected urge to comfort the girl, but she ignored the compassion and held stubbornly to her anger. "She was my mistress for more years than I can remember," Miriam said. "I won't have her spoken of with disrespect. Especially now."

Isha, rubbing her wrist, stood up. "Nothing will be said," she told Miriam. "I'll be as quiet as you wish."

This sudden docility after so much arrogance was more

than Miriam could endure. She had been forced to swallow her tears when she had found Hapithet's body and during her terrifying walk home. But now they gushed out in a flood, and she covered her face with her hands.

At first, Isha stood quietly, and neither Zipporah nor Elisheba moved from the corner of the hut where they had huddled in silence ever since Miriam had come in. Then, suddenly, Isha wrapped her arms around her aunt, and Miriam felt herself being held against the sturdy, young body.

"Don't weep so," Isha whispered. "I'll try to be wiser. Honestly I will. Here. You're tired. I'm sure you never slept a wink last night. Mother, put a pallet on the floor. Come and lie down, Dodah. I'll sit and hold your hand until you fall asleep."

Still sobbing, Miriam allowed herself to be led to a dim corner and helped down onto one of the thin, woven mats. Isha, as good as her word, sat beside her, held her hand, and gently wiped away her tears.

"I don't seem to know anyone any longer," Miriam gasped at last. "You're one thing one moment and something else the next. Even Moses goes from sternness to gentleness. I'm so confused."

"It's because we're all changing," Isha said solemnly. "We're learning that we're Israelites, a nation of people— not just slaves. But some of us forget. Sometimes we think of ourselves as slaves, worthy of nothing but the lash. Even you, Dodah."

Miriam opened her swollen eyes to look up at her niece. "I?"

"Yes. You've been completely divided in your loyalty. One minute, you're hanging on my uncle's words—and the next you're grieving over events in the Egyptian homes. You've got to be one or the other."

The words were not insolent. Nor, Miriam felt, had they come from Moses or Aaron. Isha was stating her own convictions with the rare courage it took to speak so plainly to one of her elders. And Miriam reluctantly recognized the truth of what the girl had to say.

"Now that the princess is gone," Miriam said hesitantly, "there's nothing to draw me back to the palace."

"Nothing, Dodah? You don't have a longing for the children or grandchildren of the princess?"

Miriam shook her head against her pallet. "None of them. I was concerned only for her. When I cared for her children, I did it to help her. Now that she's—." Her voice broke and she could not go on.

Isha's face brightened. "Then we can work together, you and I. We can help my uncle lead our people from slavery."

Miriam met Isha's eyes. "Yes," she replied. "Yes, I suppose we can."

Isha became brisk. "But for now, you must sleep. I know you're exhausted. When you wake up, we'll talk. There are many frightened women." She glanced scornfully at Zipporah and Elisheba. "Many frightened women," she repeated, "who must be persuaded that Yahweh will save us."

"Just as he kept everyone from seeing me when I left the palace," Miriam said in a tone of discovery.

Isha nodded gravely. "Just like that," she agreed.

Stillness washed over Miriam. For that moment, all fears and jealousies were gone, and in the sudden peace of their absence, she slept.

In the days that followed, Miriam felt a new closeness toward her niece. Although Miriam had always been fond of the girl, she had been repelled by Isha's arrogance and pride. Now, for the first time, she saw virtue in the girl's strength. And as Miriam's understanding of Isha grew, the girl's love for her aunt also increased until the two of them found that theirs was a warm and pleasant relationship.

Even Moses commented on it. "You make a good team," he said one night. "With Miriam's wisdom, experience, and understanding, and Isha's courage and fervor, we'll have a combination that will be an inspiration to every Hebrew woman."

Miriam and Isha smiled at each other. Words of praise came so seldom to women that when they did, they were to be treasured and cherished.

Even so, it came as a total surprise to Miriam when Moses announced that she and Isha were to attend a meeting of the tribal leaders which was to be held that night at the home of Pagael.

"Why not here?" Isha asked.

"Two reasons," Moses answered. "First, Pagael's house is a little bigger, and second, he must feel important to my plans. As he is. As every one of us is important."

"But women don't ordinarily attend the meetings of tribal leaders," Elisheba said more in curiosity than opposition.

"Ordinarily, each woman has a man—husband, father, brother—to look out for her, to see that she is cared for and protected. But now, with so many of our men dying under the whips of the taskmasters, there are many women who will need leadership. I plan to put Miriam in charge of the single women. By that, I mean the widows, the orphans. Unmarried girls like Isha can still be the responsibility of their own fathers or brothers."

Isha looked so crestfallen that Moses laughed outright. "No, now, never fear. You'll be assigned as your aunt's helper. Between the two of you, you'll keep the single women safe."

"I'm glad, then, that I still have a husband to look out for me," Zipporah muttered, more to herself than to anyone else. "A man's care is a great comfort."

"You're right, my dear," Moses agreed. "But my own duties will be so great that I'll probably assign you as well to help with the column of women." And before his wife could reply, he spoke again in such persuasive tones that Miriam began to understand how he managed so often to get his own way. "For me, my love? Surely you will do this for me?"

Zipporah's submission was plain in her eyes, but her pride must have shaped the stiff words that came out. "As my lord wishes."

Moses smiled, drawing her into his arms, while Miriam looked away in embarrassment and disgust. "Your obedience touches me. Now, my dear, keep the children safe while Aaron, Miriam, Isha, and I go to the house of Pagael."

There were representatives of all the tribes gathered in the single room of Pagael's house. They had come silently in the dusk, and now they sat on the floor and looked at Moses, who stood before them. Each of them had glanced with surprise and suspicion at the corner where Miriam and Isha sat alone, and then none of them looked that way again.

Moses greeted the leaders, but his tension revealed itself in the way his words tripped and stumbled. After only the briefest of remarks, he signalled to Aaron to speak, then moved to the back of the room. Miriam wondered, seeing the gesture, if this were a bitter thing for Moses or if he were so caught up in his mission that he did not think of his disability as a hindrance.

"My brothers," Aaron began. "There is much that must be said to you. First, let me apologize for the presence of the women, but it is my brother's belief that they will be needed to help lead the people out. Thus, they must be acquainted with our plans."

None of the men glanced their way, but Miriam and Isha felt a lessening of the antagonism that had been so evident at first.

"The Lord, our God," Aaron went on, "blessed be his name, has spoken again and again to my brother. You have all seen evidence of this. You have seen my brother's staff, his leprous hand, a river of blood, and plagues of frogs and lice and flies. And you should know that, even now, the cattle of the Egyptians are suffering from a dreadful malady."

One of the men interrupted. "The Egyptian cattle? What of ours? Some of them are in adjoining fields."

"They'll be spared," Aaron replied. "You can trust your God."

The men glanced at one another, and Miriam saw apprehension in their faces.

"Now," Aaron went on, "you must know exactly what will happen. You must be prepared for that time when our God grants us freedom from slavery. But first, there will be other plagues to torment the Egyptian people—plagues of locusts and destruction and death—until finally, the pharaoh will give his permission for us to go."

"Why do we need his permission?" another man demanded. "Why don't we just go?"

Moses spoke quietly from the back of the room. "And if we did that, what then? Without the pharaoh's permission, we would be pursued and seized before we got beyond the boundaries of the city. With his permission, we will be able to get as far as the wilderness and there he won't be able to take us. His permission is essential."

"But how will we ever get it?" cried still another man.

"You must leave that to Yahweh," Aaron replied in a strong, sure voice. "Our God will humble the pharaoh's spirit and bend his neck. What *you* must do is prepare to leave the moment word comes. Every man in your tribe must be ready. There will be no time to pack our possessions when the hour to depart arrives, because we will be leaving in such great haste. So before that time comes, there are certain things which must be done. And it will be your responsibility to do them."

"Tell us, then!" Pagael called out. "Tell us what we have to do."

"We must gather up riches," Aaron said, "and we must plan a feast that will become a festival our people will observe for as long as there is memory of this place."

Whispers ran across the room. Even Miriam was astonished and she turned to Isha. "Riches? A feast?" she asked.

"Listen," Aaron said, "and I will tell you exactly what you must do."

= 10 =

The short walk from Pagael's hut to Aaron's started out in silence. Miriam sensed that her brothers were exhausted from the strain of the meeting, while Isha seemed to be in a cloud of feverish anticipation. But although Miriam ached from the labor of the day, her mind was whirling so rapidly that she felt no desire for sleep. Nor did she feel any of Isha's simmering excitement. What she felt instead, Miriam thought sullenly, was anger. It wasn't fair. Everyone had been given tasks of magnitude to do before they left Egypt—and she hardly realized how all of them had come to accept the fact that they *would* be leaving the land where they had been enslaved—but *she* had been told to cook a meal!

The silliest woman among them could prepare a meal, Miriam thought, but Aaron and Moses had told her that the task was to be hers. Not Elisheba's or Zipporah's, but Miriam's.

Anger coiled and bubbled in her mind as they walked along, and suddenly escaped from her lips with a short, exasperated sound.

"You said something?" Moses asked. He had been walking closer to her than she had realized, and he had heard the sound. "What did you say?"

"I didn't say anything," Miriam snapped. She longed to add, "And if I did, what's it to *you?*" But she knew she did not dare.

Moses was mild but insistent. "No. Now, you said something. Or meant to. And you've looked like a storm cloud ever since I explained the preparations for the meal. What's the matter?"

"It seems a stupid task to give to me," she sputtered, her vexation overcoming her discretion. "You gave everyone else important things to do—telling them how to wheedle gifts of gold and jewels out of the Egyptians, explaining how the men could build up a supply of arms, instructing Isha in the method of teaching our people how to get ready to leave this place. But me—the sister of the leaders—you tell to cook a meal. As if any woman couldn't do that."

"You're proud of that, aren't you?" Moses asked.

"Proud of what?"

"Proud of being the sister of the leaders."

"Why not?" she cried. "Yahweh had forgotten us—he had turned his back on us. And then you came back, and Yahweh remembered us. You've proven it a dozen ways, and why shouldn't I be proud that it was to my family that Yahweh spoke?"

"Grateful, maybe," Moses conceded. "You might be grateful that it was to the sons of Amram that Yahweh spoke. But not proud, my sister."

Miriam listened, and all her years of automatic submission to the princess, even when insolence had clamored at the back of her tongue, enabled her now to bow her head and lower her voice. "Yes, my brother," she murmured, but there was no submission in her heart.

"Did you want to be the one to maneuver riches out of the Egyptians? You who are known to so many Egyptians? You who might arouse suspicion more quickly than anyone else?"

This was an entirely new idea to her. "I suppose not," she said dully.

"Listen, sister," Moses said. "The task I've given to you is neither menial nor unimportant. This meal that you will prepare is no ordinary meal."

"I don't understand."

"Yahweh has told me what we are to eat and how we are to eat it. He has even given us the exact date. Just as I told the men at the meeting. The sacrificial lambs are to be brought home on the tenth of the month of Nissan, and they are to be killed and roasted on the night of the fourteenth as our last meal in Egypt."

Understanding hit Miriam with the force of a blow. "You mean," she gasped, "that we shall leave on the fourteenth of Nissan?"

"Exactly. And this meal, which is to be prepared precisely as Yahweh has commanded, will be your responsibility. Not only will you cook it for our household, but you will see that the other women know exactly what to do. How to fix the bitter herbs, how to shape the loaves, how to roast the lamb with the bones unbroken. This is no casual thing I've asked of you. So long as our people live and have memory of this thing we do, they will go on eating this meal."

Miriam's anger had completely left her, and now shame colored her voice. "I'm sorry, my brother. I had not understood."

"You are used to giving commands and to having your own way," Moses replied, and she could not tell if there was compassion or regret in his voice. "At the palace, you were a person of some prestige because of the princess. You probably feel that you deserve the same thing here. But we are all servants of the Most High God."

"I'll try," she said meekly. But even as she spoke the words, her mind darted ahead, planning what methods she might use to teach the other women.

"Good," Moses said briefly, and the rest of the trip was made in silence.

As Aaron had predicted that night in Pagael's house, the plagues continued to harass and torment the Egyptians who lived in the city of Raamses. And as the plagues waxed and waned, the Hebrews went on with their preparations to leave. They became subtle and sly, and each day the Hebrew women would report how they had received some gift of a jewel or gold, as the Egyptians attempted to buy for themselves the security that kept the children of Yahweh safe.

The tenth of the month of Nissan arrived, and although the pharaoh had not granted Moses' request, the men of each family obeyed Aaron's instructions and brought home an unblemished lamb or kid. It was impossible, of course, to keep the little animals quiet, and so the word was allowed to drift through the city that the Hebrews had grown tired of waiting and would probably hold their sacrificial ceremony near their homes. The Egyptians, who found this idea repellent, turned their faces away as the butchering was performed and the meat made ready for roasting. They were, therefore, unaware of the anxiety that mounted in every Hebrew home.

As darkness fell on the evening of the fourteenth of Nissan, the tension had reached an unbearable pitch, even though there were those who said it was foolish to believe Moses and Aaron, foolish to imagine that the pharaoh would ever grant them freedom. But in Aaron's house, only ordered silence reigned as the women hurried to complete the last tasks.

"Is everything packed?" Elisheba asked.

"Everything of value," Isha responded. "You know we can't take everything."

"Not that we have that much," Elisheba said dully.

"Still, there's more than we can take," Isha insisted. "Each person can take a mat or a shawl, a bowl to eat from, and either a basket of grain or a jug of oil. The 'gifts' we have received are packed in skins and will be hidden under bags of grain on the backs of donkeys. There is no room for anything else."

"Our spindles and looms," Elisheba suggested.

"Of course, if at all possible," Miriam said, seeing the impatience on Isha's face. "But all will depend on how quickly we have to leave and how many animals we will have for carrying the heavier things."

"Today is the day my uncle said we would leave," Isha said. Her voice was strained. "But there has been no word from the pharaoh. Nothing."

"If Yahweh has said this is the day, then this is it," Miriam stated flatly.

Isha looked at her aunt. "You haven't always been so sure," she said.

Miriam made no attempt to explain. For how could she explain what she herself did not understand? "I know," she answered.

Moses appeared at the door, looking tense and ashen. Miriam considered the intolerable burden he was carrying. If nothing happens today, she thought, if we're not released, then he will be made a fool in the eyes of all our people.

"Is the lamb roasting?" Moses asked abruptly, his eyes going immediately to Miriam.

"Yes, my brother. Can't you smell it? It's been on the fire for several hours now. Your sons are keeping watch and turning it so that it won't burn."

"And the bitter herbs? The bread?"

"I haven't set the bread to rise," Miriam confessed. "If I do it too soon, it will be ruined."

Moses shook his head. "It doesn't matter," he said." If we have to, we'll eat it unleavened." He looked around the room. "Everything is ready? Every person knows exactly what he or she must do? You've told the single women?"

"Yes, Dod," Isha answered. "They all know precisely where we are to meet and what order they are to walk in. I don't think any army could be better prepared." She smiled at the last words, but Moses took no notice.

"Aaron is visiting as many of the tribe of Levi as possible. Just as all the tribal leaders are doing. I don't think there will be any problems."

"But it's already dark," Miriam said at last. "And we haven't received any message. What are we going to do?"

Moses stared at her in astonishment. "Do? Why, we'll go to sleep, so that we'll be ready to go when the time comes."

Without further comment, he walked to the corner of the room, pulled his robe around him and lay down on the bare ground, ignoring the rolled and stacked pallets that stood by the door.

The women looked at him for a minute and then at each other.

"Call the boys in," Miriam told Zipporah. "If they bank the coals carefully, the meat will be safe."

Even as she said the words, Aaron arrived at the door, a small nephew on either side of him. "So we'll sleep now," he said without expression.

What greater demonstration of faith could there be, Miriam thought, than simply to lie down and go to sleep? For she knew that if daylight came with no word from the pharaoh, the people would never again believe anything Moses had to say. She considered this idea for a moment, and then she, too, lay down on the dirt floor and fell asleep.

The night was dark. Even the stars seemed to have disappeared, so that the sentries of the city found it easier to stay at their posts than to move out into streets that were pockets of blackness. Around midnight, a soft, clammy wind began to blow, and a sound that was no ordinary sound drifted eerily through the streets and over the thresholds of the Egyptian homes. Even those who slept in the palace, with its rich hangings and elaborately carved furniture, grew restless, and the palace guards found excuses to stay close to their braziers that burned in the pitiless dark.

In the center of the city, an Egyptian mother woke, her breasts full of milk, and wondered why her infant son had not cried out in hunger. Overcome by an odd sense of fear, the woman got up from her pallet and moved across the dark room to where her baby lay on his soft sheepskin. She reached out, anticipating the curved warmth of the baby's body, and touched only a chill and rigid form. Frantically, she scrabbled through the sheepskins, but found only this cold travesty of the child she had sung to sleep.

Her scream pierced shrilly through the walls of her house. And other mothers, waking to the pure terror and grief of that scream, hurried to comfort their hands with the living bodies of their own children. But every Egyptian mother, from the poorest, dirtiest peasant along the river to the royal queen in the palace of the pharaoh, found only a dead son. The agony grew and such sounds of horror spilled out onto the streets that even the priests in the temples shrank back from their carved gods who had once seemed to offer protection against the threats of the Hebrew who had promised this ultimate evil.

The cries of anguish woke Miriam, and she lay stiffly, listening.

"It has happened as our God promised," Moses said in a soft, excited voice. "And from the feel of things, it is still the middle of the night. I wonder—."

But Miriam was never to know what he wondered. At

that moment, the door curtain was ripped from its rod and cast onto the floor, and an Egyptian soldier strode into the hut, guided by the dim light of a small oil lamp.

"You!" he said roughly, fear and grief grating in his voice. He pointed a shaking finger at Moses. "You. Come at once. The pharaoh wants to see you."

Moses' eyes gleamed, and he shot a swift glance at Aaron. "May my brother come with me?" he asked.

"What difference does it make?" The soldier's teeth were clenched against the powerful emotions that shook him. "Just come. At once."

Moses stood up and arranged his robe and shawl. Aaron did the same.

"Bake the bread," Moses told Miriam. Then he took his staff in his hand, turned, and strode out of the hut, followed by Aaron and the soldier.

Miriam heard a sharp command and had a quick glimpse of the flare of torches. Then there was nothing to be seen but darkness again, and nothing to be heard but the terrible wave of grief that swept over every Egyptian house in the city. The promise of the Lord must have come true: the firstborn of every household in Egypt had been touched by the angel of death.

"Should we get up?" The voice was that of Gershom, Moses' firstborn son, and the sound of it was blessed proof that Yahweh had caused the angel of death to pass over the homes of his chosen people.

"Yes," Miriam said briskly. "Get up and gird your robe so that if you must, you can run more swiftly than a hare." She smiled through the darkness at her small nephew. "Then go and poke up the fire so that we can bake some bread. The lamb should be roasted by now."

"But the bread hasn't risen yet," Elisheba said. "Can't it all wait until morning?"

"Listen, my sister," Miriam said. "Even now, at this very

moment, Moses and Aaron are in the court of the pharaoh. I believe—and I hope you do, too—that they will receive permission to leave this land, to shake the dust of the Nile valley forever from our feet. We have no time for waiting. When they come back, the roast meat must be laid out on a mat, the bitter herbs set in a bowl, the bread, no matter that it's unleavened, beside it. Then when we've eaten, we shall gather up our belongings and leave. And our God," she said, her voice dropping to a whisper, "our God will lead us forth until we come to the promised land."

"You make it sound like a party," Zipporah snapped. "You haven't the least idea of what it's like to cross the desert. To be scorched by day and frozen by night. You haven't struggled along in terror that some nomad will come up behind you and slit your throat. You haven't been so thirsty that you would sell your soul for a swallow of water."

Miriam stared at her sister-in-law in astonishment. Never had she heard Zipporah so outspoken. Yet, oddly enough, Miriam felt no anger. Instead, she sensed the truth of her sister-in-law's words.

"You're right, my sister," Miriam said slowly. "I haven't experienced any of those things. And I don't question what you say. You have crossed the desert and you know. But I believe, I truly believe that Yahweh will go with us."

Zipporah shrugged. "What difference does it make?" she asked in a dull voice. "My lord has said we'll go—so we'll go. Just as we did before. There's nothing for me to do but follow."

"We'll do more than follow." The speaker was Isha and her words blazed with certainty. "We'll also lead. Here, let me take the unleavened bread and put it on the stones to bake. It should be finished by the time my uncles return."

It was almost as though Isha had a small gift of prophecy, Miriam thought in amazement. The flat, unleavened loaf of bread, hot and crisp, had lain on the mat for only a few minutes when Moses and Aaron came in the door.

"We have notified the tribal leaders," Moses said, "and the message is going from house to house, just as we had planned. The people are already beginning to eat the pre-scribed food, and in less than an hour, just at daybreak, we will start out."

"And the pharaoh?" Miriam breathed.

Moses' expression held both triumph and utter fatigue. "It is just as our God promised. The pharaoh now urges us to leave his city—insists on it, in fact. He has sent word to all of his troops, all of his sentries, that we are not to be stopped or hindered in any way. When we go, we'll be completely unmolested."

"His son?" Miriam questioned.

"His son is dead," Aaron said, "and his grief is as great as any man's. If he'd listened before—."

Moses interrupted. "It had to be as our God decreed. So I've explained, over and over. If the pharaoh had submitted to our first demand, no one would have believed. Not the Egyptians and certainly not our own people. Now, no one can help believing. No one."

He stared at his brother until Aaron finally dropped his eyes and shrugged. "I forget sometimes, my brother," Aaron murmured, "that it is to you that the word of Yah-weh comes. I say so many words of persuasion that some-times I think they come from me."

Moses did not smile. "I didn't choose Yahweh," he said. "Yahweh chose me. I may not understand, but I believe."

His glance swept over the people who stood in the small room. "I did not wish to set myself up as your leader," he went on. "Nevertheless, I *am* your leader. You must trust me—and obey me."

Why does he find it necessary to say these things, Miriam wondered, when he's said it all before?

"Come, my brothers," she urged. "The food is prepared."

Moses and Aaron had already pulled the skirts of their robes up between their legs, so that they could move freely. After assuring himself that his sons had also girded their robes, Moses took his place beside the roast lamb. He washed his hands in the bowl that Isha had provided, and lifting his dripping hands above his head, he called upon the Most High God to bless their going forth.

Then, as he tore the roast meat into pieces and began to distribute them, Gershom spoke up:

"Why are we eating like this, in the middle of the night, Father?"

"We're eating like this, my son, to honor Yahweh, our God, and to praise him for setting his people free. As long as there are men who follow him, this meal will be eaten. The angel of death has passed over this house, my son, and you are alive to prove his passing." Moses dipped his hand into the bowl of bitter herbs. "This will remind you and your sons and your sons' sons of the miracle of this night. So—eat, my son."

Gershom picked up his meat and herbs and ate eagerly. For the children, at least, there was no fear for tomorrow, Miriam thought. Only the adults could know that when they finished this meal and left this house, they would be setting forth on a journey of incredible danger. She leaned forward to ask Moses if he thought there was any chance the pharaoh might change his mind and send his soldiers after them. Then, seeing the expression on her brother's face, she sat back again and closed her mouth. No, she would not borrow trouble on this night of hope. Tomorrow would be soon enough to think of what the pharaoh might do when the first sharp pangs of his grief eased and his fury rose.

And the sons of Israel said to [Moses and Aaron], "Would that we had died by the Lord's hand in the land of Egypt, when we sat by the pots of meat, when we ate bread to the full; for you have brought us out into this wilderness to kill this whole assembly with hunger." Then the Lord said to Moses, "Behold, I will rain bread from heaven for you. . . ." Then all the congregation of the sons of Israel journeyed by stages from the wilderness of Sin . . . and camped at Rephidim. . . .

Exodus 16:3, 4a; 17:1a

= 11 =

A pale strip of green light suffused the edge of the sky as Moses and Aaron led the people of Israel away from the city of Raamses. Among those who followed were women who wept at leaving the only homes they had ever known, and children who protested the strangeness of the early hour and the fact that playthings were left behind. But for every one who wept or protested, there were a hundred others who went with joy. Wasn't this the moment for which their souls had longed during all their years of captivity?

There was no attempt at secrecy in the actual going forth. The pharaoh's permission had been reported all through the city, and the Hebrews walked unmolested through the dark streets that still echoed with the wails of grief.

Miriam and Isha took the positions they had been assigned—Miriam at the head and Isha at the rear of the column that consisted of several hundred women and their children. There was probably more weeping among her group than anywhere else, Miriam thought sourly. Wives and daughters would be obliged to smother their sorrow so as not to anger their husbands and fathers. But because her women had no one to consider except other women, they felt free to lament and complain.

Yet in spite of the freely expressed grief—much of it prompted by fear—the women walked in an orderly enough fashion, and all of them, even those burdened with small children or by old age, managed to keep up.

As the day brightened, Miriam looked about to familiar-
ize herself with their position in regards to the main proces-
sion of people. She and her group of women had been
placed at the rear, she realized. Only the shepherds and the
flocks of sheep and goats were behind them.

"See," Miriam said to Elisheba, who walked beside her,
"we've been given the safest place. Here in the back, we
are protected by the people in front and by all the flocks and
shepherds behind."

Elisheba glanced over her shoulder and replied, "I confess I don't feel much comfort in knowing that there are
only sheep behind us. The chariots of the pharaoh could run
them down like so many shrubs in their path."

But Miriam saw that her usual gloom and worry of recent
days had been lightened by this final miracle. All plagues
and prophecies notwithstanding, Elisheba must have been
unable to believe that the pharaoh would really let them
leave. Now, though her mouth was full of complaints, her
face looked strangely serene.

Miriam grinned at her. "No, now, I don't agree with
you. I think the fancy carriage wheels would be bogged
down in all the fleece."

Gershom, overhearing them, giggled and trotted over to
his two aunts. "Do you really think the pharaoh might come
after us?" he asked, but there was nothing but childish
curiosity in his voice.

"I don't think so," Miriam said comfortingly. "The pharaoh and all his people will be busy for days taking care of
funeral arrangements for their sons. He'll forget us soon
enough."

The child stared up at her with something in his face that
made him look strangely adult. "I'm not so sure," he said.
"I think it would be exciting if he came after us. We could
fight the Egyptians and kill them. We have swords and
knives and spears, you know."

Miriam remembered the efforts Moses had made to see that the men of Israel would be as well armed as possible. When she had asked him why such efforts were necessary if they were only doing the will of their God, Moses had looked at her with irritation.

"Yahweh will accompany us and he may defeat our enemies," he had retorted. "But he will expect us to do our share. To go out empty-handed would be to tempt our God needlessly."

Now she answered her nephew. "Yes, I know we have such weapons. I only hope we never have to use them."

He looked puzzled, then declared solemnly, "I shall watch every minute, so that when our enemies appear, I'll be sure to see them. And I'll be the one who will call for the men to take out their swords and cut off the heads of all the Egyptians."

As Miriam and Elisheba exchanged a smile, Gershom ran over to where his younger brother was walking beside Zipporah. After an animated exchange, the two boys darted away from their mother to join some other children. Zipporah watched them, and it seemed for a moment that she would call them back. But Miriam called over to her, "Let them run and play. Let them have whatever joy they can find."

So Miriam had begun the journey with a light heart.

But as the day dragged on, she grew more and more irritated with her little band. She had listened for hours to complaints and expressions of fear. For although the Egyptian sentries had all turned their faces away as the people walked by, although they now traveled in apparent safety, still the women were afraid. And they were tired, too. Their daily labors of gathering grain, grinding meal, carrying water, and spinning cloth had been back-breaking, but had not prepared these women for the exertion of walking for hours without a rest. Several brief stops were made to distribute water and some of the unleavened bread, but there was no time to stretch out on the ground and rest aching legs and feet.

The sun climbed high in the sky and then hung relentlessly overhead, while thirst grew more acute and tempers frayed. Just when Miriam had reached the point that she felt she could not endure one more hour of this misery, she saw Moses approaching her. He was riding a sturdy little donkey, and although his shawl was drawn over his head and face to protect him from the sun and dust, nothing could hide his blazing grin.

"Well, now," he called out, "I've visited every tribe except this one." The exaggeration of his words brought smiles to the faces of many women, and Miriam found herself relaxing and returning his grin.

"And are they all as weary and thirsty as we are, my brother?" she called back.

"More so," Moses replied. "Or so they would have me believe."

He threw his right leg over the donkey's back and slid to the ground. "Here," he told Zipporah. "Ride for a few minutes. It will rest you."

Her face lost its gravity almost at once. All she needs, Miriam thought with scorn, is a little personal attention, an assurance that someone cares. Well, all women were not so fortunate.

Moses fell into step with Miriam. "I'm sorry," he said quietly, "that I must push so hard, that we have had to go so far in one day. But I feel we cannot rest until we are safely away."

She stared at him in shock. "You think we might be followed?"

"We might."

"But the pharaoh promised!" Miriam cried.

Moses shrugged. "He promised us many things. Who can depend on promises?"

"The promises of Yahweh?" Miriam dared to ask.

"Without fail," Moses declared. "You'll see. But, listen, I came back to ask you to do something."

"Anything," she replied, wondering at her own willingness to comply.

"When we stop for the night," Moses said, "make every effort to keep the women in good temper. Perhaps Isha could get them to sing a little—or make a little music. Did you manage to bring any musical instruments?"

Miriam smiled, remembering the care she had taken to make sure that no one should see her packing the tambourines and the small drum. Evidently, she had not made a mistake in bringing them.

"Yes, I brought them. A few. I thought the time might come when you would want music made to the Most High God."

Moses nodded with pleasure. "Excellent. Music will lift our spirits. We'll make camp tonight near Sukkoth, and if all goes well, we should reach Etham tomorrow. Then we'll be close enough to the wilderness to be safe."

Before Miriam could answer, Moses had turned and was walking away from her. "Don't forget the music," he flung over his shoulder. "Your task is to keep up their spirits. Don't fail me."

Then she saw him speak to Zipporah and help her down from the donkey's back. Miriam noted with what gentleness he touched his wife before he left her to go on to his next duty. He spoils her, Miriam thought. No wonder she's so timid and so worried. She needs more responsibility.

"Listen," Miriam called to Elisheba, "will you and Zipporah take over my task of leading while I go back to speak to Isha? Just follow those ahead of us. It's important that you keep up the pace so that no one lags behind. And make sure that no one falls or gets hurt. I'll be back in a few minutes."

Maybe if Moses treated Zipporah like *that* more often, Miriam thought with satisfaction, things would go better. She strode briskly to the rear of the column of women, taking notice of those who limped, those who still wept, those who walked with a bright look of expectation on their faces. Within minutes, she was at Isha's side. The girl was carrying a child who slept heavily against her shoulder.

"How are you getting along?" Miriam asked, falling into step with her niece.

Isha smiled broadly. "I doubt that there were as many tears shed in all of Egypt last night as have been shed in this group. The children cry because they're tired or thirsty or bored. The women cry because they aren't bending over gathering up straw for bricks." Her young voice was sharp with scorn. "I haven't seen too many tears of happiness."

Miriam nodded in sympathy. "It's our job to keep up their spirits, your uncle says," she reported. "When we make camp tonight, we're to make music and to make them all glad that they're without a roof or a cooking pot."

"A huge task," Isha said. "What are we to make music on? A water gourd?"

"Well, it's not an impossibility," Miriam conceded, "if you'd be willing to do the blowing."

They laughed together, and Miriam felt a sudden prick of pleasure at the exchange of words. Just so had she and Hapithet talked. It was reassuring to find that Isha was capable of humor as well as loyalty.

"As dry as my throat is," Isha said, "I'd never be able to produce a single note."

"It won't be necessary anyhow. I packed some tambourines and a small drum."

Isha grinned. "When I imagined this escape from Egypt,

when I dreamed of how it would be, I never thought of things like making music and carrying someone else's baby." She glanced down at the child in her arms. "I had something much grander in mind."

"You may have grander things to do before it's all over," Miriam admitted. "Who knows what tomorrow will hold?"

Without waiting for Isha to answer, Miriam moved quickly away to take up her place at the head of the column of women. Zipporah and Elisheba dropped back a little with relief. They talked quietly together, but neither of them made any attempt to retain any of the leadership that Miriam relished.

Miriam walked along briskly, shutting her mind to the chattering of the women and children near her, letting her thoughts move as rapidly as her feet. She considered the many changes that had taken place in her life during the past few months. She looked back on her days with the princess as though someone else had experienced them. How could she have guessed, while laying out cosmetics in the palace, that she would ever be here, walking through dust and heat with no promise of shelter or sufficient food?

If it weren't for Moses, she thought soberly, I'd think we had all gone mad. It seemed to her that Moses had somehow taken control of their minds and their bodies so that they had all become compliant and obedient to his will.

The thought was a startling one. An ordinary man could not turn a group of slaves into a band of determined, aggressive peple, she thought. And yet that is what had happened. So does that mean that Moses is no ordinary man? Miriam wondered. But he had to be—he was only her brother, after all.

Yahweh had truly touched him, Miriam realized, letting her thoughts slow to a crawl. But then—what about me?

What about Aaron? We're Levites, too. We too are the children of Amram and Jochabed.

"The people are stopping," Elisheba called out to Miriam. "See. They're forming into groups. What should we do?"

"We're to fix a place to sleep close to the tribe of Benjamin," Miriam answered. "There. See over there, where Pagael is gathering the men together. They're all Benjamites, and we're to stay near them. Come on, call the women. There's enough room for everyone."

Her voice expressed more confidence than she felt. But no one must guess, she thought fiercely, how repulsed she was at the thought of sleeping here in the wilderness with hordes of people around her. For one terrible moment, she felt such an aching homesickness for the palace and the privacy of Hapithet's rooms that she could scarcely breathe.

On that first night, they began what was to become a regular practice. The leaders, after seeing that their people were settled as securely as possible, gathered together privately to discuss the events of the past hours and to make plans for the day ahead.

"We'll never be able to find our way," one of the tribal leaders argued. Although he tried to keep his voice under control, Miriam could hear how stretched thin with worry it was.

"I have traveled in the desert before," Moses said. "Don't forget that I lived in Midian and made my home with desert nomads. I'll be able to lead the way."

"You haven't even told any of us which way you're going!" Pagael cried out.

Moses shook his head. "I'm not wholly sure. I only know that we are to avoid the established way through the north because of the danger of armies and soldiers. But somehow, some way, I'm sure the Lord will lead us."

"How can he lead us?" The question came from so deep in the shadows that it was impossible to distinguish the speaker. "Can he come down and walk along the sand in front of us? Will we see his footprints even if we can't see him?"

Moses opened his mouth to answer, but was unable to say anything for stuttering. And Aaron only stared at the questioner in confusion.

Miriam, sitting in decorous and respectful silence, saw the discomfort of her two brothers. It was the first time she had known them to be without an answer, and at first she was uneasy. Then, unexpectedly, a warm tide of conviction filled her and burst out in words that she had neither planned nor expected to say. "He will lead us indeed!" she cried out. "Yahweh, blessed be his name, will walk before us like a pillar of cloud in the day and a pillar of flame at night."

The sound of a woman's voice so startled the men that for a few minutes, no one said anything at all. Then, without exception, the leaders turned to stare increduously at Miriam. Even Isha looked at her aunt with mingled amazement and apprehension.

Miriam herself was shocked at what she had done. She had not intended to speak out. Yet the words had come, unbidden, into her thoughts and spilled out as though she had been only a channel through which they flowed.

"What do you mean by that?" Aaron asked, his voice more amazed than stern.

She planned to apologize, to offer an explanation of what had happened, but instead she found herself repeating the same words in a positive voice: "Yahweh, blessed be his name, will walk before us like a pillar of cloud in the day and a pillar of fire at night."

"What are you saying?" Moses asked, as astonished as Aaron had been.

Miriam only stared at him. "I don't know," she mumbled. "I don't—."

It was Isha's voice that cut shrilly into her aunt's words. "Look!" she cried. "There! At the end of the valley, where the first tribe is camped. See? A pillar of fire!"

There was a long, awed silence as the men turned to look.

"Maybe it's a camp fire," Aaron said at last, his voice unsteady.

"A camp fire?" Moses replied. "A camp fire that climbs to the stars and does not fade? No, my brothers, this is a sign from Yahweh."

"How did *she* know?" Pagael gasped. He did not look directly at Miriam, but she felt that all of the men were slanting frightened, perhaps even angry, glances in her direction.

"How *did* you know?" Moses demanded.

But Miriam only shook her head in puzzlement. She heard the word *prophetess* handed from man to man, and at first she felt only great surprise. They couldn't possibly mean her. Still—how *had* she known? The sense of conviction that had filled her for those few minutes had gone and left her empty.

Then slowly, subtly, her old pride began to take its place. After all, as the sister of Moses and Aaron, surely she, too, was deserving of the special touch of Yahweh.

But she knew better than to let the pride show. She bent her head with an acceptable show of modesty that hid the fact that her heart was singing. If the story of her prophecy spread—and she would see that it did—then no one could question her right to sit among the leaders of the tribes or to be the one to whom Moses spoke.

⹀ 12 ⹀

Miriam, plodding along at
the head of the column of women, saw what seemed to be
a gleam of water dancing along the horizon. A mirage, she
thought, and turned to look down the lines of women. They
were getting weary, she knew. Some were ill, and more
than one Hebrew grave marked the way they had traveled.
Even the music that she and Isha provided around the camp
fire at night did little to brighten their spirits. Oh, some of
the younger ones clapped and danced a little, hoping, Miriam was sure, to catch the attention of the young men in
nearby tribes.

"I suppose it's only natural," Miriam had muttered later
to Isha. "Every woman thinks she needs a man." She
glanced up at Isha and felt a sudden stab of sympathy.
"Even you, I'm sure. This journey of ours doesn't promise
to be a good place to make marriage arrangements. Does
your father talk about it?"

Isha had flushed at the remark. "I doubt that he has time
to think about it," she replied. "But my mother talks about
it."

"When we've reached the land of promise," Miriam said,
"in a few weeks, when we're safely past the land of the
Egyptians, then we'll think about it seriously. There should
be some suitable young man."

So their conversation had gone, and now, as she walked
toward the persistent gleam of water on the horizon, Miriam thought more seriously about the matter. Were there

really any suitable young men left? A heart-breaking number had been killed or maimed by the Egyptian overseers, and every father had his eye on the healthy, strong boys who were left. She considered the unmarried men she knew. Well, she would have to speak to Aaron about it. Elisheba wasn't really capable of making a wise decision in this area. Fortunately, Miriam thought complacently, she herself had many opportunities while in the palace to see how skillfully matchmaking could be done. She ought to be able to work out something for Isha.

Looking up again, Miriam wondered at the bright line on the horizon. For it had none of the shimmer and haze of the usual mirages. Could it possibly be real water? And if so, why on earth would Moses have brought them here—to a place where water would have to be crossed? Sometimes she wondered about Moses. She loved and admired him, of course, and she would travel to the ends of the earth for him —as indeed she was doing this very moment. But there were times, she thought with exasperation, when he might do well to listen to the practical advice of a woman who knew how tired these people were becoming.

Isha was suddenly at her side. "It looks as though we're coming to some huge body of water, Dodah," she said. "I've never seen so much water in all of my life."

"Nor I," Miriam admitted. "The Nile is wide, but that looks more than twice as wide. Is it a sea, do you think? What do you suppose your uncle has in mind?"

"You're the prophetess, not me," Isha replied.

"Watch your tongue." Miriam's voice was sharp. "You don't ridicule gifts that Yahweh gives to His children."

Isha refused to look abashed. "Do you really believe it was a gift? Truly? Or just a—a coincidence of sorts?"

"I think you're insolent," Miriam retorted and turned her back on the girl. Even so, she could not ignore the brief exchange of words that took place between Isha and her mother.

"She's changed," Isha complained.

Elisheba sounded tired. "Haven't they all?" she said. "Your father and your uncle. Now your aunt. I don't even try to understand."

Isha said something else, but the words weren't clear to Miriam. She felt an odd mixture of irritation and disappointment that Isha would find fault with her. I had almost believed, Miriam thought, that Isha was closer to me in some ways than to her mother. Until that moment, Miriam had not realized fully that her long hunger for a child had been eased a little by Isha's recent devotion.

I won't think about it, Miriam decided, then turned her attention to the fact that the Israelites had stopped and were separating into their usual groups. Immediately, Miriam took charge.

"We're stopping here," she called down the line of women. "You know what you're supposed to do. Start the fires so we can bake the bread, and be sure to keep your children close to you. Don't let them go near the water."

"Will we never have time to make leavened bread again?" someone grumbled.

"We have more important things to think about than bread," Miriam declared. "Now do as you've been told."

She looked up and saw that the sun was higher in the sky than it had been the day before when they had stopped. Why were they stopping early, and what were they going to do about getting across the water? She needed to talk to Aaron or Moses to find out exactly what was going on.

She gave a few terse orders to Zipporah and Elisheba, then started toward the shore of the sea that spread out before them.

The water, deep blue under a cloudless sky, seemed to

stretch to the ends of the earth. Even though there was no wind, small waves lapped at the shore and left a creamy foam. It would be beautiful, Miriam thought, if only it were not so wide and they did not need to get around it or across it. When she finally found Moses, he was standing with Aaron, gazing across the water.

"May I speak with you, my brother?" Miriam asked.

Moses turned and smiled at her. "And why not? Do you have any problems? Are the women able to keep up? Is Isha proving to be as helpful as I had thought she would be?"

Miriam lifted her hands and laughed. "I came to ask you a question, and instead you ask me a score of them. I'll try to answer yours first. The women are doing as well as can be expected. Some of them are exhausted, but I notice that the others help where they can. A younger woman will let an old one lean on her shoulder, and they all help with the carrying of the children. Even Isha."

"Even Isha?" Moses looked surprised.

Seeing his reaction, Miriam realized how critical she must have sounded. "I don't mean it quite like that," she said hastily. "But she's young, you know, and—."

"Yes, she's young," Moses interrupted and turned his attention back to the water in front of them. "How are we going to get across this, do you suppose?"

Miriam stared at him in disbelief. "You mean you don't know?"

"I only followed the commands of Yahweh," Moses confessed.

Aaron broke in. "I tried to tell him," he declared. "I told him that this sea was here and that it would be impossible to cross it. I told him—."

Moses interrupted. "And I've told you: I don't listen to any man. Or woman," he added with a quick look at Miriam. "Now, you had a question, my sister?"

"You've answered it," she replied. "I came only to find out why you had brought us to this place. I can't imagine how we're ever going to get across."

Moses lifted his hands in frustration. "You and Aaron are just the same. Filled with conviction and faith one minute, and filled with doubt and disbelief the next. You've had proof upon proof that Yahweh speaks to me—and yet you question. You've got to learn to trust in him."

"But what if the pharaoh should change his mind?" Miriam argued. "What if he should decide to come after us? What if the loss of so many slaves should suddenly become more important to him than anything else? What would we do here, trapped by water on one side and Egyptian chariots on the other?"

"She's right," Aaron declared. "That's exactly what I've been saying. We have no proof at all that the pharaoh won't come after us."

Miriam and her two brothers looked at one another, then turned away. All of the doubts that had troubled Miriam since the day she had taken Moses to the palace came back, swarming within her head as the plague of flies had once swarmed about her. The sense of quiet conviction that had filled her when she prophecied the miraculous coming of the fire and the cloud was gone.

At that moment, a donkey came galloping toward them, and Miriam recognized the young man astride it. Joshua, the son of Nun, had been one of the first to embrace Moses' plans, and she had noticed then how devoted the young man was to the older one. Fleetingly, the thought went through Miriam's mind that here might be the perfect young man for Isha. I'll talk to her father about it later, Miriam thought before she turned her attention to what Joshua now had to tell Moses.

"It's true, my lord," he was saying in a voice filled with

panic. "The word has come down the line, and everyone is sure it's true. I've seen the cloud of dust myself."

"Dust? What cloud of dust?" Miriam heard herself asking even though she knew perfectly well she should let the men talk.

"Didn't you hear?" Aaron hissed. "It's exactly as you and I predicted. The forces of the pharaoh are coming."

Miriam's hand went up to cover her mouth as a wave of fear went through her. "Oh, no," she whispered. "Nothing can save us. Nothing."

"Our God can save us," Moses said. But even his voice wavered.

"A long way off," Joshua was saying. "They are so far away that nothing can be seen yet, except a cloud of dust. And their chariots move slowly, my lord. I don't think they can possibly reach us before dark, and they surely won't attack until morning when they can see what they're doing."

"What difference does that make?" Aaron said. "In the morning, we'll still be here, caught between this sea and the pharaoh's chariots. We shall die beneath their wheels."

"Would our God bring us so far just to let us die here?" Moses cried defiantly. "Would he have told me to come here just to have us killed?"

But other men were already crowding around, calling out in their anger and fear.

"Weren't there enough graves in Egypt?" Pagael shouted. "Is it necessary for us to die here in the wilderness with nothing to mark our graves?"

"Be quiet!" Moses thundered. "All of you return to your own tribes. Stay with them and give them an example of courage and faith to follow. And pray. All of you pray that Yahweh will save us."

"It's impossible!" another man cried. "It's impossible!"

"And since when," Moses shouted back, "has the Most High God been limited to doing only things that are possible?"

Moses had spoken with such intensity that no one dared to answer. Miriam looked from her brothers to the men who crowded around them to the waters before them. There's no way out, she thought, unless . . . unless. . . .

Excitement rose up inside her. Moses was right. Yahweh had performed a dozen miracles already and he could perform another if he pleased. She would set an example.

"I'll go back to the women," she said simply. "If you need me, call me."

Her obedience quieted the despairing men. They fell silent, and the fists they had raised in threat dropped to their sides. With scarcely a glance at either Moses or Aaron, they walked away to rejoin the frightened people who waited for them.

When Miriam reached the women, she found that the news had preceded her. There wasn't a woman or a child who did not know that, far to the west, the ponderous forces of the pharaoh, slowed down by the heavy chariots that carried arms superior to any the Israelites possessed, were marching inexorably across the sands.

But instead of the hysteria she assumed would sweep like a raging fire among the women, she was greeted with only a dull, apathetic resignation.

"It would have been better," Elisheba said wearily, "if we had died in our homes in Egypt. At least there might have been some of us left to bury the others. But here they'll push us into the sea to drown like rats. Those of us who aren't sliced in two by the sword, that is."

Gershom was wide-eyed with horror. "Is she right?" he begged his mother. "Is that really what's going to happen?"

Zipporah stared blindly at her son. "I don't know," she muttered. "I don't know."

Miriam spoke up briskly. "You're terrifying the child," she snapped. "His father doesn't believe that we're going to die here. Why should you?"

"His father," Zipporah replied, "hasn't given a thought to us or our safety since the day he claims he saw a bush that burned but was not consumed. Ever since that day, he's been driven by some—some passion that hasn't taken us into consideration at all."

"That's not true," Miriam declared. "It's just that he has more to consider than two little boys and one woman. He cares about *all* the Hebrew people." She turned to Gershom and spoke firmly. "Your father has promised that Yahweh will save us. That's all you have to think about."

"And what about you?" Zipporah's voice was tired and bitter. "Do you believe it, too? Are you filled with the same power of conviction as my lord?"

Miriam ignored the women's sarcasm. "Yes," she said in a loud, stubborn voice. "Yes, I believe it, too."

Elisheba and Zipporah looked at her with defeat in their eyes, then got up and began to make preparations for the baking of bread.

"At least," Miriam heard Elisheba say, "the children needn't die hungry."

Miriam turned on her heel, more angry than anything else. The first person she saw was Isha, running toward her.

"Have you heard?" Isha exclaimed breathlessly.

"Of course. Everyone's heard. Are you filled with the same terror they are?"

Isha looked surprised. "Terror? I don't hear any screams or see anyone trying to escape. They're frightened, but that's only natural."

"They lack faith," Miriam sputtered.

Isha shook her head. "It's natural to be afraid," she insisted. "I don't think faith is natural to most people. Maybe to my father and my uncle. But not to the rest of us."

"Speak for yourself," Miriam replied.

"Listen, Dodah," Isha persisted. "You're sure Yahweh will save us. Or you say you are. I'm not. I only know that it's better to die with my freedom in the wilderness than to remain alive as a slave in Egypt."

Miriam had intended to make a biting retort, but then she suddenly remembered how she had once said to Isha, "No god saves all of his children from danger. You're talking like a child."

So, then, what was the more faithful way? To believe that Yahweh would surely save his children—or to believe that it didn't matter whether or not he did, that to be free was all that mattered?

She turned away from Isha, trying to bring some order to her chaotic thoughts, and watched the huge pillar of cloud that daily went before the people. It had drifted to the west and was spreading out like a dust storm between the Israelites and the approaching Egyptian army.

"Look!" Miriam cried, pointing. "Look!"

For a few minutes, the people watched and none spoke. Then Gershom said in a high shrill voice, "The Egyptians won't be able to see us. The cloud will keep them from seeing our camp fires."

"And it's getting dark," Miriam agreed. "We'll be safe for this night at least."

Her mind was racing. Was this the miracle that she had hoped for, but not expected? Was Yahweh providing them with a means of escape? Perhaps, she thought, I should go to Moses and suggest that the people, under cover of the cloud and the coming darkness, try to get around the sea.

"It doesn't really solve anything," Isha said close to her

aunt's shoulder. "I'm told the land is marshy for long distances in each direction. We could never get so many people safely around the sea before the army caught up to us."

"Then have you made up your mind to die?" Miriam asked.

Isha shrugged. "Have you made up your mind that Yahweh will give us wings? I don't see any other hope."

"He could," Miriam argued. "If he wanted to, he could give us wings."

But the stubborn conviction with which she spoke did not reveal to her niece the fear she also felt. How *were* they going to escape? Unlike Isha, Miriam was not altogether sure that dying in freedom was preferable to living in slavery. Certainly, her life in the palace apartment of Hapithet was preferable to dying on the point of an Egyptian soldier's sword.

⸗ 13 ⸗

The wind began in the night. Miriam was unable to sleep, and so she paced back and forth beside the frightened women. She had looked often at the fire that burned on the shore of the sea and had guessed that the shadowy figures she saw walking around it were Aaron and Joshua. Moses, she had thought with asperity, was probably sleeping soundly.

The first gusts of wind, coming from the east, were refreshing and stimulating, but the gusts grew in intensity until they became a gale sweeping across the land. The women woke and huddled over their children, covering them to protect them from the sand that whipped through the air.

Miriam wrapped her shawl across her face as she had done during the plague of flies and went from woman to woman, trying to calm their rising panic. The wind whined through the air with a frightening force, and Miriam finally turned in a fit of anger to face the nebulous, hazy cloud that had formed a wall between the Israelites and the Egyptians.

"Isn't it enough?" Miriam cried, sure that no one would hear her above the shriek of the wind, "that we face death by the sword or by drowning? Must we be blown to bits on top of everything else?"

She glared at the vague, shifting heap of cloud. If the pillar of cloud by day and the pillar of fire by night were truly from Yahweh as Moses believed, then perhaps Yahweh was there in the drifting cloud bank as well.

"Do you hear me?" she shouted. "Do you hear me at all?"

"What in the world are you shouting about?" someone asked nearby. She spun around and dimly saw Aaron beside her. His hair and beard were whipping wildly in spite of the scarf he had wound about his head, and his face was only faintly discernible in the light that came from the low, hanging stars and the scattered camp fires.

"I'm talking to Yahweh," Miriam admitted. "How much are we supposed to endure—or has this whole crazy thing just been something that Moses dreamed up?

Aaron grasped her arm and shook her. "Don't be stupid. You're frightened and tired, I know, but you've seen too many signs of Yahweh's favor to give up now."

"But the sea, the soldiers, and now the wind!" she cried. "There's no help for us anywhere. Morning is nearly here —and we're going to die."

Her own words shocked her into some degree of calmness. She had been so certain, and now she was acting worse than either Elisheba or Zipporah or even the weakest and least faithful of the women. She stood, ashamed and silent, before her brother.

"Do you feel better now?" he asked. "Now that you've said the very worst thing you can say, do you feel better?"

She realized that he was smiling, and that his hand on her arm had become gentle and reassuring.

"I'm sorry," she said, her voice breaking.

"I came to get you," Aaron said. "Moses told me to come for you. You won't believe what I'm going to show you, but you're to be one of the first to see."

Without further comment, he turned her toward the shore, and Miriam, walking bent against the buffeting of the wind, followed him. By the time they reached the place where Moses and Joshua stood, Miriam was aware that the sky was growing lighter. Morning had not yet come, but it was coming.

When Moses saw her, he took her arm in a firm grip and pulled her to the very edge of the water. "Look!" he said in a voice that was hoarse with emotion.

She cast a quick glance at his face before she turned to look where his hand was pointing. At first, she did not understand what she was seeing. At first, she saw only the height of the angry waves to her right—and wondered if the sight of this stormy sea had completely unbalanced Moses. Why else would he be so excited over the fact that the waves were climbing to incredible heights?

Realization struck her. True, the waves were building up on the right, but at her feet, the sea bed was dry. As far as she could see in the dim light, a wide swath of land stretched like a dry path to the distant shore.

Well, it wasn't altogether dry, she knew, even before she had crouched and touched the ground with her hands. It was muddy and wet as the bottom of a sea would be, but the land could be walked on.

"I don't understand," she said stupidly, still crouching. "How did this happen?"

"Yahweh has provided a way for us to cross over!" Moses cried, his words singing with exultation. "What does it matter how it happened? Go and gather your women together—quietly so the Egyptians won't hear us—and perhaps we can get a head start. If we go quickly enough and quietly enough, we may find a place on the other side of the sea where we can be safe."

Her first thought was that he was wrong. There wouldn't be any place to hide on the other side.

And yet who could possibly overlook this incredible chance to get away? There was no eagerness in her as she ran to do her brother's bidding, but neither could she wholly suppress the hope that sprang up in her heart.

Word spread among the people with the swiftness of the wind, and the crossing was started without delay. Tribe by tribe, in the order assigned, the people walked across the sea bed. They carried their sandals and found the pathway cool and soft to their feet.

When it was the women's turn to cross, Miriam stood on the shore and herded her group along. The children stared, wide-eyed, at the angry water that roared away from the pathway, and yet their mothers were able to keep them silent. Their fear of the Egyptian swords must be greater than their fear of the water, Miriam thought as they passed in front of her. Isha brought up the rear, and her expression, too, was one of awe and wonder.

Just before she stepped into the wind-swept pathway, Miriam turned to look back toward the bank of cloud that still hid the pharaoh's army from sight. Gray as smoke, the cloud eddied against the lightening sky. And against its hazy, nebulous shape, Miriam saw the shepherds hurrying their sheep along, and she realized that even the creatures were silent. Or nearly so. What small confusion they made was concealed by the wind that still swept, screaming, out of the east.

Miriam started along the path that the wind had created. As she walked, trailing a little behind the women and only a little ahead of the shepherds and their flocks, she felt as though she was surrounded by a circle of silence. Or perhaps, she reflected, as the soft mud slipped and shifted under her feet, perhaps the quiet was inside of her. She felt herself suspended from all normal things, lifted up into some strange realm she had never encountered before. For these few minutes, she was safe. There was no room in her for fear or dread of what the Egyptians would do when the cloud lifted and they discovered that their prey was no longer trapped between their chariots and the sea.

"I don't know how it's going to help," she heard a shepherd grumble, his words muffled and scattered by the wind. "They'll only cross behind us and get us on the other side."

"Hush, old man," someone else said. "Just walk and hush."

The order and serenity of the crossing was dispersed when the opposite shore was reached. Seeing dry land so near at hand, the people began to run toward the wilderness, and there was nothing the tribal leaders could do to hold their ranks together.

Miriam tried to keep her group of women from scattering, but even they—at least the youngest of them—took to their heels. Suddenly Miriam was aware of a loud wail from Zipporah.

"Gershom is gone!" Zipporah cried. "He's gone!"

"Was he with you when you crossed the sea?" Miriam asked, speaking sharply in an attempt to calm the hysterical woman.

"No. Eliezer says he ran back to help an old shepherd he's taken a fancy to." Zipporah's voice was shrill with fear.

"Well, then, he's surely all right," Miriam said, too irritated to be consoling.

"But how do I know?" Zipporah wailed. "How do I dare take even one step from this spot until I know he's safe? My lord will never forgive me if I've let anything happen to his son."

Miriam felt her calmness slip away entirely in the frustration of this moment. There, before them, was a wide expanse of land, so they were no longer trapped. But instead of running toward freedom as the others had done, she was now forced to go back through the shepherds to look for one small boy. Zipporah was certainly in no condition to do it. She only stood there, wringing her hands and weeping like a lost soul.

"Don't carry on so," Miriam snapped. "I'll go find him."

She threaded her way through the surge of animals and humanity, stopping every few feet to call out in a sharp voice: "Gershom! Gershom!"

She realized gratefully that all of the Israelites had successfully crossed the sea. But far behind the shepherds, she saw, to her horror, that the cloud of Yahweh had risen and was drifting over the water. Even as she watched, the cloud became again the slender, drifting pillar to which they had all become accustomed and moved toward the front ranks of the fleeing Israelites.

As the cloud lifted, she could see the advancing Egyptians. The morning light glinted on their chariots and on their swords, and it seemed to Miriam no force on earth could stop them.

"Here come the soldiers!" she cried despairingly. Her feet felt heavy, as though rooted to the ground, and she knew she was unable to turn and run. Not only because she had not yet found Gershom, but also because she knew there was no point in running.

At that moment, she saw a small boy appear from the path that cleft the sea and stagger up to the shore. In his arms, he carried a tiny lamb, and Miriam felt a thrust of pity that this child had tried to save a lamb and now both of them would die beneath the wheels of the Egyptian chariots.

"Gershom!" she shouted, hoping to make herself heard above the wind. "Gershom, come here!"

At least, she thought, he could be held in his mother's arms at the end. She shouted again, feeling her own panic build as the first of the Egyptian chariots started across the sea bed.

Gershom heard her and came toward her, so concerned

with the lamb he was carrying, holding it high so that its dangling legs would clear the ground, that he was unaware of the danger behind him. It took him so long to climb the rise of ground toward his aunt that she could only stand and watch as all the Egyptian chariots entered the path that swept across the sea.

"Hurry!" Miriam shouted. "Hurry!" Though she knew they couldn't run to safety, at least she wanted to reach the spot where Zipporah waited.

Her voice sounded abnormally loud, and she saw that a number of people were staring at her. Then she realized that the wind had stopped. In the sudden calm, she could hear the calling of the people around her, the bleating of the animals, the metallic thunder of the chariots.

Gershom stopped abruptly and turned toward the sound of the advancing chariots. It was clearly the first he had seen them, and Miriam wondered what terror he must now be feeling. But before she could call to him again, she heard his high clear voice cry out in amazement: "Look, Dodah, look at the sea!"

At first, she could not believe it was really happening. Perhaps her eyes were dazzled by the sun's rays glittering on the angry waves. But the growing sounds of astonishment around her seemed to comfirm her own impression.

The waves, no longer swept up and held back by the steady force of the wind, were rushing across the path that had once divided the sea. And the mud, she realized, the mud which had been so cool and soft to the feet of the Israelites, had formed a trap for the chariots. The metal-bound wheels, heavy and cumbersome, had sunk to their axles in the soft sea bottom, and the chariots were held fast. Then, as Miriam watched, the waters began to flow east again, swirling about the chariots and drowning the soldiers who had driven them.

Gershom spoke up again in the sudden stillness. "They're gone," he announced. "Every single one of them is gone."

Miriam and the shepherds stared in shocked disbelief at the broad expanse of water. Only minutes before, the enemy had been nearly upon them. And now there was no enemy, and they were no longer pursued.

"Did you see it?" Gershom shrieked. "Did you see what happened? Did you see how Yahweh saved us?"

The child's words released everyone from the paralyzing immobility which had held them. A great shout broke out.

"The Egyptians are dead!" the cry went down along the columns of people. "Come and see. Yahweh has saved us!"

And all the while the news spread among the people, Gershom capered on the bank like someone gone mad. He had set the lamb on its feet, and there it stood, bewildered, staring at the little boy who leaped and cavorted and shouted in happy abandonment.

Like the lamb, Miriam stared at her nephew and then saw the rightness of his actions. How a child could understand intuitively that they had been granted one of the greatest miracles the world had ever known, she neither knew nor cared. Yahweh's intercession was clear. Who now could question the wind or the cloud that had hidden the actions of the Israelites from their enemies? Who now could dare to doubt this miracle—that a poorly armed, unmounted band of men, encumbered by their women, children, and flocks, had crossed a sea in safety while the chosen soldiers of the pharaoh had died in the midst of it?

The recognition of this truth flowed through Miriam's entire body, exhilarating her. All of her doubts of the past few months disappeared and were replaced by a certainty that burned in her now. Though she was no longer as young as Isha, she felt herself beginning to move in a rhythm with the dancing Gershom. She reached into the bag that hung at her side and pulled out her tambourine. Oh, now, she thought in a rapture of ecstasy, I will make music unto the Lord! And striking the small instrument against the heel of her left hand, she moved swiftly, exuberantly, into a spontaneous dance of joy.

"Sing to the Lord," Miriam sang, "for he has triumphed gloriously!

"The horse and the rider he has cast into the sea!"

The words rang out with the same uninhibited delight that directed her feet. She sang them again and again, and she was dimly aware that other people had started to sing the same words, that Isha and the other women were also dancing and shaking their little musical instruments.

With their singing and dancing, the people of Israel made such a din that those who had run ahead to escape the massacre began to creep back, drawn by the sounds of joy.

Gershom grabbed Miriam's skirts and spun in such a dizzy whirl that he and his aunt both dropped to the sand in a breathless heap.

"Oh, Dodah," Gershom cried, his eyes shining. "You're wonderful!"

"And why not?" Aaron stood beside them, his face flushed with excitement. "Twice now she has been given the words of Yahweh. She's a prophetess, a priestess. All Levites are priests, but few are touched by flame."

Miriam stared up at her brother. This was what she had always longed to hear, although in the midst of her singing and dancing, she had not considered it. But now, with Aaron's words ringing in her ears and Yahweh's words still singing in her heart, she knew that this moment was the supreme moment of her life, that Yahweh had touched her as surely as he had touched Moses.

= 14 =

The next two months, made up of long, bitter, arduous days, moved slowly by, and at the end of them, the Hebrews seemed no closer to the land of promise than they had been on the day they had crossed the sea.

In the heat of the sun and the desolation of the nights, Miriam had almost forgotten the ecstacy that had filled her as she watched the chariots disappear beneath the surging waters. Her skin had darkened under the constant sun, her feet were sore and calloused, and her ears were tired of the complaints of women who were as dark and sore and weary as she. The only people who were darker, she had once said bitterly to Isha, were the small band of Cushites who had thrown in their lot with the Hebrews when they had encountered them at Elim. But they were no longer in Elim with its palms and tamerisks and wells of sweet water. They were in the trackless, dry wilderness of Sin.

And Miriam, like everyone else, was hungry. She knew that their meal and oil supplies were all but gone, and what little was left had to be saved for the leaders and the children. The rest of them would just have to try to survive. Miriam could see flesh melting from the bodies of the women, and Isha, once slender, had become emaciated. As for herself, Miriam knew that it would take a long time for her to become emaciated or even slender, but still her clothes hung with slackness and the cord about her waist was no longer tied in the usual place.

And the people complained more each day. It was, in fact, the bitterness of some of their complaints that caused Miriam to pull away from her usual place late one afternoon so that she could walk alone, her thoughts uninterrupted. Instead, her mind twisted and turned in endless confusion.

She was aware of a tug at her skirt, and when she looked down, she saw Gershom trotting along beside her.

"Dodah," he whined, "I'm hungry."

"So am I," she snapped, then felt ashamed. It would never do, she thought, to let the children know that the adults were as vulnerable as they were. "But we'll be stopping before too long," she forced herself to add with a smile. "I'm sure that there will be a little bread—perhaps even a piece or two of dried fruit. You'll see."

"Honest?" Anxiety thinned his voice.

With effort, Miriam managed a light caress on the boy's tousled head. She supposed she was almost like a grandmother to Gershom, and the idea was gratifying to her. Her maternal heart had always had to be satisfied with someone else's children, she thought—the children of the princess, of Elisheba, and now of Zipporah. She supposed it had all begun when, as a child herself, she had been required to assume responsibility for her younger brother. Well, if Yahweh had seen fit to keep her childless during her brief marriage to Jehu, at least he had given her the ability to love children who had not been born to her.

"Honest!" she promised.

"I hope we stop soon," he confided.

"As soon as there's water," she assured him. "I'm sure your father will stop as soon as he finds water."

Gershom kicked up a little sand with his foot and smiled up at his aunt. "Wouldn't it be nice, Dodah, if we found a city just over the edge of the hill there—a city with a marketplace filled with food? Melons and fish and—and even pomegranates?''

She grinned down at him, entering into his fancy. "And deep wells,'' she agreed. "And fields of grain to grind into meal—even groves of olive trees.''

He grew suddenly realistic. "But there won't be, will there?'' he asked sadly.

"Probably not.'' She saw no reason to be less than honest with him. "But your father has always found a way out of every difficulty.''

"Do you think my father is magic?'' he asked abruptly. "Some of the boys tell me my father is a sorcerer.''

"No, he is not!'' Miriam's voice was harsh. "When you hear people say that, you must tell them that he is not a sorcerer, but a man to whom Yahweh speaks.''

"They say—the boys, I mean—that he'll find food for us,'' Gershom argued. "They say that my father will work a magic spell.''

"He'll do nothing of the sort,'' Miriam snapped. "Don't listen to such nonsense. Your father's abilities are not magic —they're gifts from Yahweh.''

But even as she spoke, she knew that unless something happened soon, they would all starve. So something *had* to happen. Perhaps not today nor tomorrow, but soon. Their supplies were nearly depleted, and there seemed to be no hope. They would never find Gershom's dream city in this wilderness—or, for that matter, the fields and groves that filled her own fantasies. There was nothing here but dried, cracked earth, angular hills, and parched valleys.

As she had predicted, the people were brought to a halt while the sun was still high in the sky, and the routine of camp-making was begun. Rough cloth shelters were erected by those who had been farsighted enough to bring lengths of woven material, and camp fires were started from the coals that had been carefully carried from the last camp-site.

Miriam urged Gershom to find Eliezer and play with him, so that their mother might have some rest from her fretful younger son. Then she went in search of Isha. She found her niece crouched on the ground, staring vacantly into a small piece of burnished metal.

"Look at me," Isha wailed. "I'm as black as any desert nomad or even some of the Cushites. My hair is like straw —and look at my hands. Who would ever guess that I was once fair with hands softened by the most expensive oils in Egypt?"

Miriam stood looking down at her niece. It wasn't like Isha to be so concerned about her looks. "No one cares how you look," she said gently. "Everyone looks the same."

"It doesn't matter to you or my mother," Isha said bluntly. "You're too old for it to matter. But I'm young and—."

"You're hungry," Miriam declared. "Everything seems worse because you haven't had enough to eat for days."

"I ought to be able to stand that," Isha cried. "If I really care about our freedom . . ."

"An empty belly doesn't leave much room for dreams and visions," Miriam replied. "At least in Egypt, we had—."

"Don't," Isha begged. "Don't you be one of them, too."

"One of them?"

"One of the people who are constantly saying that we would have been better off in slavery. Food isn't every-thing, and my injured vanity over how I look is wicked. It's —it's just that . . ."

"Just what?" There was something in Isha's voice, Miriam realized, that suggested the girl was truly disturbed.

Isha's head drooped. "It's just that no man would desire me now. Not the way I am."

Miriam made a sharp noise of exasperation. "It's not fair," she said. "It's just not fair to young people like you who are ready for marriage that we have no time for match-making. But don't worry—every girl in every tribe looks as you do, and the men will care more about who your parents and grandparents are than how you look."

"The Cushite girls are dark," Isha mourned, "but their skin is soft and smooth."

"The Cushite girls are foreigners. They're not children of Abraham."

"Some of them are starting to worship my father's God," Isha argued. "Oh, I agree that they're foreigners, that they don't look and think as we do, but my father says that if they worship Yahweh—."

"Well, what does *that* matter anyhow?" Miriam interrupted her. "The boys of our tribes will prefer our own girls. Don't think about it. The thing that's important now is food."

But Isha wasn't listening. She was staring at something in the distance. "Look," she said. "Over there, see? Several men coming on donkeys. They're surely not one of us."

Miriam shaded her eyes and squinted at the strangers. "No," she agreed. "They look different. But they can't be enemies—just three men like that. Or are there more of them?"

"Four, I think. But they're leading extra donkeys."

Isha dropped her small piece of metal into a pouch she wore about her neck and stood up. "They're coming toward the women," she announced. "And they seem to be making signs of friendship. I wonder who they are."

The men were close enough now that Miriam could see

their faces. They were dark and wore the burnooses of nomads, but their teeth shone in wide smiles.

Miriam heard a shrill cry and then saw Gershom racing toward the strangers. "It's my uncle!" she heard him shout. "It's my uncle from Midian."

Immediately, Zipporah and Eliezer got to their feet and joined in the race across the sand. As Miriam watched, the leader jumped from his donkey and threw his arms about his two small nephews. Then, standing erect again, he embraced Zipporah and kissed her cheek.

Miriam spoke softly to Isha. "Had she said anything to you about being so close to her home?"

Isha shook her head. "No, but now that you mention it, I've noticed that she has seemed more cheerful lately. Maybe she was hoping for something like this."

Zipporah, laughing excitedly, came toward them, followed by the tall bearded man with Gershom and Eliezer hanging on his hands.

"This is my sister's husband, Boz," she announced. "And this, my lord, is my husband's sister, Miriam, and his niece, Isha. Boz has come to take me home for a short time," she concluded.

"Does my brother know of this?" Miriam demanded after she had bowed her head courteously to Boz.

"It was he who sent a message to my father-in-law," Boz explained. "We are staying not too far from here, and Moses found out about it somehow. He always did have an uncanny ability to tell who was where in the wilderness."

"It will mean three fewer people to feed," Zipporah said, her face puckering anxiously. "For just a few weeks."

It seemed things were always made easy for Zipporah, Miriam thought with a stab of jealousy. Why was it that some women were protected and cherished, while others had to claw and scratch for everything they had?

But she only asked politely, "The children will go, too, of course?"

Zipporah nodded. "Maybe by the time my father brings us back, my husband will have found a place where food is plentiful and everyone has enough water to drink."

"And are you leaving right away?"

"As soon as we can find my husband to tell him that Boz has come."

"With donkeys to ride, you should be able to find him in a short time," Miriam said, trying to keep the bitterness out of her voice. She was glad, she told herself, that the little boys would be taken to a place where they would be fed and sheltered. And surely she didn't begrudge Zipporah this time of relief and peace? Yet she could not suppress her resentment altogether. Zipporah's loyalty to her husband, she felt, ought to have been so great that nothing else would matter.

But Zipporah, in her excitement, seemed not to notice the edge in Miriam's voice, and she threw her arms around Miriam, then Isha. Her face was shining. "I wish my father had enough to feed everyone," she whispered. "But there's hardly ever more than enough for the family."

"Don't worry about it," Miriam managed to say. "Go in the peace of Yahweh."

Gershom hugged Miriam. "Come with us, Dodah," he begged. "My uncle will show you where the best springs are and there's always enough to eat. Even quail sometimes."

"No, my place is here," Miriam said, her voice stiff with pride. Then she looked down into Gershom's face and softened. "I'll be waiting for your return," she said, smiling. "Maybe you'll be able to bring me a small piece of bread. Would you do that for me?"

"I will," Gershom promised before he ran to where his

uncle was holding a donkey in readiness. Clambering up on the beast's shaggy back, Gershom waved at Miriam and Isha. "I'll miss you," he called, then turned his donkey's head in the direction his uncle indicated.

A few minutes later, they were gone, and Miriam turned to Isha with a sense of desolation. "It doesn't seem fair," she began, but Isha spoke up resolutely.

"Don't forget, Dodah, that it was my uncle who made the arrangements. He must have wanted this."

"I suppose," Miriam conceded. "Evidently they're the only ones that matter to him. He doesn't care how hungry *I* get, or you—or how much extra work we shall have to do now with Zipporah gone," she added.

"She wasn't made for hardship," Isha said. "And the boys are still very young. Besides, they aren't necessary here. It's more important to my uncle, I'm sure, that they be safe. But he *needs* you and me. He needs us to lead the women and to—well, to do whatever has to be done."

"You're probably right," Miriam said slowly. "But it's not fair that some women have more than others."

Isha nodded. "I understand, Dodah. But you know what I think? I think you were right when you said everything seems worse just now because we're so hungry. No wonder we're both jealous of Zipporah. Tonight she'll be eating hot leavened bread and maybe soup with leeks in it."

Miriam was aware of the way her mouth watered at the thought and of a sudden grinding pain in her stomach. Unless something happened, she thought bitterly, they would all end up as corpses in this wilderness. Then nothing would be left of Moses and his vision but his two sons who, safe in their grandfather's care, would soon forget their father's dream.

≈ 15 ≈

Although Moses had not spent much time with either his wife or his sons since leaving Egypt, it seemed to Miriam that he was strangely lonely after they had gone to be with Zipporah's family. He seemed to seek out the company of both Miriam and Isha, as though he needed human closeness even though he walked intimately with his God.

Miriam grew to look forward to seeing her brother each day and exchanging ideas with him. To her delight, he seemed to have unusual confidence in her, and he was willing to express his doubts to her as well as his hopes. She was soon able to tell, even before he spoke of it, when Moses had been in communication with his God. There was a luminous look to his face, a glow in his eyes that spoke more vividly than words. And she discovered that after he had spoken with Yahweh, Moses' confidence could not be shaken by any worries that might torment her. She also learned, however, that Moses could not always choose the time when Yahweh would speak to him. He was, as he admitted to Miriam, forced to wait upon the Lord. She was sure she could never have matched her brother's patience, and she was equally sure she could not have been as humble as he was. If the Lord would speak to me, she thought in her despair over their lack of food, I would demand his attention whenever *I* wanted it.

One morning, shortly after daybreak, as Miriam was helping to distribute the pitifully small amount of food they had left, she looked up to see Moses striding toward her. She knew that he ate no more than anyone else, and yet he moved with the vigor of a young and healthy man. She herself felt as though she were a million years old, and she knew that when she walked, she shuffled her feet in the listless, weary way of the aged.

"Come," Moses called as soon as he was within speaking distance, "Come and talk with me. I have something to tell you."

She opened her lips to suggest that he wait until all the food had been distributed, but before she could say anything, she caught a clear look at her brother's face and was shaken by the blazing joy she saw there. Not only has he spoken with Yahweh, Miriam thought, but he has received good news. She thrust the jar she was holding into Elisheba's hands and turned to follow Moses away from the throng of hungry women.

They walked, without speaking, for a short distance and then Moses pointed to a spot where a jutting ledge of rock threw an elongated wedge of shadow on the ground. Even though the sun was just rising over the rim of the sky, the air was already hot. Miriam dropped gratefully to the ground, hardly aware that she had grown so comfortable with her brother that she dared sit down before he did.

"I've spoken with Yahweh, blessed be his name," Moses announced. "And he has promised great and wonderful things. I've told Aaron and the other tribal leaders about it, and now I want to tell you."

She nodded wearily, waiting for her brother to go on.

"Yahweh has promised that we won't be hungry any longer," Moses said with suppressed excitement. "He's going to meet our every need."

"How?" she asked at once.

Her question was too abrupt for courtesy, but Moses

seemed hardly to notice. "The Lord has told me that he will rain down bread for us every morning—and that for at least one evening, there will be flesh to eat."

Miriam looked at him, feeling almost embarrassed by his exuberance. "Rain bread?" she asked skeptically. "Oh, come, my brother, you can't really expect us to believe anything so—so incredible. So impossible."

"Everything that has happened to us has been impossible," Moses replied. "Everything."

"But to *rain* bread," Miriam argued. "I can't even imagine loaves of bread tumbling down from the sky." She could not refrain from laughing a little. "Will it be leavened or unleavened bread, my brother?"

Moses frowned at her levity, and after a second or two of his level scrutiny, her eyes fell.

"Don't be childish," he rebuked her. "Just be grateful for the promise of bread."

"I—I guess I find it hard to believe," she admitted.

"Well, it won't be loaves, anyhow," Moses said, "because Yahweh told me that we are to gather it up in baskets or jars. Each family is to gather up an omer of it—that couldn't be loaves—no more, no less."

"That sounds as though it might be grain." In spite of herself, Miriam felt again the faint wash of hope that Moses always implanted in her and in all the people. "Could grain fall down from heaven?" she asked.

"I have no idea." His words were clipped and impatient. "I only know that for six days, we are to gather it up, and on the sixth day, we must gather a double amount."

"Why?"

"Because the seventh day is to be a sabbath unto the Lord," Moses announced in a voice of hushed wonder. "A holy day set aside for worship."

Miriam felt bewildered. True, Moses had insisted ever since they left Egypt that one day out of seven must be a day of rest and silence with some sort of small sacrifice made to the Lord. But she had thought of this as her brother's whim —or perhaps some strange notion he had picked up from the Midianites. Now he was saying that the Lord had decreed it.

"I think you'll have a hard time persuading the people that they must not go out to gather up this heavenly bread on the seventh day," she demurred. "I can't imagine that they will be willing to let it lie there on the ground while they observe a time of sabbath."

Moses' eyes twinkled. "I notice you're beginning to accept the fact that there *will* be something lying on the ground."

She felt her face flushing. "It's hard to remain skeptical around you, my brother," she replied.

"And it is impossible to be skeptical when the Lord has spoken," Moses said. "Besides, you won't have to worry about the people's greed on the seventh day. There won't be any rain of bread on that day."

She was sure her face reflected her doubt. "None on that day?" she repeated after him. "Well, if that's true, then I suppose we won't have to worry about that particular greed. But what of the other six days? What's to prevent some ambitious person gathering up two or even three omers?"

Moses shook his head. "I don't know. That much hasn't been made clear to me. I only know that we're to gather up what the Lord provides before the sun gets too high. Tonight we'll have flesh to eat, and tomorrow morning, bread will rain down from heaven."

Maybe the sun and his worries have addled his thinking, Miriam thought, but somehow she forced herself to smile as though she accepted every word. "What do you want me to do?" she asked.

"Nothing particularly. I just wanted to tell you about it.

I wanted you to know that it's going to happen."

"I'm grateful for your confidence," she admitted honestly. "And you don't want me to tell the women?" she asked finally.

"Oh, that? Yes, yes, I do. Tell them that tonight we will eat flesh. Tonight there will be a feast in the wilderness. No one will go to sleep with an empty belly tonight." He laughed like a child who has been entrusted with an exciting secret.

"I'll tell them," Miriam agreed, "but I don't think they'll believe it."

"Fortunately," Moses said dryly, "the actions of the Lord do not depend on whether or not people believe."

The words were not said with the tone of prophecy or revelation, and yet Miriam was shaken by the profundity of the statement her brother had made. If one could truly believe that, she thought—but she knew that she did not possess such simplicity of faith.

The two of them had been sitting comfortably in the shade. But now Moses stood up and extended his hand to help his sister to her feet.

"When there is food and to spare," he said, "then I can send for my wife and sons to return."

Miriam kept her eyes lowered so that her brother would not see the disappointment that she felt. If it were possible, she thought regretfully, for just the little boys to come back —especially Gershom—but not their mother. When Zipporah is here, Moses will no longer seek me out for company. Maybe he doesn't actually confide in her, but he finds enough contentment in her presence that he doesn't need me.

Without talking, they walked back toward the camp. The taste of envy was in Miriam's mouth, and even the promise of food could not remove it.

The flock of quail flew out of the north late in the afternoon. At first, it looked like a long, low cloud, but everyone knew that this was not the time of year for rain clouds to climb up over the horizon. Some of the people cried out in fear that the Lord had sent yet another column of cloud to confuse them. But as the flock came closer, they saw the movement of thousands of wings and soon heard the whirring sound of the small birds in flight.

"They're flying so low," Isha called out to Miriam. "Look, Dodah, you could almost reach up and catch them with your hands."

Miriam's lethargy fled as she gazed overhead. "Look over there!" she cried. "See the way the women are throwing scarves and shawls up in the air to knock the birds down. We can do that, too."

Hastily, the two women unwound the shawls that covered their heads and began to fling them wildly into the air. The small birds, flying close to the ground and fluttering their wings in exhaustion, were easy prey. Stunned and bewildered by the flailing scarves, the quail blundered into the hands that reached out for them or simply fell to the ground. The women wrung the small necks with quick efficiency and dropped the feathered bodies into their pouches. No one talked or cried out, but each woman worked as fast and as competently as she could. Miriam could see that the flock of birds spread over the whole width of the camp, and she was sure that the women of every tribe were working as enthusiastically as her women were working to catch this bounty before it could escape.

Then, as suddenly as they had come, the birds were gone. Most of them had been caught, Miriam decided, as she watched the tattered remnants of the flock disappear over the southern horizon.

With the others, Miriam began the task of plucking and salting the small carcasses. But it was odd, she thought, looking around, that everyone seemed to have the proper number of the little birds. Those women who had the largest piles of birds in front of them were the women who had the greatest number of children.

"Will we roast them?" Isha called, her face flushed and happy as her nimble fingers plucked away at the tiny brown feathers.

"Who will be willing to wait for that?" Miriam responded. "Besides, hardly anyone cooked them in Egypt. Lightly salted and fresh as they are, they'll be simply delicious raw."

"I can almost taste them now," Isha agreed, but she, like the others, seemed willing to wait until the birds were all prepared so that the people could hold some semblance of a feast.

Each tribe held its own celebration of the unexpected gift of flesh, but not until after Moses had offered the first and most perfect birds to Yahweh. In grateful silence, the people watched the thin trickle of smoke from the sacrifice rise into the air and mingle with the column of cloud that stood always above the tribe of Levi. Then when it was no longer possible to distinguish sacrificial smoke from the cloud of Yahweh, they turned to their feasting with laughter and conversation. The flesh of the quail was moist and smooth and fresh to lips and throats parched from desert travel, and the people ate until they were sated.

"And in the morning," Moses called out to the people, who had grown sleepy from their full stomachs and were turning away from their fires to find places to sleep. "In the morning, Yahweh will rain bread upon us. I tell you this, my people: you won't be hungry any more."

No one even questioned his words. Replete and safe, the

children of Israel were willing to concede, for this hour at least, that Yahweh could well supply their needs.

In the morning, a white substance, looking a little like frost, covered the ground. Miriam, one of the first to wake up, took a few grains of it on the tips of her fingers and touched them to her tongue. She hadn't known what to expect, but the sweet, delicate taste of honey that filled her mouth came as a complete surprise. Who would ever have dreamed, she exulted within herself, that Yahweh would give them such a delicacy? We would have been content, she thought with a humility that was foreign to her, to have received even a tasteless sort of seed, if it had satisfied our hunger. But to have been given something so delicious! For a moment, she was tempted to sing and dance as she had done on the shore of the sea, to fill the morning with the sounds of praise. But she remembered that Moses had said they must gather up the substance before the sun got too high.

"Wake up, everyone!" she cried. "Wake up and see what the Lord has provided."

The women rose with exclamations of joy and contented clucks, and Miriam could see how quickly excitement swept through the camp.

"There's so much of it," Miriam gasped as she worked beside Isha to gather up the small coriander-like seeds from the ground. "Why should we be limited to only one omer? Even leaving enough for everyone else, we could gather up two or three omers of it. It looks as though it could be boiled like meal or made into loaves. We could prepare enough for tomorrow, in case there isn't any then."

"But you said that my uncle told you—" Isha began.

"My brother is not a woman," Miriam interrupted her. "What do men know of the necessity of planning ahead, of the importance of storing food? I think we should gather more. I have several baskets over there.''

"I'm sure my uncle would say that if Yahweh provided for us last night and today," Isha protested, "then he will surely provide for us again tomorrow.''

"And what about all the days he didn't provide?" Miriam asked bluntly. She took hold of Isha's arm. "See how skinny you are. No one was providing for us when you were getting so skinny.''

Isha had no answer to that, and she and Miriam stood looking at the white seeds on the ground.

"We wouldn't be depriving anyone else," Miriam argued. "Surely if Yahweh provided so much, he didn't intend that it should go to waste.''

"All right," Isha said in sudden capitulation. "All right, then. Bring the other baskets and we'll gather more.''

That day, the women worked zealously, boiling some of the strange stuff into meal and forming more of it into loaves which they baked on the hot stones around their fires. The people ate with thanksgiving and pleasure, and that night, once again, the camp slept heavily, contentedly, filled with food which the Lord had sent.

The next morning, Miriam woke early and discovered that the ground was again covered with the miraculous little seeds. But she had not begun to gather them when she heard Isha call out in a soft, sleepy voice, "Don't hurry, Dodah. We still have plenty from yesterday, remember?''

"Yes, of course," Miriam replied, but an unexpected surge of guilt sent her to look in the baskets that she and Isha had hidden among their possessions. She uncovered one and recoiled in disgust. The basket was filled with a mass of loathesome maggots. The seeds were utterly ruined.

"What is it?" Isha asked, for she had come hurrying when

she heard her aunt's gasp of horror. Then she, too, looked into the basket and shuddered when she saw its contents.

"It's because we disobeyed," Isha declared. "We disobeyed the instructions of my uncle."

"Maybe it's the nature of the seed to rot," Miriam suggested, unwilling to accept too much blame.

"Well, whatever it is," Isha responded, "we'll have to throw this mess out, clean out the baskets, and start all over again."

Miriam nodded and bent to the task of gathering the seed. There was, she realized regretfully, less praise and joy in her this morning than there had been the day before. Her decision to gather more than an omer of the seed yesterday had seemed wise and practical at the time. Must Moses always be right and she always wrong? It's not fair, she thought. Yahweh spoke to me once—how else could I have known about the coming of the cloud and fire?—so I have every right to believe that he should speak to me again.

"We should be moving on."
Moses's voice was loud and insistent.

"Why?" The question was abrupt to the point of insolence, and Miriam could not tell, from her position in the
outer circle of leaders, which man had asked it.

"Because we must press on toward the promised land,"
Moses answered angrily. "I am the leader of these people,
and I say we must go."

"And I, my brother, say we ought to stay a little longer."
Aaron spoke quietly, respectfully, but he was no less stubborn than Moses. "There is water here—not as much as at
Elim, but enough—and the manna falls every day. What
guarantee do we have that it will fall anywhere else in the
wilderness?"

"But this wretched place isn't our destination," Moses
sputtered.

"How do you know? Maybe it is," Pagael argued.

"Yahweh never told me that it was," Moses answered.

"Has Yahweh spoken to you in the past few days?"
Pagael persisted.

"No, not so recently as that," Moses admitted.

"Then how do you know we're to go on?"

Moses glared at the little man, scowled at Aaron who
seemed on the verge of speaking again, then looked around
at the assembled group.

Maybe, Miriam thought, this is a time for me to speak.
She usually remained silent when the leaders met, but this

night she felt she might have an answer that would pacify the leaders and still help Moses save face.

Timidly, she put up her hand to attract her brother's attention.

"Well?" he barked.

"Please, my lord," she began, "I don't mean to be bold, but sometimes women have practical ideas—because it's their responsibility to provide food and shelter for everyone. Might it not be a good idea, my lord, for us to stay here just long enough to shear the sheep and goats, spin the thread, and make the tents that we so desperately need? If we're going to be in the wilderness for any length of time, that is."

"We already have some tents and smaller shelters," Moses protested, his voice rising against the murmurs of approval that followed Miriam's suggestion.

"Yes, my lord, we do," Miriam agreed. "But the people prepared for only a week or two in the wilderness. We didn't know—" she said, then caught herself. "We didn't understand that we would be here so long. Decent goat's hair tents, warmer shawls for these desert nights—such comforts might make the people more content, my lord, and there might be less complaining."

She lapsed into silence, and all about her the sounds of approval went on.

"The people are weary, my brother," Aaron added. "They went hungry a long time. Perhaps here, where there is food enough and where the work our sister has suggested could be done, we might build up a new courage, a new faith."

Moses turned and walked away from the group. The men watched him go in silence. No one turned toward Miriam, and she kept her eyes decorously on the ground. She had planted the seed—it was up to Moses now. But she knew her brother was a man of logic as well as a man of vision, so she was not surprised when he turned again and resumed his place in front of the leaders. The anger was gone from his face.

"All right, then," he said. "We'll stay for awhile. I warn you, though, that if the Lord calls to me and says we must move on, we'll move."

Isha leaned toward her aunt and whispered, "Look, Dodah, even the cloud over there—the cloud of Yahweh, as my uncle says—isn't moving away from us as it does sometimes. It's just resting on that hill as though to say it's right that we should stay awhile."

Miriam followed Isha's pointing finger with her eyes, and a thrill ran through her body. Her words had not come out of any flaming conviction, but had been only a normal, practical suggestion as she might make to her column of women or to either of her sisters-in-law. Yet they seemed to be words sent from Yahweh. She felt warm with self-confidence and pride.

Moses nodded to dismiss the leaders. Miriam, heading for her accustomed place, walked by her brothers.

"They forget," Moses was saying, "that this is more than just a journey. They forget that Yahweh leads us and has a plan for us."

"But the cloud, my brother," Miriam dared to say. "It's not tugging us on as it sometimes does. See?"

Moses glanced at the cloud and then at his sister. "There was a time," he said slowly, "when I would have demanded that the cloud and the people and Yahweh himself move as *I* wanted them to. You, of all people, should remember what an impatient youth I was. But you also know how the years in Midian changed me—how the solitary hours in the desert made me hear the voice of my God louder than the voice of any man."

"Yes, I know," Miriam said, nodding, wondering what he was getting at.

"So—I just want you to understand. We're not staying here because of what Pagael or Aaron said or because of your clever words of persuasion. We're staying here because Yahweh has not specifically told me to move on."

"Perhaps he has reason for us to rest and gather our strength," Miriam suggested.

"Perhaps. I know he will make everything clear in time. For the present, I'm going out alone. To pray." He flung the last words over his shoulder as he walked away.

Miriam and Aaron stood and watched their brother go.

"He *has* to listen to us sometime," Miriam said softly.

"It's not always possible to catch his ear," Aaron answered.

"Well, we caught it this time." Miriam's words were smooth with satisfaction.

Aaron only smiled and looked over to where Isha was standing, evidently waiting for her aunt. But even as he and Miriam watched, they saw a young man, one of the Cushites, hesitate beside the girl. He spoke a few words to her, and Isha was certainly proper enough, never looking directly into the young man's eyes or speaking out in a brazen sort of way. Still, alarm flashed through Miriam.

"She needs to be married," Miriam said bluntly, forgetting all the clever arguments she had concocted. "She's at an age where she should be married."

"Out here?" Aaron asked. "In a strange land with nothing but wilderness about us?"

"What has wilderness got to do with it?" Miriam snapped. "Listen, my brother, I've been thinking. We should begin to look for a husband for her. Elisheba is too upset by all that is going on to give the matter proper consideration. But you and I—we're used to dealing with problems."

Aaron sighed. "And where will we find such a young man? Even if I agreed to give thought to the matter without consulting her mother."

"What of Joshua, son of Nun?" Miriam asked. She had not planned to present this name first, but to keep it as a final prize. However, Aaron's concern for Elisheba had pushed his sister into impulsive action.

"Joshua? But he's of the tribe of Ephraim."

"People sometimes marry into other tribes."

"I'd rather have her marry a Levite," Aaron insisted.

"Then try to find her a Levite," Miriam replied. "But you better not waste any time. Do you want her to fall in love with a Cushite—a foreigner?"

Aaron, gentle Aaron the dreamer, looked down into his sister's face with a shrewd expression on his own. "You always want to get your own way, don't you, my sister? Well, you can't have it—not all the time. Moses says these Cushites have accepted Yahweh's sovereignty better than some of our own people have. And, furthermore, Isha is *my* child."

She knew then that she had gone too far. She and Aaron rarely quarreled, but when he finally stood up to her, she knew enough to back down and do it humbly.

"Forgive me, my brother," she whispered meekly. "I didn't mean to interfere. It's just that the girl means much to me."

"Well, she means much to me, too," Aaron responded. "And to her mother. If we need your help, we'll come to you."

"I'm sorry," Miriam repeated.

Aaron's anger dissipated as quickly as it had come. "No, now, it's all right. I'll give some thought to young Joshua, but I wouldn't count on it if I were you. He was betrothed once, I understand, and the girl died. Since then he has been obsessed by only one thing—this dream of our brother's."

"Then he might like the idea of the fact that Isha is Moses' niece."

"And he might not like the idea at all," Aaron cautioned. He looked again at Isha, and even at that distance, they could see the flushed, rapt look on her face. "But you're right about one thing," Aaron conceded. "She's ready for marriage. I should have been thinking of it, but Moses has left me neither time nor energy to think of anything except this journey from Egypt."

"Tell me," Miriam demanded suddenly, "do you ever feel that Yahweh speaks to you, too?"

Aaron did not answer at once, and when he finally spoke, there was a curious dignity in his voice. "Yes, of course. You know that I've had dreams and what I believe to be visions. You know that Yahweh told me that Moses was coming home. We are of the tribe of Levi. Why do you ask?"

For a second, she was tempted to ask, "Do you think he speaks to you—to *us*—as much as he speaks to Moses?" But she did not say it. Instead, she mumbled, "I only wondered."

"You're foolish to wonder about such things," Aaron began, but his words were cut off as one of the men hailed him. He turned immediately and left his sister without even a word of farewell. She shrugged indifferently, knowing that since this was the way with men, there was no point in taking offense.

Then Isha called out, "Are you coming? I've been waiting."

Miriam strode briskly over to her niece, aware of how

much better she felt now that she was getting enough to eat every day.

"I had business with your father and your uncle," Miriam explained.

Isha stood up and walked along with Miriam. "I'm glad you spoke up about staying here at this oasis," she said. "I don't think the women are ready to move on. And your suggestion about the tents was a good one."

Miriam looked at the girl suspiciously. Was she being so agreeable in the hope that her aunt would not comment on the fact that she had been seen with a young man? And a Cushite at that?

"Thank you," Miriam told the girl, then said tersely, "I saw you talking to that Cushite. Your boldness shocked me."

"He was talking to me," Isha protested. "I merely listened."

"You could have told him to go away."

"Perhaps he doesn't understand our customs," Isha murmured.

Miriam snorted. "You're just making excuses. What did he want?"

Isha looked defensive. "Nothing. He didn't want anything. He was just saying how grateful they were—his people, that is—for the security of traveling with us. For the manna that falls every day."

Miriam looked at her niece in astonishment. "To you? He said all that to *you?* Why didn't he say it to Moses or even to your father?"

Isha raised her eyes bravely. "I don't know, Dodah. Perhaps he just wanted to speak to me."

"I certainly didn't think I'd have to stand guard over you," Miriam cried.

"You don't," Isha retorted. Then she added, defiantly,

"It was good to see admiration in a young man's eyes. As thin and dark as I am, I never expected anyone to even look at me again as though—as though I were a woman."

Miriam did not reply at once. She was slowly realizing that the girl should not be scolded. After all, Isha had put aside all the thoughts that girls her age usually have of beauty and marriage and children. She had given herself for months now to a cause, to a passion that was surely not normal. Even in the strictest homes, girls had always peeped through the door when the boys walked by. Isha could hardly be blamed for feeling hungry for admiration.

"Well, you mustn't feel that there's no hope," Miriam said as she took Isha's arm. "I'm sure we'll find someone who wants to marry you. When the tents are made, when there's some hope for a roof over our heads so that it will seem as though we have a home again, then we'll begin to look. All right?"

But Isha's arm was stiff and resistant under Miriam's hand. "His name is Zarim," she said.

"Whose name?"

"The Cushite. His name is Zarim."

"What possible difference does it make?" Miriam protested.

"He believes," Isha went on, speaking in a soft, stubborn voice as though nothing her aunt had said had affected her in the least. "He believes in Yahweh and that we are being guided. He believes that."

Miriam dropped the girl's arm. "He certainly said a lot in a very short time," she exclaimed.

"It isn't the first time he's spoken to me," the girl said. The words were defiant, but her eyes were filled with pleading.

"It's none of my concern," Miriam said. "You're not my responsibility."

"I thought you would be the one who would understand," Isha insisted. "You've seemed to understand so much about me."

"Understand? I understand that you would be brazen enough to allow a man to seek you out—to—."

"Oh, Dodah, not brazen. But I've been treated almost like a man for months now. Put in charge of people, given responsibilities. How can I now suddenly become a woman again with no mind of my own? I thought you, of all people, would understand this."

Miriam was silent. She hadn't thought of it like that. But there was truth in what Isha said. I should have realized, Miriam thought, that I am no longer the meek little woman who once bent myself to every whim my husband had expressed? Haven't I been almost glad lately—in a secret, ashamed way—that I am a widow with no one to answer to? Except my brothers, of course, who assumed responsibility for me, but who also encouraged me to be a person of some consequence? Oh, yes, if I were fair, I would understand.

She slipped her hand through the crook of Isha's elbow again. "I'm sorry," she said. "Life isn't normal anymore. You know how it is. I have to make adjustments in everything I do—everything I think. I won't scold again. Tell me about this—this Zarim."

She saw the way the girl's eyes lit up, and she tried to smile in response. But all the time, she was promising herself that she would see to it more suitable arrangements were made. After all, although life might be different now, they still hadn't reached a place where a girl could choose the man she would marry. Before they moved away from this oasis, she would see that Aaron had approached Joshua about the possibility of marrying Isha.

= 17 =

The days fled by in a blur.
Mornings were marked by the fall of manna, and the daylight hours were filled with the homely tasks of shearing, spinning, and weaving. Although much of this work was women's work, the men, too, were kept busy with the herds, the repair of the looms, and small forays into the neighboring land to search for water or wood. And some of the men, under Joshua's instruction, practiced military action.

"Is he trying to frighten us?" Miriam demanded of Moses one day. "Are we supposed to turn into an army?"

"No, of course not. But we're strangers in this land. We never know when we'll need to defend our own."

"What do you think of this Joshua?" Miriam went on. This might be just the time she had been waiting for.

Moses' face lit up. "A fine man! Brave and wise and, even more important, a man of faith. I'm very much impressed with him."

"Well, I've been wondering," she began, but before she could say anything more, Moses was called away. Miriam shrugged and made her way to where Elisheba and Isha were working. In the relative stability of this time, they had drawn a little away from the other woman and had established a place of their own where even Moses and Aaron came for sleeping and eating. Rocks formed a natural cave and animal skins provided a roof against the sun.

"Do we have enough cloth yet for a tent?" Miriam asked, squatting down beside the loom and preparing to take over the shuttle that Elisheba had been throwing back and forth.

"Almost enough," Elisheba answered. "What with the other heavy cloth we had, we can create a decent tent, I think."

"Well, then, we don't have any excuse to beg to stay here, do we?" Miriam said and reached over to take the shuttle.

Elisheba sat back with a sigh. "I dread to think of moving on, and yet I know we can't stay. Besides, the men are growing restless. My lord is restless. He feels that it's time to move on."

"Sometimes I think it will be years instead of months before we finish this journey," Miriam said bitterly.

"Oh, surely not," Isha cried in quick protest. "Won't there ever be a place to make a lasting home—to marry and raise children?"

"And to bury our dead," Miriam added, unwilling to discuss marriage with Isha at that moment. "We've scattered our dead across the desert like—like garbage. It's not decent."

"It's the way nomads live all the time," Elisheba offered. "Zipporah told me that they never have a permanent home, that they move with the seasons and with the flow of water. I guess that's what we've become. Nomads. Nothing but wanderers."

"That's not what my brothers intended," Miriam argued. "Nomads don't have any destination. They aren't heading anywhere. We're heading for the land of promise."

"And in the meantime, what?" Isha said, her voice sullen. "In the meantime, we wander."

An angry retort crowded to Miriam's lips, but she bit it back. After all, she herself had just expressed the fear that their journey might take years.

"But at least we wander with a goal," Miriam finally said

in a gentler tone. "At least we know where we've been and where we're supposed to be going."

She glanced at Isha to see if the girl were agreeing with her and was just in time to catch a quick light that crossed Isha's face. Miriam knew, even without looking beyond her niece, that Zarim had just walked by.

Roughly, Miriam thrust the shuttle back at Elisheba. "Where's your husband?" she asked. "I must talk to him."

Elisheba shrugged. "It's not my place to know where my lord is every minute of the day." Then she added quickly, seeing the dark expression on Miriam's face, "He might be back with the shepherds, though he tries to go from group to group to encourage and to teach."

"I'll look for him," was all Miriam said.

Isha, dreamy-eyed, made no sign that she even noticed her aunt leaving.

Aaron, when Miriam had found him, seemed glad for a respite from his duties.

"They never seem to understand," Aaron grumbled to his sister. "No matter how many times I tell them that being free is a blessing, they still complain. They can't seem to grasp the fact that we can come and go as we please, that we no longer have to dread the knock of the Egyptian overseers on our doors."

"They're not all dreamers, my brother," Miriam protested. "They're realistic men with little or no vision in their lives. But they understand practical things. They know that we're not really free. We're still prisoners of—well, of the way things are. We're held captive by such ordinary things as springs with water in them."

Aaron nodded heavily. "Yes, of course. Still—." He stopped and squinted at his sister. "You didn't seek me out just to tell me what I already know."

She smiled. "No, of course not. I've come to you again about Isha. She still smiles at that Cushite boy—that Zarim."

"Is that his name? Zarim?"

"You mean you haven't even found that out?"

Aaron looked apologetic. "I've been so busy. You can't understand how much is on my mind, how much I have to do."

Miriam nodded abruptly. "I understand. I have many burdens too, you know, but I'm still concerned about your daughter."

"I'm not entirely indifferent to her," Aaron said stiffly. "I've made some inquiries among the men of the tribe of Levi."

"And?" she prompted him.

"There aren't any young men whose families would go well with ours. Either too closely related or too distant. The only good thing is that none of the fathers are demanding a huge dowry. We're all reduced to poverty here, and they know it."

"Well, not exactly poverty," Miriam demurred, remembering the gold and silver and turquoise that they had hidden in saddle bags and grain sacks before they left Egypt.

"Perhaps not, but you know what I mean."

"What about Joshua? Have you inquired about him?"

"Not yet," Aaron confessed. "If we get desperate, I'll go to Nun and talk to him. Or to Moses. Not," he added, "that I think it will do the least bit of good."

"You can't know for sure until you've tried," Miriam said.

"True enough," Aaron admitted. "Well, I really will try to do something soon. I'll talk to either Nun or Moses in a day or so."

So Miriam had to be content with that, although she felt

sure that every time Isha saw young Zarim, her heart was becoming more firmly entangled with his. Considering the way Elisheba and Aaron doted on Isha, they would never force the girl to marry someone she hated. And if the girl lost her heart to one young man, it would be easy for her to hate all others, Miriam realized. Didn't she herself know? Hadn't it been that way with her after she'd seen Jehu? She had known, even then, how blessed she was that her heart had gone out to a boy who was suitable, who came from the proper tribe. It wasn't going to be as easy for Isha.

Before Aaron was able to talk to either Moses or Nun, Moses announced that they were going to move on. Yahweh had spoken and Moses would no longer listen to any suggestions from anyone else. Laboriously, regretfully, the people prepared to leave. And yet, disappointment and regret were only a part of what they felt. There was also a sense of excitement, a feeling of hope, among the people, and these were heightened when they discovered, after the first day's journey, that the manna continued to fall regardless of where they camped. As long as they had the pillar of fire by night, the column of cloud by day, and the daily miracle of the manna, the Israelites could believe in the presence of their God.

And yet this belief crumbled and twisted itself into violence when they reached the oasis of Rephidim and could find no visible springs. Those who arrived first had seen the bushes and trees and had hurried forward in anticipation only to discover that there was no water to drink.

All the frustration, despair, and anger that had so often been repressed by the people since they left Egypt now boiled up in a great fury that was aimed directly at Moses.

"You told us to come in this direction!"

"Isn't it enough that we have starved and roasted and frozen?"

"Are you so anxious to see us die, then?"

"We'd have been better off in Egypt. At least there was water to drink!"

To Miriam's horror, some of the men bent to pick up rocks. And the look on their faces as they advanced resolutely toward Moses was ugly.

Moses did not retreat, but Miriam could see the despair in his eyes. Then Moses did something he had never done before in front of everyone: he cried out to his God in a loud and vehement voice.

"Yahweh, my Lord!" he cried. "What am I to do? These people are about to stone me, and I don't know what to do."

The shock of this shout, uttered not in some silent, isolated spot where communion with the Lord might seem proper, but brashly, without shame in front of everyone, stopped the angry horde. The men, holding stones in their hands, stood as still as if they had been carved from rock.

Would Yahweh answer? Miriam wondered. Would all of them now hear the holy voice of the Most High and would it come thundering out of the sky in a wave of purple sound? She listened, half afraid, half excited, but the air was undisturbed. Far down the lines of people, a child wailed, and its cry was clear in the silence.

Miriam, watching her brother intently, saw his face change. The look of despair left his eyes, and a radiant certainty turned up the corners of his mouth in a smile of satisfaction. He bowed his head, whispered a few words, and then turned to Aaron.

"Come," he announced in a loud, steady voice. "Yahweh, blessed be his name, has told me where water can be found."

"I didn't hear anything," one man muttered, and Miriam saw that the rock did not drop from his fingers.

Moses looked serenely at the speaker. "Why should you? He was speaking to me."

Grasping his staff firmly, Moses turned away from the threatening crowd and strode over to a rocky hillside. He lifted his staff high and cried out in a loud voice that carried great distances in the still air:

"Come forth, I say! Be obedient unto Yahweh and come forth!"

The staff smashed down on the rock, and there was a sudden splintering sound. The rock split beneath the blow and a bubbling, gushing stream of water poured forth.

Moses cupped his hands under it, and when his palms were full, he cast the water in a sparkling cascade into the air. "Blessed be the name of our great God!" he shouted.

Only then did he scoop up another handful of the water and touch his lips to it. "Sweet," he announced, grinning. "Sweet and pure. Get your water skins and fill them. Don't waste it. Although," he added quietly, "I don't think the flow will diminish. Not while we have need of it."

Stunned and chastened, the people moved quickly to obey this man who, it seemed, had worked yet another miracle. The men who had picked up stones dropped them and cast looks of shame at their neighbors. Obediently, quietly, the people went for their water skins as they had been commanded to do.

Miriam made her way over to her brothers. "I was very frightened," she confessed.

"I, too," Moses admitted. "Without Yahweh at my side, I would be carrion now."

Aaron nodded. "They can't remember for a single day. At every difficulty, they resort to despair and anger."

"They've been slaves," Moses said. "All of their lives,

they've been slaves. And slaves live only for the next meal, the next skin of water. They forget their yesterdays and are afraid to hope for tomorrows."

While listening to them, Miriam was struck with a realization: Moses no longer stuttered. Indeed, he hadn't stuttered since—since when? At least since the crossing of the sea. Had Yahweh healed Moses of his problem because of his faith? And did that mean that if they all had more faith, they, too, would be changed? It was an impossible question to answer.

"Don't you ever get angry at them?" Aaron asked. "Sometimes I wish I had one of the overseer's whips in my hand."

Moses laughed and then his face sobered. "Yes, I get angry. So far, Yahweh has given me patience and understanding. It may be that someday they'll push me too far. I don't know."

Miriam ventured to speak into the silence that fell between her brothers. "When Yahweh spoke to you, my brother, did you hear his answer in words? I—we—heard nothing."

Moses shook his head. "No, not words. Not words as I use them to talk to Aaron or you. But something. I can't explain what. I only know that it was made clear to me what I should do."

"Well," she said, hesitating, and then blurted out, "Do you realize you don't stutter anymore?"

Moses' eyes twinkled. "The Lord, our God, is merciful and mighty."

Miriam smiled in reply, but Moses was looking beyond her at a young man who hurried toward them.

"Trouble?" Moses called out.

"I'm not sure," the young man said. "Someone reported seeing a cloud of dust behind us, but it may only be that raised by the flocks."

"Better send someone to be sure. Someone mounted on a fast donkey." Moses turned to Miriam. "How about the women? Are any of them lagging behind?"

A cold uneasiness touched her. Some of the women had been walking so slowly that they had fallen back with the flocks.

"I'll go and see," she said and hurried away.

She called out to Isha when she saw her, and the girl came quickly to join her aunt.

"The shepherds and some of the women are still out in that valley," Isha said. "It's getting harder and harder to make them keep up. They seem to feel it's perfectly safe to just take their time."

"Well, it isn't safe," Miriam snapped. "Sometimes I wonder if we'll ever be really safe. Come on. Hurry."

It was as though her own fears had caused the dreaded thing to happen, Miriam thought, as she and Isha rounded a hill of stone. There, in the distance, was a haze of dust that could be raised only by the hooves of many donkeys. And, faintly, but coming closer, she could hear the shouting of men and the clear, metallic sound of arms. Even as she looked, she saw, in the distance, the women and the shepherds start to run. However, the men on their donkeys were swifter, and they quickly cut off the straggling women, shepherds, and flocks.

Foolishly, impulsively, Isha and Miriam ran toward the women who were their responsibility. We should be running toward the men of Israel, Miriam thought in despair. What can we do—two frightened women? Yet something pulled her on toward the screaming, terrified women and the glinting swords that flashed in the sun.

Then Amalek came and fought against Israel at Rephidim. So Moses said to Joshua, "Choose men for me and go out, fight against Amalek." . . . So Joshua overwhelmed Amalek and his people with the edge of the sword. . . . And Moses went up to God, and the Lord called to him from [Mount Sinai] saying, "Thus you shall say to the house of Jacob and tell the sons of Israel . . . if you will indeed obey my voice and keep my covenant, then you shall be my own possession among all people." . . . So Moses went down to the people and told them.

Exodus 17:8, 13; 19:3a, 5a, 25

⸗ 18 ⸗

"Come back, come back!"

Miriam heard the distant shout through the muddled chaos of her fear and tried to check her headlong pace, but it was too late. A donkey plunged toward her and cut off any possible retreat in the same way that the Amalekites had so adroitly cut off the women and shepherds from the rest of the Hebrews.

"You seem very eager to throw in your lot with ours," a mocking voice shouted, and Miriam looked up to see a rider coming toward her.

Gasping for breath, frightened and angry, Miriam tried to come to a dignified halt. It would never do to let this pagan Amalekite realize just how frightened she was. She cast one quick glance toward Isha, guessing that she, too, had heard the call to come back too late to obey.

"I'd rather die than throw in my lot with the likes of you," Miriam retorted.

The fellow grinned maliciously. "That could be arranged," he sneered and rode toward her with his sword ready. Isha screamed, and the fellow, glancing over at her, checked his mount.

"Don't waste your breath on this old woman," he snarled. "And you needn't worry about your own hide either. At the moment, anyhow. You're too young to waste on swords!"

He laughed and turned again to Miriam. Although her legs felt weak with fear, she somehow held herself erect and glared back at him.

"You wouldn't dare talk so if our men were here," Miriam snapped.

The man lifted his sword and then, with a twist of his wrist, brought the blade down flatly on Miriam's shoulder. The force of the blow drove her to her knees, but she realized almost at once that the Amalekite had deliberately chosen not to kill her.

"You have an insolent tongue," he spat out, "but maybe that means you can control the other women till we decide which ones to kill and which ones to keep. Now shut up and get over there with the others." He turned his donkey's head and flung a few words over his shoulder. "Remember, you cause any trouble—and you'll be the first to die."

Still kneeling, Miriam caught the look of terror on Isha's face when the hungry eyes of the man on the donkey raked over her. For Isha's sake, Miriam realized, she would have to be submissive, though anger burned through her body.

"I'll do what I can," she muttered, then got to her feet and walked over to where Isha stood. "Come," she told her niece in a steady voice. "Come and help me do what has been ordered."

Isha's arm was tense and trembling in Miriam's grasp, and Miriam could hear the girl's breath rasping in her throat.

"Don't even look toward him," Miriam hissed. "Maybe in all the confusion, he'll forget he ever saw you."

Isha lowered her eyes, bowed her head, and moved obediently with her aunt to where the women were crowding together, pushing their children into the center of the rough circle they had formed. Most of them were weeping or uttering breathless cries of fear, but Miriam was comforted to see that they had not wholly lost the discipline that had been instilled in them during their journey from Egypt. Outflanked by a superior force they could not possibly hope to combat, they still moved with purpose and courage as they made a shelter of their own bodies to protect their children.

"What do you think will happen?" Isha asked breathlessly.

Miriam shrugged in a gesture of hopelessness. "How can I tell?" she replied. "If my brothers and the tribal leaders think we're worth saving, I suppose there will be a battle."

"Worth saving?" Isha's voice was outraged. "I'm the niece of the leader, the daughter of the chief priest. My mother is somewhere among this crowd. What do you mean worth saving?"

Miriam spoke grimly. "I confess I had forgotten your mother. The wife of one of the leaders might be considered that important. I'm not sure that Moses would risk his whole tribe for a sister or a niece."

Isha stared at her aunt and then smiled wryly. "I'm not sure we have to worry, anyhow. They'll think the sheep are important enough."

Miriam felt laughter bubble in her throat. "You're right," she agreed cheerfully. "The sheep and the shepherds are important enough. For now—we have simply to concentrate on being as quiet as possible so that no one will pay any attention to us. Maybe we can keep ourselves alive until we can be rescued."

When she could do so without attracting attention, Miriam cast a glance back toward the tumble of hills where most of the Israelites were halted. Although the Israelites were a fair distance away and although a scattered line of mounted Amalekites formed a rough barrier between them and the captured women, Miriam was still able to see the flurry of activity that was taking place among her people. The thing she had feared—a hasty packing up and moving out—was not taking place. Faintly, she could hear commands being issued, and it seemed that the men were moving into some sort of order. At the same time, a large portion of Amalekites were advancing cautiously but purposefully toward the Hebrews.

"Can you see what they're doing?" Isha asked. "Are they getting into battle formation?" When Miriam nodded, she added, "Zarim told me once that if we were ever attacked, plans had been made to fight the attackers. They must think we're worth saving, after all."

Elisheba had worked her way over beside them. "Of course they'll fight to save us," she said. "I'm Aaron's wife, and besides, how long could they survive in the wilderness without the wool of the sheep, the milk of the goats? They'll fight for us, all right, but can they win? Look at the swords these Amalekites have."

"Zarim says—" Isha began, but Miriam interrupted.

"What does a foreigner know? It's young Joshua who knows of the plans and how a battle should be fought."

Isha shrugged and turned away. Miriam felt irritated with herself. Why was she concerned about such trivialities when their lives were threatened? How could she possibly quarrel with her niece under these circumstances?

"What do you think we ought to do?" Elisheba asked anxiously. "Is there any chance at all that we could escape?"

"Don't be silly," Miriam replied. "Any action that drew the attention of the Amalekites would only get us into deeper trouble. Our only hope lies in staying alive until our men can rescue us. If we cause any trouble, the Amalekites will kill us simply to get rid of us."

"She's right," Isha said, returning to the conversation. "They'll probably kill most of us anyhow—at least, the very old and the very young. Let's not do anything to call attention to ourselves in the meantime."

Miriam was sure that Isha was thinking to herself that, being neither very old nor very young, she was in quite a different kind of danger.

"Let's keep the women close together," Miriam proposed, "and persuade them to be as quiet as possible. Everyone of us should be praying every minute."

Elisheba and Isha nodded in agreement, and the three of them moved unobtrusively among the other women, soothing, comforting, and assisting them. Gradually, all the women were quieted. A calmness settled upon the group, and though it was not the serenity of hope, at least all panic had been dispelled.

An old shepherd named Reuben had been observing the actions of the women, and now he crept over and whispered to Miriam. "You give us courage, you do. No use our fussing and squalling. Maybe if we're still enough, the dirty devils will pay no attention to us either. Who knows what can happen?"

Miriam smiled into the brown, wrinkled face. Praise from any man was a heady thing for a woman. "It's our only hope," she agreed. "Can you get word to the other shepherds?"

"I can try. The Amalekites might think we're not worth worrying about—just women and old men. I'll try."

She watched him shamble away, ignoring the mounted guards, stopping to sooth a lamb or lead a sheep away from some rocks. And even though she knew what he was doing, Miriam found it difficult to tell that he was, all the while, also speaking to the other shepherds. And yet, the calm sense of resignation that had fallen upon the women began to spread throughout the uneasy ranks of men as well. The captives waited in silence, and those who guarded them relaxed a little and turned to see what was happening on the plain between the Amalekites and the children of Yahweh.

Moses, accompanied by Hur and Aaron, left the place of encampment and climbed to the top of the hill that overlooked the plain. It was not fear for himself that pulled

Moses away from the battleground, but a sense of compulsion. He had seen Joshua take command, had watched the steady, skillful actions of the younger man, and he knew that he was not needed in that place of impending war.

But he felt himself needed on this hilltop, even though he was not sure what he was to do. So, silently, breathing hard, the three men climbed away from the sounds of the gathering of arms and found themselves at last on a high outcropping of rock where a single tree raised its gnarled branches to the blazing sky. Here they dropped thankfully in the sparse shadow cast by the tree, and, shading their eyes from the sun, gazed out across the plain.

The Amalekites could be seen easily from this vantage point, and Moses watched anxiously as the enemy drew closer and closer to the Hebrew forces. Yet he also saw that Joshua had formed his ranks well and that the Hebrews had positioned themselves in a location that was not readily accessible.

But military strategy would not be enough to defeat the Amalekites, and Moses knew that. A greater power than any Joshua could summon was needed. Moses bowed his head to pray. But before he could begin the impassioned plea that he had planned, he heard the sounds of conflict and looked up to see the Hebrew forces fall back from a sudden, fierce onslaught of the enemy.

Moses leaped to his feet and thrust his arms up in an instinctive gesture of supplication. "Yahweh, my God, my Lord," he cried out, "be with your children! Strengthen their arms so that they won't be defeated."

To his amazement and joy, he saw the Amalekites waver and draw back.

With a great sigh of relief, Moses let his hands fall to his sides. Almost at once, the enemy seemed to gain strength. They surged again into Hebrew territory, and the faint, faraway sounds of battle rose from the plain.

"Raise your hands again," Aaron gasped. "Perhaps your prayer and blessing will give our people strength. Raise your hands again, my brother."

Moses stretched up his arms and saw with gratitude that once more the Amalekite forces were pushed back to their original stand.

This, then, was his duty—to stand on the hill and keep his arms raised in humble supplication to Yahweh.

Hours passed, and at times his arms ached so cruelly that he felt he could not endure it. But each time he let his hands drop, the enemy forces pushed forward. Finally, Aaron and Hur brought a rock for Moses to sit on, and they gently lowered his body until he was comfortable. Then each of them took one of Moses' hands and held it aloft. And though Moses groaned with the agony of holding up his arms, he would not allow Aaron and Hur to lower them. His fingers were numb, and pain spread like fire through his shoulders, but he bore it and only prayed for the courage and strength to remain as he was until the forces of Joshua could be victorious.

Some hours later, Elisheba came noiselessly to Miriam. "Can you see up there?" she whispered. "Can you see how the battle is raging?"

"Yes, I can see," Miriam admitted, "but I've been trying not to look."

"It's horrible," Elisheba agreed, "but we have to know how the tide of battle is going. Look, there in that valley. I'm sure it's our men in the valley. When they come out of it—see—like a wave—I think they must be winning. But then, can you hear that dreadful yelling? The Amalekites seem to gather up strength and surge in toward the valley. It's been going on like that for a long time."

"Then neither of them is winning."

"No, not constantly. It's almost more frightening than it would be if things were all in favor of one side or the other."

Miriam tried to smile at her sister-in-law. "Nothing in the world could be more frightening than to know positively that the Amalekites were winning."

"I suppose so," Elisheba admitted. "But watching the way things go back and forth is awful. I feel such hope when our men rush out of the valley—and then I nearly die of fear when the Amalekites push them back again."

"The Amalekites must need every available man," Isha contributed, coming up to her mother and her aunt. "I've noticed that there are fewer and fewer men keeping watch over us. Every once in a while, one of them rides away to where the fighting is going on. If only they would all go."

"Then there'd be no reason to fight," Miriam reasoned. "After all, the battle is being fought because we're prisoners—the women and the sheep. If we were allowed to escape, there'd be no cause for battle."

"And so we must endure just standing here," Isha cried. "We're helpless and useless. If only we could *do* something to help."

"We can watch," Elisheba offered.

"And pray," Miriam added.

"What good does that do?" Isha protested. "From here, we can see that men are falling and dying, but we can't tell which men. For all we know . . ." Her voice trailed away in misery.

"I suppose," Miriam suggested, "that the one we should be most concerned about is Joshua. He's the nearest thing we have to a general. He probably needs our prayers most of all."

"Yes, probably," Elisheba agreed.

But Isha didn't answer, and Miriam could see that the mention of young Joshua's name had not brought any change to her niece's face. Only thoughts of the Cushite, Zarim, could light Isha's eyes.

But if we're all killed, Miriam thought, or taken into a worse kind of slavery than we ever knew back in Egypt, then what difference will it make who holds Isha's heart in his hands? She won't be able to marry anyone. Even if they let her live, she'll be used by any Amalekite who wants her. And when they're done with her, what then? Perhaps they'll put out her eyes or cut off her hands. Or flay her alive. Haven't we heard of the terrible things done by these men who roam the desert, killing and torturing?

These and other dark thoughts writhed through Miriam's mind, and she realized that what mattered now was Isha's safety, not whom she thought herself in love with or even whom she eventually married. The important thing was that she be kept alive until a marriage could take place. Even, Miriam thought somberly, a marriage with Zarim of Cush.

A baby cried, and the piercing sound sliced through the afternoon air. A guard whirled toward the women, raising his sword in a threatening gesture. The child's cry was silenced, and Miriam could see with what terror the young widow had pulled her baby to her breast. The courage of the women must be wearing thin, but the quick irritation of the guard might very well indicate that things were not going well for the Amalekite forces.

Miriam moved slowly away from the huddle of women and sat by herself on the hot ground. She bowed her head and let her despair spill over into prayer. She was incapable of forming articulate petitions. She merely felt her whole being crying out, "Yahweh, my Lord. Yahweh, my God."

And though she felt no real sense of comfort in that, still somehow she was given the strength she needed to remain quietly in that place and not plunge blindly, hysterically at the Amalekite sentry who sat on his donkey, glaring malevolently at his captives.

⸗ 19 ⸗

The first indication Miriam had that the Israelites might be winning the battle was the sudden appearance of a single Amalekite who came pounding by them, shouting some sort of warning. His words were garbled and spoken in a strange dialect, so Miriam was not sure what he said. However, the reaction of the sentry who had knocked her to her knees when they were first captured spoke clearer than words. At once, he swung his donkey back toward the shepherds, and it was obvious that he was either frightened or angry or both.

The old shepherd, Reuben, tried to warn his fellows not to agitate the angry sentry, but one burly, hot-tempered young shepherd shouldered the old man aside and stood defiantly before the Amalekite sentry.

"Did you get word that our forces are beating your forces, then?" the young shepherd shouted. "Maybe if you let us go, our men will have mercy on you."

The Amalekite's face darkened with rage, and without a word of warning, he spurred his donkey forward and ran his sword through the shepherd's chest.

Blood gushed out over the Amalekite's hand as he wrested his sword free, and the shepherd sprawled in a grotesque heap on the ground. He had not had a chance to cry out in either fear or prayer, and now his blood ran red on the dry ground.

Miriam felt nausea and protest crowd up into her throat, but she struggled to maintain the passive silence that she had urged all the women to display. She did not look again at the fallen shepherd, nor did she allow her eyes to go toward the Amalekite. She suspected that this sentry was the sort of man who had to be goaded into killing, and she did not want anyone else to give him an excuse to use his bloody sword.

The older shepherds moved slowly, cautiously away from the body of their friend and sat down with their backs to the sentry, facing away from the battle. With the slightest of gestures, Miriam indicated that the women were to do the same, and no one, not even a child, cried out in fear or revulsion because of the bloody body on the ground.

The sentry rode a short distance and sat staring toward the valley where the Israelites and the Amalekites still battled bitterly. Even though Miriam could not see everything that was happening and even though the sounds of the fighting drifted so thinly through the hot air that they could scarcely be heard, she knew that the ground would be littered with bloody and grotesque bodies like the one before them. She could only hope and pray that she had correctly guessed the meaning of the sentry's action. Surely, if the Amalekites were winning, the reaction to the messenger's shouted words would have been one of delight, and the sentry would have herded the women and shepherds together for the march back to the Amalekite encampment. Or for the slaughter, she reminded herself honestly. She wished more than anything, that she could kneel, stretch out her hands in supplication to the God of Moses, and beg with approved words for their safety. But such actions, she knew, would certainly cause the sentry to attack her as he had attacked the young shepherd.

I wonder, she thought, if Yahweh might hear the words of my heart, words not said with my lips? The idea was a strange one that seemed almost ridiculous to her. But fear shaped her thoughts, and her unspoken prayers rose like smoke into the air. She bent her face into her hands and concentrated on her God.

If we are your people, O Yahweh, she reflected, *and if you want us to go into a land of our own where we can worship you as a free people, then strengthen the arms of our men and give us victory. If you truly spoke to my brother from the burning bush and brought us out into this wilderness, then defeat our enemies.*

The words ran like fire through her body, and for a time, Miriam was unaware of her surroundings and the people around her. Never before had she turned to Yahweh with such total concentration.

A touch on her arm brought her back and reminded her of where she was. She looked up, dazed, and saw Isha's face close to her own. The girl's eyes were blazing with excitement, but she had wrapped her head scarf so that the rest of her face could not be seen.

"What is it?" Miriam asked in a whisper.

"Zarim has come. And our men have won the battle. Most of the Amalekites have been killed, and in only a little while, we'll be rescued."

Miriam's mind caught on the first word Isha had said and seemed unable to go any further. "Zarim?" she said in amazement. "Zarim has come?"

"Don't look now," Isha begged, "but in a minute or two, let your eyes drift over to the shepherds. You'll see a very ragged fellow huddled between old Reuben and Kodash. It's Zarim. He dressed like a shepherd and managed to creep along the ground without being seen—hiding among the sheep, he said—until he found us."

"But why did he risk his life like that?" Miriam asked.

"He wanted to save me," Isha said simply.

Miriam waited for a time and then let her eyes drift over to the two shepherds Isha had named. And there, between them, sat a young man in tattered robes, his face nearly hidden by the scarf he had wound around his head. She could, however, see enough of his cheek to recognize the color of Zarim's skin.

"Isn't he afraid the Amalekites will see that he's dark?"

Isha shrugged. "So are they, some of them. They won't even notice."

Something stirred in Miriam, some reluctant admiration for this young man's courage that would allow him to risk entering the enemy's camp for the sake of a girl. Such devotion could not be ignored. When they were all together again and safe, she would have to discuss this whole problem again with Aaron.

"What does he plan to do to save you?" Miriam whispered.

"At the right moment, Zarim will kill the sentry before he can kill any of us or join the few who will escape."

"But the Amalekite has a sword," Miriam protested.

"And Zarim has a knife," Isha said.

"How does he plan to get close enough to use a knife?" Miriam asked.

"It's better that you don't know," Isha whispered. "Don't worry, though. We'll work it out."

"We?" Miriam repeated sharply. "You're not planning to do anything foolish?"

Isha smiled and, rising from her knees, drifted quietly away from her aunt. Miriam wanted to cry out to stop her, but she knew she dared not risk inflaming the sentry.

And then a new fear caught at Miriam. If those Amalekites who had been spared called to the sentry to join them, what would he do? For the sake of his pride, certainly, he would not just ride harmlessly away. More likely, he would kill again, or—the idea hit Miriam like a blow to the stomach—he would try to capture Isha. How easy it would be, she imagined, for him to grab the girl, pull her up onto his donkey, and ride away. What chance did a young man with a knife have against an action like that?

In the midst of these frightening thoughts, Miriam was suddenly aware of an even more frightening reality. Isha, was walking casually away from the other women. At first, the Amalekite sentry seemed unaware of her, but before she had gone far, he swung around and shouted in a furious voice, "Where do you think you're going?"

Isha turned and looked at him, her eyes wide with surprise. "Why, I was only stretching my legs a little, my lord. Surely you don't object?" Her voice was properly humble, but there was a subtle note of teasing in it, and a smile indented the corners of her mouth.

The fellow rode his donkey over to Isha. His attention was entirely on her, and so he was unaware of Zarim, who had gotten to his feet and was drifting closer, moving no more substantially than a shadow behind him.

"I do object," the sentry snapped. "If anyone moves, it's only with my permission. And you haven't asked for that."

Isha looked up demurely. "May I walk a bit, my lord?"

The man swung himself off his donkey and grabbed Isha's arm. "If you do anything at all," he declared, "you will do it with me." He jerked her toward him, wrapped his arms around her, and pushed his dark, sweating face into hers. Then he kissed her greedily. "No need to wait any longer for you," he sneered before he pushed her down and fell sprawling on top of her.

Even though Miriam knew that Zarim was closing in on the Amalekite, she felt a scream of protest building up in her throat. But before she could make a sound, she realized that Isha was screaming enough for two as she thrashed, struggled, and fought under her captor. He tried to hold his hand over her mouth, but jerked it away when the girl's teeth sank firmly into his thumb. The man raised his injured hand with the obvious intent of smashing it into Isha's face.

In a flash, Zarim was directly behind the pair, and he grabbed the man's hand and wrung it viciously. The Amalekite howled in pain and twisted toward his attacker. As he looked up, his throat was exposed. Zarim's hand moved with the swiftness of a snake striking, and blood gushed across Isha. A cry gurgled in the Amalekite's slit throat and bubbled into silence. Isha wriggled calmly from under the body of the sentry and stood up.

"Thank you, my lord," she said breathlessly to Zarim. "For a few minutes, I was afraid our plan wouldn't work."

"Even if there had been no plan," Zarim said, his teeth glinting in a grin, "I would have killed him with my bare hands."

Elisheba came cautiously toward her daughter. "Are you all right?" she asked. "When he knocked you down, my heart nearly burst with fear. What were you thinking of to move so brazenly and attract his attention like that?"

"How else could we have gotten him off his donkey?" Isha said. "My lord Zarim could not have used his knife against a man on a donkey. Not against an armed man with a sword."

Elisheba's face was filled with amazement. "Did you know it was the Cushite?" she whispered to Miriam. "I thought it was only one of the shepherds."

Zarim pushed back the ragged scarf that bound his head and smiled at both Elisheba and Miriam. His black eyes and white teeth shone in his lean, dark face. For the first time, Miriam understood why her niece felt as she did.

Miriam smiled at her sister-in-law. "I knew he had come with the intention of rescuing Isha. But I had no idea how he meant to do it. We have much to be grateful for." She spoke loud enough that Zarim and Isha might hear her where they stood, and she saw them both brighten at her words. Well, then—that was that. If they escaped unscathed, it seemed that Isha's future was settled.

"Now, my lady," Zarim said, coming closer to Miriam, "it's very important that you move as quickly as possible away from this end of the valley. If any Amalekites escape, they will probably ride this way. And in their fury, they will ride you down like so many sheep. Can you get the other women to hurry? I'll round up the shepherds."

Without thought, Miriam accepted the young man's suggestion. "What direction should we run?" she asked.

"There. Toward the east. Quickly. The battle was nearly over when I left—just a few nomads trying to get away with their skins still whole. We'll have to hurry."

Freed from the surveillance of the sentry, the women and shepherds ran swiftly to huddle behind an outcropping of stone where the ground was too rough for donkeys to cross. Giddy with relief, the women would have broken into a babble if Miriam had not hushed them.

"Don't attract their attention," she warned. "Who knows what they might do if they discover we're here?"

She noticed then that some of the younger shepherds had not joined in their flight. They were busy rounding up the sheep and goats and driving the animals into another rocky area. But before all the animals were safe, the remaining Amalekites broke away from the Israelites and came pounding toward them. The Israelites followed, brandishing their swords.

The men herding sheep continued their task even in the face of danger, and Miriam saw that one of them was Zarim.

"Why isn't he trying to escape as he told us to do?" she demanded of Isha.

"The sheep have to be rescued," Isha said simply. "Without the herds, we're lost. You know that."

Miriam silently watched the young men in their desperate attempt to salvage the flocks. Then, with anger and frustration, she watched the Amalekites deliberately knock down the scurrying shepherds and stab the frantic sheep with their swords. For a few minutes, there were anguished sounds of pain, but almost immediately the scuffle was over.

The last few Amalekites were overtaken by the pursuing

Israelites, pulled from their donkeys, and killed. Jubilantly, the Israelites took arms and water skins from their fallen enemies and kicked their bodies aside. Leading the donkeys, the men came back in triumph. The women, sobbing and laughing with relief, ran from the sheltering rocks and sang praises to their victorious men.

Miriam, looking around, discovered that Isha was not among the rejoicing women, and a quick panic filled her. Then, over where the sheep were milling around, still bleating with terror at the scent of blood, she saw Isha crouched on the ground beside one of the fallen men.

Miriam ran to join her niece. She knew, even before she reached Isha, who would be laying on the blood-drenched earth.

"Zarim?" Miriam gasped. "Is it Zarim?"

Isha's face was stricken as she looked up at her aunt. "It's Zarim," she cried. "They rode over him as though he were one of the sheep. And there's a terrible wound here—in his back."

"Is he dead?" Miriam demanded.

"I don't know." Isha bent weeping over Zarim, unable to hide her grief.

Miriam knelt beside her niece and placed her hands on Zarim's face. He was warm to her touch, so she bent swiftly and put her cheek close to his mouth. She felt his breath soft against her face.

"He's alive," she said to Isha. "Stop crying and help me bind up this gash in his back before he bleeds to death. Call Reuben to get someone to help us carry him back to camp. Don't waste your time crying, girl. Not if you want to save this man."

Isha's face was streaked with tears, and her lips trembled. "Oh, I do," she sobbed. "Saving him is the most important thing in all the world."

= 20 =

Their concern over Zarim and with the problem of getting him back to the camp absorbed all of Miriam's and Isha's attention for the balance of the day. They were hardly aware of the results of the battle and scarcely took notice when Moses and Aaron came back to the camp claiming that the protection and mercy of Yahweh had given them the victory over the Amalekites. Miriam and Isha concentrated entirely on the young man who had risked his life to save them.

It was Elisheba who went in search of Zarim's family and brought his sister, Tarbis, back with her.

"His parents are dead," Elisheba explained to Miriam who was crouching over Zarim, trying to rouse him. "There's only his sister."

Miriam looked up to see a startlingly beautiful woman. Tarbis was tall, slender, with the same oval face as her brother. Her black eyes were long-lashed and expressive, and her features were regular and noble.

"He's very badly hurt," Miriam said. "He was cut down by the escaping Amalekites, and I don't know if he can be saved."

Tarbis knelt swiftly beside her brother and laid a long, narrow, dark hand along his cheek. "Just so was my husband killed," she said in a husky voice. "He died almost at once, just after he was stabbed. But my brother is still breathing, so perhaps there is hope for him." Her eyes were brilliant with tears.

"Could a priest be found to use some healing oil or herb?" Miriam asked.

"The priests are all busy with the wounded men of Israel," Tarbis said. "They shouldn't be called away from their duties to aid a foreigner."

"My father is the chief priest," Isha said. "He'll come if I call him. He'll come if I tell him—."

Then she stopped and stared at her aunt, stricken.

"I'll go find him," Miriam announced. "I'll explain everything."

She found Aaron almost at once.

"Can you spare a minute?" she begged. "I know there are many claims on you, but it's for the sake of your daughter."

"Has she been hurt?" he asked, turning to follow her.

"No, not Isha. But Zarim has."

"Zarim? The young Cushite?"

"Yes. He came to rescue us. He saved Isha from being raped, probably from being killed as well. Then he went on trying to save the flocks, and he was attacked by the escaping Amalekites."

"But Isha?"

"She loves him. They love each other. So it's as though the sword had gone through her."

"But you don't approve," Aaron said.

Miriam shrugged, trying to make her weary legs move as rapidly as Aaron's were moving. "I've learned a great deal this day."

"Then we'll try to save him," Aaron said.

Miriam saw the comforting way Aaron's hand slid across Isha's head when they got to where Zarim was lying. Quickly and efficiently, Aaron anointed the young man with oil and adjusted the clumsy bandage. Finally, he knelt beside Zarim and lifted his hands to pray for life and health for the wounded Cushite.

Tarbis was the first to speak. "My brother will get well," she said. "I know it. Yahweh will hear your prayer, my lord, and he will grant your wish."

"I wish all of us had as much faith as you seem to have."

The speaker was Moses who had come up behind them and heard Tarbis's remark. The Cushite woman only smiled and lowered her eyes humbly. Moses looked at his brother.

"Another victim?"

Isha's head came up quickly. "Not a victim, Dod. I mean, he's going to live. I feel it."

"I hope so," Moses said and turned to Miriam. "Will you walk with me a minute, my sister?"

Wearily, Miriam stood up, but though her body was heavy with fatigue, her heart was light. When Moses sought her company, she was always filled with joy.

They walked awhile in silence, and then Moses told Miriam of his experience on the hill and how his upheld hands had given victory to the Israelites. But when he spoke of the way Aaron and Hur had supported his aching arms, Miriam spoke abruptly.

"Then it wasn't you alone, my brother? Yahweh let ordinary men assist you?" The words were out before she had considered how they would sound.

Moses halted and frowned at her. "What do you mean?"

She tried to laugh. "Nothing. I didn't mean anything. I'm so tired that silly words come into my head. Did you recognize the young man Aaron was ministering to?"

"One of the Cushites. I don't know his name."

"His name is Zarim. He risked his life to save Isha and, as it turned out, all of us. They're in love, those two. At first, I was strongly opposed—."

Moses interrupted her with a quick gesture. "There's nothing to oppose. These Cushites have accepted our God with a faith that is astonishing. Did you hear how the woman spoke?"

"But the color of their skin."

"It's nothing. Some of us, too, have become very dark since we left Egypt. It's nothing."

"Well, I've come to see that," Miriam confessed. "But I had hoped that maybe someone a little more influential—Joshua, perhaps."

"Joshua isn't interested in marriage," Moses said firmly. "If the girl is ready for marriage, and the Cushite is eager to have her—provided he lives, of course—then we'll have a wedding ceremony. It will be good to celebrate."

Miriam smiled. "We have much to celebrate. We've won a great battle."

"But at a terrible cost," Moses replied. "The men are digging graves for many of our people."

"At least we have living men to dig the graves," Miriam insisted. "There are still many of us who hope to reach the promised land."

Moses looked at her with affection. "You're always a comfort to me. Even when I don't agree with everything you say, I find your thoughts refreshing and good."

Warmth spread through Miriam as they walked on, Moses' approval was a heady thing to her. And maybe someday, she hoped, she would be one of the ordinary people used by Yahweh to do something marvelous to assist her brother.

The following days were busy with nursing the wounded and burying the dead and re-establishing the ranks that once had been so well formed. To Isha's great joy, Zarim improved steadily after Aaron's ministration, and Elisheba confided to Miriam that she and Aaron had been discussing a wedding and were working toward that happy event.

A few days after the battle, Zipporah's brother-in-law, Boz, returned to the camp, bringing his sister-in-law and nephews with him. Caught up in the work of the battle's aftermath, Miriam paid little attention to her sister-in-law's arrival and felt none of the resentment she had feared she might feel. Zipporah and her sons quickly settled into the camp routine, and in a short while, their presence seemed normal and ordinary again.

When the tribal members were once more able to travel, the Israelites broke camp to journey through the southern wilderness. The land became more and more mountainous, and it seemed to Miriam that the rocky, golden hills thrust themselves up into the very heavens. Sometimes clouds covered the tops of the hills, and while rain seldom fell, an atmosphere of somber mystery surrounded these cloud-wreathed flanks of mountains.

The terrain became so difficult to cross that when they finally reached an oasis in a wide valley, Moses and Aaron agreed to stop for a longer duration than usual, perhaps even long enough to grow a few leeks and herbs for both cooking and medicinal purposes. The manna still fell like a blessing every morning, but a few leeks would go very well, some of the women had suggested wistfully, and Moses, hearing of their desires, gave in and ordered the establishment of a camp.

"It's amazing," Miriam said to Elisheba as they pitched their tent and set up the small portable looms that enabled them to weave whenever fiber was available, "how quickly some of us have adjusted to this wild way of living. Only a few months ago, we lived in civilized, rich cities—with walls and roofs and gardens. Now we live under the sky with nothing but wool cloth or goat skins to shelter us. And yet somehow we survive."

Elisheba nodded. "Though not all the people are content, of course. You've heard their complaints."

Miriam shrugged. "People are born to complain. If the

sun shines, they're too hot. If the sun sets, they're too cold. The manna becomes monotonous, they say. They forget what it felt like to have an empty belly."

"I haven't forgotten," Elisheba said simply. "I'm glad my children are as old as they are. I don't think I could have borne that time if I'd had babies or small children crying for food and nothing to give them."

"I thought of that, too," Miriam confessed. "I was almost glad to have been barren."

"You weren't married long enough to know that you were truly barren," Elisheba argued. "Less than a year. Yahweh might yet have blessed your womb with children if Jehu had not been killed."

"It comforts me to have you say that," Miriam admitted, feeling warmer toward her sister-in-law than she usually did. "In the meantime, I've comforted myself with your children. Which reminds me—this is a good place, don't you think, for us to plan a wedding for Isha?"

"Is Zarim well enough? He still limps badly when he walks."

"He may always limp. But he's well enough. They look at each other with the look of silly sheep. Why don't you speak to your husband? Ask him to pick out an auspicious day, and we'll have a celebration. The people will welcome a chance to sing and dance and rest from their troubles."

"I'll ask him," Elisheba said. "It's a good idea. And now that she has returned, Zipporah will be able to help, too."

Miriam's forehead creased in a slight frown. "She doesn't look well. Have you noticed? Her face is flushed, and her arms are thin. I thought she'd come back from her father's looking plump and healthy. But she looks worse than when she went away."

"I hadn't noticed. I'll look at her more closely."

"Well, whether she can help or not," Miriam said, "you and I can handle everything. You speak to your husband, and I'll begin to think of ways we can celebrate. There must be something we can fix that will resemble a feast. And we must weave or find something pretty for Isha to wear. Even here in the wilderness, we must make a celebration that will bring joy to the people."

Elisheba's eyes shone. "I'll do it right away," she promised. "And one of us, I suppose, should speak to Isha. She's become so independent and wild that she's almost like a boy. She needs a little calming down."

"I'll talk to her," Miriam promised. "She'll be willing to calm down, I'm sure. She'd be willing to do anything to become Zarim's wife."

The day chosen for the wedding arrived. Miriam had spent hours gathering enough water that Isha might bathe herself from head to foot and even wash her long black hair before a handful of perfumed oil—an unexpected gift brought by Zipporah from her father's home—would be rubbed into its dark length. Isha wore a simple white tunic that fell straight from her armpits to her knees, but over her glossy hair she wore the sheer Egyptian shawl embroidered with gold thread that had been given to Miriam by the princess.

Properly, decorously, although her eyes were dancing, Isha sat in a small shelter and waited for Zarim to come from the crowd of laughing, drinking men. Miriam and Elisheba sat on either side of Isha, and Zipporah waited quietly nearby. Tarbis, Zarim's sister, sat modestly away from the bride's family, but her dark eyes were warm and friendly when she met Isha's glance.

Miriam considered the Cushite woman. She and Tarbis were alike, Miriam realized, in that they were both widows, both childless, and both concerned about their brothers. But there the similarity ended. Tarbis was still young and beautiful, while Miriam had grown old and tired.

Why do I even think about her? Miriam chided herself. She is nothing to me, nothing to this tribe. So her brother is marrying my niece—what is that? Why do I feel, when I look at her, that she is a threat? I'm being foolish.

She turned her attention from the lovely Cushite woman and looked toward the sound of masculine merrymaking. The men were dancing and clapping, shouting bawdy songs to young Zarim who only laughed. It was time for him to claim his bride, to take her to the tent that had been prepared for her.

Miriam watched his approach. He still walked with a limp, but his eyes shone with gladness at the sight of Isha.

So short a time ago, Miriam mused, Isha's only thought was for freedom, for escaping from the Egyptians. Now she thinks only of this young man and of the children she may bear. Perhaps it's that way with all of us. We left because we thought we were doing the will of Yahweh, but now we think only of getting enough food or having a shelter.

Then she saw Moses standing alone to one side, apart from the other men. He seemed hardly aware of what was going on around him. Instead, he had that shining, lofty look that was his whenever he had spoken to Yahweh. Even on this day of completely human concerns, Moses was in touch with his God.

At least Moses hasn't changed, Miriam decided with satisfaction. Moses still cares about the thing that has driven him all along. So we are not just nomads stopping briefly to celebrate a marriage. We are a people who are led by their God in search of a promised land.

⸗ 21 ⸗

The settlement at the foot of the cloud-topped mountain quickly took on the appearance of home. Not, of course, the sort of home that all of them had known since birth—not the streets and houses and shops and fertile fields of Egypt. Miriam, who well remembered the sights and sounds and smells of the palace, the fine meats served even to slaves, the delicate oils she had rubbed into the skin of the princess, the rich drapes hung on the walls, understood why the people grumbled and complained and longed for their lost comforts. It was difficult in this harsh world of sand and sun to remember the cruel side of the life in Egypt—the forced labor, the beatings. In some strange way, only the past pleasures of Egypt now came readily to mind.

Miriam discovered, as the days went by, that the women had adjusted better to this new life than the men. She heard of the constant complaints that Moses' chosen leaders were forced to deal with, but the women settled in with docility. As long as their children were not hungry, as long as no enemy lurked near them, as long as there was water to carry and the manna meal to shape into loaves and bake, as long as there was thread to be spun, the women were content.

There were periods of illness, when some minor plague would sweep through the camp, leaving suffering and death in its wake. But this was nothing new to the women. There had always been illness.

"I believe," Miriam confided to Elisheba one day, "that

the thing I miss most about Egypt are the medicines. They knew so much, those priests who stayed at the palace to look after the pharaoh and his family. They could heal almost anything."

"Not everything," Elisheba answered. "When the firstborn sons were struck down by our God, the priests were helpless."

"That's different," Miriam replied impatiently. "I mean common illnesses—like the one that is eating at Zipporah. She's just wasting away."

Elisheba's face sobered. "Yes, I know. Her cheeks are always red and her eyes so bright, but she coughs all the time and her flesh is just melting off her body."

"Has Aaron tried to help her?"

"Yes, several times. He's poured holy oil on her and has given her cassia tea to drink. But she's no better."

"I know," Miriam said, feeling only pity now for the woman who had once created such jealousy in her heart. "And Moses doesn't act as though he even realizes that she's so ill. Maybe I ought to talk to him."

"Better you than me," Elisheba said with a shrug. "Moses hardly seems of this earth since we've been here by this mountain he calls Sinai. Even Aaron says that his brother has become totally withdrawn. And Gershom and Eliezer run freely all day with neither father nor mother able or willing to correct them."

"They don't go uncorrected," Miriam said grimly. "I watch them when I can, and they've learned that when I speak, they either obey or feel a switch on their legs."

Elisheba laughed. "Yes, I suppose. Isha watches them sometimes, too. But she's so caught up in her marriage that she isn't as much help as she used to be."

Miriam smiled, but her thoughts were busy. "Maybe you're right," she said abruptly. "Maybe I should talk to

Moses. I know he loves his wife and surely he has some influence with Yahweh."

"You can try," Elisheba agreed, but there was doubt in her voice. "I suppose it wouldn't hurt to try."

Miriam got resolutely to her feet. "He's often out by the foot of the mountain," she murmured. "I'll go look for him there."

At first, she didn't see any sign of her brother. She walked closer and closer to the foot of the mountain, feeling the heat parch her mouth and burn the soles of her feet, but Moses was not to be seen. The men who watched the sheep had taken their flocks out into the valley that lay in the opposite direction where there was a bit of grass for their grazing, and all of the other men and women were busy in the area close to the tents. Here, where the land broke into jagged angles and steep ascents of stone, there was nothing. Silence hummed in the air, and Miriam began to be afraid. She had come too far. It wasn't safe here. There was nothing for her to do but turn around and go back to the camp.

A sound stopped her, and she waited without moving, her heart hammering against the walls of her chest. The sound came again, and she recognized it for what it was. Moses crying out in prayer, speaking to his God.

Miriam hardly dared to breathe. Except for that one time when Moses had cried out for water, she had never heard her brother speak to Yahweh. Now, she bent her head and listened, aware that she had no right to remain there. But she had always been curious about what Moses said when he spoke to his God and whether or not anyone else could hear Yahweh's reply.

Moses sounded both bewildered and stubborn. "But how can I persuade them, my Lord and my God? Even though they finally agreed to leave Egypt, they have never stopped complaining. How can I convince them that they should agree to a covenant? A covenant with the Most High God?''

It was as though he were arguing with Aaron, Miriam thought in amazement. There's nothing formal or awed about the way he's talking at all. Anyone could tell that he expects an answer.

She stood silently, her hands clasped at her breast, her breath almost suspended as she strained to hear the answer that Moses obviously anticipated. But she heard nothing—no mysterious vibrations in the hot, still air, no sudden thunder, no echo floating from the mountain's flanks.

Moses' voice grew sharper. "I know that. I understand, my Lord God. I know what you want me to tell them. It's just that I'm sure they won't listen."

Another thrumming silence, and then Moses spoke in a calmer, quieter tone. "No, of course not, Lord God, blessed be your name. I don't want to turn the leadership over to Aaron again. You've healed me of my stutter, and I know you'll give me the words. It's just that—."

Once more, stillness flowed through the morning air. Miriam realized that she was nearly strangling from her effort to be quiet, and she drew a deep breath. The air tickled her throat, and she coughed.

"Is someone there?" Moses asked in a startled voice.

"It's only your sister," Miriam managed to say. "I must have choked on a bit of sand."

Moses appeared suddenly from behind the pile of rocks that had hidden him from her. "What do you want?" he demanded irritably.

"I'm sorry, my brother." She bent her head in a gesture of humility. "I don't mean to interrupt you. It's just that I need to talk to you and I rarely see you these days."

Moses moved toward her. "Come away from here," he

said sharply. "This is hallowed ground where the Lord of Israel speaks to me. Don't you see that my feet are bare and my head is covered?"

"I'm sorry," she mumbled and backed hastily away. In her effort to move quickly on the rough ground, she stumbled and fell. Moses made no effort to help her up. It was almost as though he didn't see her. He had not fully returned to the concerns of the ordinary world, Miriam thought, as she picked herself up. He's still—still—wherever he is when Yahweh speaks to him. He did not, she noticed, uncover his head or slip on his sandals.

She felt a keen sense of desolation as she brushed the sand from her bruised hands. Not only was her brother unaware of her and her needs, but no matter how hard she had tried, she had not heard the voice of the Lord. She had been so sure that if only she could be close enough when the voice of Yahweh came down from his heavens, she, too, would hear and understand. Oh, perhaps not hear syllables and sounds, but certainly she had believed she would feel an awareness of something. But she had heard and felt absolutely nothing in the silent morning.

"If it's inconvenient," Miriam said stiffly, allowing her hurt to show, "I won't bother you now. I'll seek you out another time."

Moses spread his hands wearily. "No, it's all right. Our God speaks to me all the time lately. There's no getting away from his presence. Even if I wanted to," he added hastily. "So tell me what you want. When I've finished talking with you, I have only to go back to my sacred place. Yahweh will speak to me again."

There were a hundred things she wanted to ask, but she dared not ask them. Even though Moses sounded almost as though he felt beleaguered by Yahweh, she knew he would not tolerate any questions about why Yahweh chose to speak as he did.

"I will only stay a minute, my brother," she said. "It's about Zipporah, your wife. Have you noticed how ill she is?"

Anger and frustration swept across Moses' face. "What do you mean, have I noticed? She's my wife, after all."

"But you are so caught up in other matters, my lord." Her address was more formal than she had intended, but she was suddenly uncomfortable before this stern-faced man. "I wondered—." She stumbled over the words and then plunged on. "I wondered if you had prayed for her?"

Moses struck one fist into the palm of his other hand. "Do you take me for an insensitive fool? Of course, I've prayed. When she first came back from her father's, I thought the color on her face and the brightness of her eyes were signs of pleasure at being back with me and our people. But I know now that she is dying of the wasting illness. And Yahweh has chosen not to hear my prayers that she recover. Even though my sons need her. . . ." His voice trailed off.

"I can care for your sons," Miriam said.

"I just don't know why Yahweh has refused my pleas," Moses admitted.

Miriam searched her thoughts for the right words. "If he said yes to everything we wanted," she said slowly, "we would have been given our freedom right there in Egypt and would still be living in the city of Raamses."

Moses stared at her. "And the people no more aware of the greatness and mercy of Yahweh than they were before I came," he murmured. "I do know that. I do. But sometimes I need to be reminded. Thank you, Miriam."

His kindness moved her as his anger and irritation never could. "I would do anything to serve you," she whispered.

He laid a gentle hand on her shoulder. "Then comfort

my wife," he said. "She's going to die, and I think she knows it. Ease her pain and give her all the love you can. Even in this time of her terrible need, I'm enslaved by my God and I can't give Zipporah the care and attention she needs. Can I count on you?"

Miriam felt the hot rush of tears in her eyes. "Oh, yes," she breathed. "You can count on me."

As Zipporah grew frailer and weaker, Miriam found that her longing for Egyptian medicines increased. She woke up at night, remembering the smoky incense burning in front of the small golden bull that had been the princess' own idol for worship, and she wondered how the priests had worked their healing magic. It never occurred to her that she might be hungering after more dangerous things than the riches of Egypt.

All of the old resentment and jealousy that Miriam had once felt for Zipporah disappeared in the wash of pity and compassion that swept over her as Zipporah coughed her life away. Miriam washed out the blood-soaked bedroll, comforted the dying woman with her touch and with words, and saw to it that her nephews were well behaved and properly disciplined.

Every day the boys came obediently to Zipporah's bed-side. But they were too young for compassion, and they were obviously relieved when they could run again to play or to perform duties for their father and other men in the tribe. Miriam took over more and more of their care, so it was at her hands that Zipporah's sons were punished and comforted, disciplined and cleaned, fed and clothed. She was a bit uncomfortable at how swiftly their loyalty switched from their mother to her.

Zipporah seemed hardly to notice, and yet not a day passed that the dying woman did not murmur her gratitude to Miriam for the care lavished on her and her sons. One day, it was on the tip of Miriam's tongue to confess the jealousy she had once felt, but something stopped her. There was no point in putting yet another burden on this woman's shoulders, Miriam told herself, and besides, perhaps she exaggerated the jealousy in her own mind. Surely she had always been more loving to her sister-in-law than she remembered.

Zipporah's death came more swiftly than anyone had anticipated. One minute she was alive—flushed and coughing, but alert and conscious—and the next minute she was gone. There was not even time for her to call out for her husband or her sons. She merely twisted in a spasm of coughing, put out her hands to Miriam in a curious fluttering gesture, and died.

Miriam knelt beside her sister-in-law for a few minutes, then began to prepare the body for burial. The spices had been brought to the tent some weeks before, so that their fragrance might give pleasure to the dying woman, and a basin of water stood waiting. Quickly, deftly, Miriam bathed Zipporah's body, washing away the last traces of the blood that had gushed from her lips. A clean robe, saved for the purpose, was wrapped snugly around the body, and the spices were scattered among the folds of the cloth.

By the time Miriam had finished, Moses and his sons had been summoned. Gershom, as the elder son, knelt and kissed his mother's cheek, but he was unable to prevent himself from shuddering when his lips felt the strangeness of the dead flesh.

"She's cold," he whispered hoarsely and scrambled up to move closer to his aunt.

Miriam felt his hand in hers and knew it must have taken real courage for him to risk the scorn of anyone who observed his reaching out for comfort. She clung to the small hand with a feeling of mixed affection and satisfaction. This child, bereft of a mother, would surely belong to her as none of her other nieces or nephews had. Even Isha had not been as close as this boy would be.

The growing circle of mourners pulled her thoughts away from Gershom. This is a time to weep, Miriam told herself. There will be other times to think of the children who will be mine.

She lifted her voice in a loud, keening wail, and Gershom, after a quick glance up at her, joined her in weeping. At first, he only made the noise of weeping, but in a few minutes, Miriam saw that real tears were coursing down his face. She put her other hand on his head and pressed his face against her. For a long time, he wept with true abandon.

Miriam kept herself from saying words of comfort to the child. Weeping was a normal and proper thing. Even Moses wept loudly and ripped the neck of his robe to bare his chest.

The comfort will come later, Miriam thought with a sudden sense of certainty. Now they grieve, but before long, they will be coming to me for care and comfort, and I will finally be needed as every woman wants to be. No longer just a widow. I'll be a real mother at last.

= 22 =

The months drifted by, and the family's grief over Zipporah's death changed slowly to acceptance. Moses himself seemed almost to have forgotten her as he became more and more absorbed in the instructions of his God. Frequently he left the camp, seeking the isolated heights of the mountain he called Sinai, and when he returned, his eyes were glazed and unfocused, and he sometimes stumbled as though he did not see the earth under his sandals.

One evening he gathered the leaders together and spoke to them sternly.

"You must prepare yourself to receive the word of the Most High God. For three days, while I seek Yahweh's guidance, you must purify yourselves by staying away from your women, and on the morning of the third day, you must come to the place of assembly and hear what our God has to say."

He did not wait for questions, but stalked hurriedly away so that no man dared to bid him stay. For once they voiced no complaints as they made preparations to carry out Moses' instructions.

On the third day, the morning sky had none of the luminous light that usually heralded the rising of the sun. Black, heavy clouds were smeared across the horizon, and above Mount Sinai, flashes of lightning shot through the clouds followed by rolling thunder. And the people cringed in fear before the fury of sound and fire from the mountain.

Miriam found herself crouching at the opening of her tent, staring up at the fiery sky. She was so filled with awe and apprehension that she felt no sense of the comfort that the sweet, ordinary tasks of recent weeks had given her since she had taken her small nephews as her own sons.

"Surely you're going to attend the meeting my uncle has called?" Isha said, appearing suddenly. She had become more subdued and docile since her marriage, but this morning there was a look of fervor on her face again. "You and I can slip into the back of the crowd."

"I'm not sure," Miriam said. "I don't know if we should."

"Even some of the women who have no special position are going," Isha insisted. "My husband's sister is one of them. Tarbis feels that Moses is going to reveal great things to us. Things we'll all need to know. Even the women. And who will tell the women in our group if you and I don't go?"

Miriam shot a quick look up at Isha. "Our group?" she asked. "You belong to your husband now."

Isha made an impatient motion with her hands. "You know what I mean."

"Aren't you afraid?" Miriam asked, looking into the angry sky.

"No, not afraid. Nervous, maybe, but not afraid."

"Then," Miriam said, getting to her feet, "I must not be afraid either. But who will be responsible for the boys if I go over to where the men are gathering?"

"I have already spoken to my mother," Isha said, slipping her hand into Miriam's arm. "Come on, Dodah, let's find out what's going on."

Miriam felt the ground tremble under her feet as they walked toward the place of assembly, and fear and excitement rose in her. Were they to witness another manifestation of Yahweh's power—or would they all be swallowed up by this unstable earth?

Isha found some flat rocks where she and her aunt could sit and yet not be too close to the men who had come together at Moses' command. They barely had time to seat themselves when Moses stalked into the gathering. There was about him an air of such vibrancy, such authority, that for a minute Miriam hardly recognized him. The pharaoh, she thought dazedly, had never appeared more regal, more touched with grandeur.

"You know that I have asked you many times in the past if you will submit to the Lord God," Moses began, "and you have agreed. To a man, you have said that you would follow the laws of the Lord and be his people. Are there any among you now who would disagree?"

Does he never tire of asking this same question? Miriam thought to herself. Ever since he first came from Midian, he has told us over and over that we must be loyal to Yahweh. And yet he asks this question again.

There was a murmur of assent, and several men cried out loudly that they had promised to obey and had not changed their minds.

"You know what it means," Moses announced, his words clear and loud with none of the old stuttering. "It means that our God is our king and we are his vassals. It means that we must obey the laws he gives us to earn his protection. Do you understand?"

"Yes!" came the cry.

"But how do we know what his laws are?" As usual, it was Pagael who dared to ask the questions that others were afraid to ask.

"The Lord God of Israel has told me what they are," Moses replied. He reached into the bosom of his robe and pulled out a thick roll. "I have heard his voice and he has told me to write down these laws. Will you sit to listen?"

The men sat obediently, looking expectant. They were utterly still as they waited for the laws to be read. Even the mountain had stopped its fearful noise and seemed to be waiting to hear the word of Yahweh.

"The Lord God has said," Moses intoned, "that he is the God who led us out of Egypt and he gives us these laws to follow. Listen, to his commandments:

" 'You shall have no other gods before me.'

" 'You shall not make for yourself any graven image.' "

As he went on, outlining vividly the instructions that must be followed if there was to be no dispersion of the holiness and might of the Israelite God, Miriam thought fleetingly of the gorgeous gods of Egypt—the gold and bronze, the silver and jewels. And she remembered the comfort the Egyptians found in the beauty and the touch of their little idols. These Israelites, she thought, glancing around her, are used to that, too. These first laws will be hard laws to follow, she realized.

" 'You shall not take the name of the Lord in vain,' " Moses declared. His voice was decisive and stern as he delivered each of the laws.

The law regarding the observance of the Sabbath was lengthier than the others, as though its importance could not be overstated.

" 'Honor your father and your mother that your days may be long in the land which the Lord will give you,' " Moses read, and the next five laws came out quickly. " 'You shall not kill. You shall not commit adultery. You shall not steal. You shall not bear false witness against your neighbor. You shall not covet anything that is your neighbor's.' . . ."

Miriam felt as if she were in shock. Oh, the laws were not all brand-new, perhaps. There had been similar laws in

Egypt, laws about killing and stealing and lying, but never before had there been laws that would force the people to acknowledge that the Lord God was their ruler and king and that he was above all other gods and that to obey him was imperative.

Moses went on to read a great many lesser laws, based on the first ten commandments, and Miriam saw that the men were still listening intently.

"And if you will accept your side of the covenant," Moses cried out at last when he had finished reading, "then Yahweh will honor his half of the covenant. We will be his people for all time, and he will be our God."

Moses paused and nothing broke the silence. But when he spoke again, his voice was softer, gentler, almost coaxing.

"What do you say, men of Israel? What do you say to the proposed covenant of your God?"

For a few moments, no one said anything, and then the affirmation thundered from the throats of the assembled men.

"Yes!" they shouted. "We will accept the covenant. We will obey the law. We will be his people and he will be our God."

Aware of her position, Miriam kept silent, but she felt the affirmation swelling in her heart as well. Oh, yes, these might be difficult laws to accept, to follow, to understand, but they were laws that would make life safe and dignified.

"I will go up into the mountain," Moses announced when the shouts of the men had died down. "I will take your decision to the Lord, our God, and I will tell him that we are ready to be his people. Then I will bring you word again."

The meeting broke up, and Miriam hurried back to her weaving, without even speaking to Isha on the way. But she was not as she had been before the reading of the law. She could not put Moses' words out of her mind. Especially the first law: no other gods before him. And the second: no graven images.

Her mind flashed back to the jeweled face of the goddess on the princess' mirror, to the golden bull that had gleamed in a dim corner of the palace room. She remembered that even she, a child of the tribe of Levi, had been unable to resist the pleasure of just looking at so much loveliness. She felt sure that many other Israelites had also recognized and admired such beauty, and that they had not altogether forgotten the Egyptian gods. She wondered if they would ever be able to forget.

As he had promised, Moses climbed up into the mountain the next day, taking Joshua with him. After he disappeared into the swirling mists, the people turned away from watching and fell to speculating about what might be happening up there and how soon Moses would return with Yahweh's covenant. If indeed, some said doubtfully after the excitement of the meeting had passed, a god would make a written covenant with a people.

Time passed and still Moses did not come back. Over and over, Miriam told Gershom and Eliezer that, no, their father had not died as their mother had, that he would soon return to them. But as day followed upon day, the reassurance in her voice wore thin, and she saw her own growing sense of panic reflected in Aaron's face and in the faces of the other tribal leaders.

One morning Gershom asked, as he always did, "Will our father come down from the mountain today?"

Miriam gazed up at the clouds that wreathed the mountain, and for once was unable to offer a gentle answer.

"He'll come down when he's ready to come down. Go and do your chores."

The boys went obediently enough, but she saw them exchange a look of dismay. Well, she could understand how they felt. Moses had been gone far too long. What was he doing up there? Was it possible that something had happened to him? Perhaps he had lost his footing on some steep rock, perhaps—but no, she mustn't allow herself to think about such things.

"Wait, sister. I want to talk to you."

She looked up to see Aaron coming toward her. He looked as worried as she felt, almost harassed.

"Is something wrong?" she asked.

"It's Moses. He's been gone for so long. The people are getting restless. They insist that he must be dead by now—and therefore, they say, the covenant is not binding because Yahweh has not given a sign of his agreement."

Miriam stared at Aaron. "Dead?" she asked. "Oh, don't even say it. Surely Yahweh wouldn't let anything happen to him."

Aaron watched the clouds and smoke swirling around the mountain. "He's been gone for so long," he repeated. Then he said abruptly, "The people want a small god to worship. They want—."

"But the law," Miriam began.

"I know," Aaron admitted. "But what can I do? They're determined to have what they want, and if I am to retain some authority as their priest, I don't dare block their wishes too much."

Aaron had always been softer than Moses, Miriam reflected. Gentler, more easygoing.

"Well, then, make them some sort of little statue," Miriam suggested, wondering if she were justified in what she was saying. "Only if they want to worship it, tell them it represents the God of Israel. That way, you can be true to Moses and still please the people, too."

Aaron's eyes held admiration. "A clever idea," he agreed. "If they choose to misunderstand me, that won't be my fault. But where can I get precious metal for the making of an idol?"

"The women have earrings," Miriam said swiftly. "If the men want their idol badly enough, then let them give of their own gold. Let them take the earrings from their wives and daughters and sisters. It will be enough. Believe me, it will be more than enough."

When Isha heard what her father and her aunt had agreed to, she was furious.

"Didn't you listen to the law?" she stormed at Miriam and Aaron. "Didn't you listen?"

"How dare you talk so insolently to me?" Miriam blazed. "I'm your aunt, after all."

"I beg your pardon," Isha replied stiffly, with no contrition in her expression. "I know you and my father should have my respect. But why are you letting the people do this dreadful thing?"

"Now, listen," Miriam said, trying to hold back her own anger, "it's not so terrible. The people are frightened and weary, and they need a little celebration. If a small golden calf will—."

"Golden calf?" Isha interrupted." Don't you mean bull? Aren't you letting them have the gods of Egypt all over again?"

"I mean *calf*. Just a small, innocent calf, but shaped with beauty. The people will appreciate such a creation. And they can still think about Yahweh while they're looking at it."

Isha turned away, and Miriam could see her swallow as she fought for control. "You're wrong," Isha declared at last. "The law says that the people must not make any graven images. That's what Dod said."

"This isn't an image. Your father wouldn't have permitted the making of it if it were an image. It's just a statue. Truly."

"My husband says—" Isha began, but Miriam interrupted.

"What does your husband know? He's a Cushite. Your father is a Levite. *He* knows."

Isha stared at Miriam for a moment, then walked away, her sandals striking the rocky ground with a staccato sound. Miriam returned to her weaving feeling both angry and ashamed. Perhaps she should never have made the suggestion to Aaron. And yet, Aaron was a priest. He was the one who ought to know. So she wasn't really to blame.

When the statue of the calf was finished, it was placed, gleaming and golden, on a block of stone, and the people gathered to admire it. With longing, they reached up to run their fingertips along its smooth, glittering legs, and the look on their faces was one of admiration and approval.

The beauty of the calf seemed to release something in the people. When they gathered in the evening, their laughter was louder than it had been since they left Egypt. They danced and made music around the campfire until the camp rocked with a raucous, almost lewd spirit. Miriam noticed that some of the young widows disappeared from their tents at night, but when she accused them of wrongdoing, they only said defiantly that they were going out to admire the golden calf in the moonlight. Too late Miriam realized that she and Aaron had allowed a truly wicked thing to happen.

On his fortieth day after leaving camp, Moses stood upon Mount Sinai, feeling as though he was no longer walking on solid earth, but was being lifted up into the habitation of his God. He was giddy and dizzy from all that the Lord told him, and it seemed to him that his mind and body were not large enough to be a repository of the immense law of Yahweh.

I am only a man, he wanted to cry out in a voice that he knew would tremble. Have pity, my Lord God. Have pity on me.

Gasping a little for breath, weakened by the many days he had gone without food—for who could eat when he was face to face with the Most High God?—blinded by the lightning, and deafened by the thunder, Moses crouched on the trembling earth and waited for what would happen next.

He knew that the words of Yahweh had been engraved on his heart, but he also knew that this alone was not enough. He must have something that he could show to the people. The parchment scroll that he had taken to them with the covenant proposal had been helpful, but he had brought neither parchment nor stylus with him on this journey. He had come to his God empty-handed, and it would seem, he thought sorrowfully, he was to return the same way. If, indeed, he could even survive the immensity of this Presence and go back to the earth where ordinary men lived and walked.

A blaze of lightning raked a fiery trail across the sky, and the thunder that followed shook the mountain as though it were nothing but a pile of dust.

"Look, my son! Look and see!"

Moses lifted his head. By now, the voice was as familiar as to him the sound of his own breath. At first, he was too dazed to see clearly, but gradually his vision grew steady, and he saw tablets of stone lying before him on the ground. The ten great laws were engraved on them, traced, Moses was sure, by the moving finger of the Most High God.

Now he could return to the valley. The decision was

made without fumbling or hesitation. Yahweh had known Moses' and the people's needs, had known them before a request could be formed. Now Moses had something with which to shake their hearts into the kind of submission that Yawweh demanded.

Moses took up the tablets and began the long journey down the quaking mountain. He had nearly reached the bottom when the setting sun threw rays of such brilliance across the valley that Moses was able to see the encampment as clearly as if he had been standing beside it. The slanting sunlight sent back a reflected gleam of gold, and Moses saw around it the dancing, capering figures of the men he had trusted. Anger and grief burst painfully in his heart, and clutching the tablets against him, he ran toward the camp and the children of Israel.

Miriam and Aaron stood with their backs to the mountain, staring in horror at the men and women who groveled or pranced before the golden calf.

"We shouldn't have let them do it," Miriam whispered.

"I didn't think they'd get carried away like this," Aaron admitted. "I wish Moses were here to control them. But what if the people are right? What if he really is dead?"

"He's not dead," Miriam said fiercely. "He's not!"

"I don't know," Aaron began doubtfully. But he was interrupted by a roar of anguish that swept across the camp, a roar so intense, so terrible that even those who were crowded around the golden calf stopped to stare.

Moses strode into the firelit scene, and his eyes burned with such horror and rage that Miriam felt herself shrinking back against Aaron.

"You infidels!" Moses shouted. "You breakers of the law! You destroyers of the covenant! You—you—." He lifted his arms above his head.

There was something in his hands, Miriam saw. Something heavy that shone dully in the flickering firelight. She watched, stunned, as Moses held up the tablets of stone for all to see.

"This is the covenant," he cried in despair, "the covenant written by the Lord our God, and you have broken it."

His hands swung down and the tablets smashed onto the ground.

"Oh, my God, my God," Moses wept and buried his face in his hands while the people stood and stared at the holy law of Yahweh which lay in fragments at their feet.

Then Miriam and Aaron spoke against Moses because of the Cushite woman whom he had married . . . and they said, "Has the Lord indeed spoken only through Moses? Has he not spoken through us as well?" And the Lord heard it. . . . Then the Lord came down in a pillar of cloud and stood at the doorway of the tent, and he called Aaron and Miriam. . . . So the anger of the Lord burned against them. . . . As Aaron turned toward Miriam, behold, she was leprous.

Numbers 12:1, 2, 5a, 9a, 10b

23

The touch of the morning light pressing against her eyelids filled Miriam with a sense of despair. For a few seconds, as consciousness filtered through her, she thought she could not bear to face another day.

Every morning since that moment when the heavy tablets had crashed to the ground, she had awakened to the inescapable memory of her brother's fury. Every morning, whether she willed it or not, she was forced to relive those first terrible minutes of Moses' anguish and the dreadful hours that followed in which he had melted down the golden calf, ground it into powder, sprinkled it into water, and then made the people drink the physical evidence of their folly. And worse than this, she knew she could never forget how the sons of Levi, led by Aaron, had been forced by Moses to go throughout the camp killing those Israelites who had bent their knees to the calf of gold. The sight and smell of blood could never be erased from her mind, Miriam thought as she awoke.

The final, searing guilt that stabbed at her each morning, no matter how many ways she tried to justify her actions, was her memory of their lie—the lie that she and Aaron had told.

"I only threw the gold into the fire," Aaron had babbled when Moses had accused him, "and it came out in the shape of the calf."

Miriam's head, of its own volition, had nodded sturdily in agreement.

Even as she nodded, she had half expected the fire of Yahweh to strike her down and kill her. But no fire had fallen, and she saw, when Moses looked at her, that he was more sad than angry.

"Even you two," Moses had said. "Even you whom I had trusted."

"You were gone so long!" Miriam wailed.

"Leave us," Moses had commanded his sister. Then he turned to Aaron. "As for you, you shall help me smash this abomination."

So humbly and shamefacedly, Aaron had bent to the task, using his hammer like a slave instead of a priest, matching his blows to those of his brother. And since then, Aaron had been able to find comfort for himself in his submission to Moses' commands. But for me, Miriam thought as she awoke, there is no comfort.

"Are you awake, Dodah?" Gershom was sitting cross-legged on his pallet and staring at his aunt.

The child's voice was her salvation, Miriam thought gratefully. Every morning, it was Gershom's or Eliezer's voice that distracted her from her tormenting memories and gave her the sanity of a new day to be lived.

"Yes, I'm awake." She sat up and smiled at Gershom.

Eliezer pushed his tousled head out from under the shawl that covered him and grinned at his aunt. "Should we gather the manna, Dodah?"

"You can gather manna," Gershom said in a lofty tone. "I'm going out to watch the sheep with Zarim."

The child's friendship with Isha's husband was so intense that Miriam was inclined to be jealous. She kept reminding herself that Gershom had been cheated out of a father's care because of Moses' devotion to Yahweh, that the boy needed a man to shape his thoughts into a man's thoughts. But still she was unable to control the irritation she felt when Gershom voiced his desire to be with Zarim.

"Tarbis has taught Isha how to flavor the manna cakes in a new way," Gershom confided as he pushed back his unruly hair.

Miriam got to her feet and drew the little boy closer to her so that she could comb his hair with the bone comb that the princess had given her. He struggled away from the pulling, but she held him fast. Only by immersing herself in such homely tasks could she escape the memories of Moses' return from the mountain, only through devotion to duty could she endure the waiting for his second return.

"What kind of flavor?" she asked.

Gershom wriggled. "I don't know. Something that takes away the plainness. Something that makes it more exciting."

"Some foreign herb or spice, no doubt," Miriam said, dismissing the importance of the flavor. "You should be content with what the Lord gives you."

"I'm contented," Gershom declared, freeing himself at last. "Only Tarbis is clever and she's teaching Isha to be clever, too."

And that was as it should be, Miriam thought. A bride belonged to her husband's family and learned from them. Then why did this resentment always spring up in her when Isha's sister-in-law was mentioned? Tarbis was good to Isha and always respectfully courteous to Miriam, but Miriam's resentment remained. There was something about the woman, Miriam reflected in the brief time between Gershom's scampering away from the comb and Eliezer's being caught by it, that bothered her. She wasn't even sure what it was.

Part of it might be that Isha had so obviously fallen under the charm of her new sister-in-law, Miriam thought honestly. Part of it might be because the tall, slender, dark

Cushite was so lovely to look at. Whatever it was, it added an unpleasant dimension to Miriam's life. As if I didn't have enough to bear already, Miriam grumbled to herself, and she pushed Eliezer out into the day.

"Now, you can gather up the manna," she announced, dismissing her thoughts about Tarbis. "Take the basket there that we always use and fill it exactly half full. You know how."

Eliezer, too young yet to think this task demeaning, trotted out to where the ground was whitened with its daily sprinkling of the grains that looked like coriander seed and melted like hoarfrost when the sun was high.

Miriam shouldered a water jar and headed for the well at the center of the camp. Maybe today, she told herself, as she had told herself every morning since Moses had gone back up into the mountain, maybe today he will come back with another set of tablets. Maybe today we'll be given another chance to accept the covenant of the Lord.

But by the time Moses finally returned to the campsite, forty days had gone by. He called the people together, and they came obediently, humbly, all eager to avoid the punishment which had been meted out the first time Moses had come down from the mountain.

Miriam needed no urging from Isha to attend this gathering. She went quietly, unobtrusively to her place behind the circle of men, looking for Moses with a mixture of apprehension and anticipation.

When he first strode into the clearing, she could not see his face, but only the stone tablets which he held up before him. Not broken this time, she thought with a rush of gratitude, not smashed on the ground, but whole and perfect. Yahweh had given them another chance. Yahweh had forgiven them. Yahweh had set his seal upon the promised covenant.

Then Moses lowered the tablets, and the assembled people gasped sharply. Moses' face shone with a luminosity that seemed to reflect the sun. Aaron, standing nearest his brother, put up his hands up as though to shield his eyes from a brilliance that could not be endured.

"Your face," Aaron said in shaking voice. "Your face shines as though the sun were burning through your skin."

"I'm not surprised," Moses answered calmly, "for I have seen the Lord."

Moses faced the people who waited in silence now for him to speak. "Hear, O men of Israel!" he cried out in a voice of such intensity that Miriam found it hard to breathe. "Yahweh has spoken to me. He has told me that he is the Lord our God, merciful and gracious, slow to anger, and abounding in steadfast love and faithfulness, keeping steadfast love of thousands, forgiving iniquity and transgression and sin."

He paused as though to force a closer attention to what he was saying. "Now hear the commandments of such a God," he cried, and then slowly, emphatically, he read the laws that were engraved upon the tablets of stone. The people remained silent until he had finished and then, with in a single mighty voice, cried out their affirmation and approval.

"You are committed to obedience," Moses told them sternly. Then relenting and drawing the end of his head covering up over his face so that the people could look at him in the old comfortable way, he went on, "It's time to hear what the Lord has said about the building of a tabernacle."

And he began to describe the ark that was to be built of acacia wood, the tent that was to be made of poles and rods and woven linen curtains, the lamps and ornaments. Miriam listened and was filled with dismay that bordered on anger. Where would they get such treasures? They were nothing but a group of wanderers who had once been slaves. How could they furnish brass and gold and silver, embroidered cloth and polished wood? If the Lord wanted such a rich repository for his holy law, he should have chosen a richer tribe, a people of substance and wealth.

"Here!" The young voice belonged to Isha. Without giving thought to the stares of disapproval she drew because she was only a woman and a young one at that, she hurried to where her uncle stood. She had stripped her gold bracelets from her arms, bracelets that had been given to her in the Egyptian court. They were the equivalent of a dowry, Miriam thought. They were all that Isha possessed of wealth.

"Here, my lord," she said. "Take what I have."

This formal address brought a gesture of approval from Moses, a warm touch on his niece's shoulder.

"I, too," Tarbis said, less impulsive and quieter than Isha, but her outstretched hands held the gleam of gold, the sparkle of jewels. "And in addition to this, there are lampstands among our possessions," Tarbis went on in a low, husky voice. "And fine linen cloth. You shall have it all, my lord."

Moses spoke with gratitude. "These two women," he told the assembled men warmly, "have given and will continue to give of what is theirs. With such generosity as this, the tabernacle of the Lord our God will be built."

Isha's and Tarbis's actions seemed to spark a response that ran among the people like a grass fire. Men disappeared into their tents, and the women followed them, not in protest but to urge them on. In an amazingly short time, jewels, precious metals, and rich fabrics lay piled on the ground beside Moses.

Miriam gazed with astonishment at the heap of richness. She would never have guessed that the people had managed to acquire so much in Egypt, or that they had been able to bring such treasure along without losing it in the sea or along their dusty travels from one oasis to another.

Moses looked upon the precious things with satisfaction. "The sons of Levi will guard this treasure," he announced. "From this time on, they will be guardians of the temple." Then he looked out over the heads of the people.

"I'll put Bezalel and Oholiab in charge of the metalwork, the woodwork, and the hanging of the curtains. And there are dozens of men in the tribes who will help them, who are clever and gifted with their hands."

But what about me, Miriam thought. I know I can't guard the treasure or work with metal or wood. But, as a sister of the chief priest, as a sister of the man who has seen the Lord, surely there is something I should be allowed to do.

As though he had read her thoughts, Moses turned to her with eyes that were dark and filled with compassion. "And you?" he asked finally. "What do you want to give?"

She stared at him. That hadn't been what she had been thinking at all. She had been wondering what opportunity was to be given to her.

Moses' eyes crinkled at the corners and she knew he was smiling. "Now that you're a fulltime mother, do you have time to give to the building of the Lord's tabernacle?"

Miriam found her voice. "I can weave," she said. "I can weave linen finer than any other woman in the camp. I learned how from some of the weavers in the Egyptian court. And I can work fruits with embroidery thread—fruits that look so real one almost wants to eat them." Her voice came out high and shrill, and she had to force herself to remain calm. "I could weave some of the cloth. I could embroider pomegranates around the border."

Moses' eyes grew sober. "How did you know that I wanted pomegranates embroidered on the hems of Aaron's robes? The robes that Aaron and his sons will wear?"

Miriam felt joy surge through her. What had seemed like an impulsive suggestion must have been the word of Yahweh. So she had not been overlooked. She, too, was to be given a position of honor.

"I just knew," she said, her voice sturdy with conviction. "Somehow I just knew."

"Well," Moses said, "if you can weave linen as fine as that used in the court of Egypt, if you can fashion pomegranates of scarlet and gold to be fastened to the hems of the robes when they are made, then I assign you to do it."

"I can do all that, my brother," she promised, daring to be less formal than Isha had been. "I can do all that and still take care of your sons."

Moses' eyes crinkled again. "I'll count on you," he replied. "During these days of doing the will of Yahweh, of learning his laws and following them, I can survive only if I have people to trust and depend on. I am grateful that you are one of them."

"My lord," Miriam murmured and knelt before her brother.

But it was not humility which had bent her knee. She knew that. It was gratification and pride that Moses had recognized her worth and had admitted it before the assembled people. She was to continue to be the mother of Moses' sons, and yet she would also be one of the artisans who helped to build the tabernacle. Surely now, the people would look up to her and pay her rightful homage.

≈ 24 ≈

When the tabernacle was fin-
ished, the people were filled with awe as though it had been
made with angelic hands. Each person had offered up his or
her own skill, but when the work was completed, when the
gleaming ark of acacia wood rested on its pedestal behind
the woven, embroidered curtains, lit by the flames that
flickered in brass lamps, the people could only stare rever-
ently. No one could see the individual result of his or her
own skill—the entire tabernacle shone with a perfection
that must, the Hebrews whispered to each other, have come
directly from Yahweh.

But Miriam could not take her eyes from the robes worn
by Aaron and his sons. Woven of the fine linen thread that
she had managed to bring from the city of Raamses, the
robes were as beautiful as those worn by any Egyptian
priest. Around the hems, scarlet pomegranates and small
bells of pure gold gave richness to the garments. Jewels, set
in the breast plates and in the shoulders of the ephod, shone
with a splendor reminiscent of the palace. No one, she
thought with satisfaction, could look on the sons of Levi and
not be aware that here were men who had been chosen to
represent their God.

The sacrifices were made, the sacred smoke rising toward
heaven, and when the ceremony was over, the people knew
that somehow, here in a wilderness, they had been allowed
—no, enabled to build a tabernacle that was fit to hold the
tablets of God's own law.

Miriam returned to the tasks that gave shape to her days: the weaving of ordinary cloth for Gershom's and Eliezer's robes, the preparation of manna for eating, the filling of water jars from the well. She had thought, while creating the glory of the embroidered pomegranates, that perhaps everyday tasks would seem tedious by comparison. Instead, she found more satisfaction in the routine and security of her duties than ever before.

Moses, too, she discovered, was slowly changing, becoming again the man he had been when he had first come from Midian. The awesome luminosity of his face faded, and his total absorption with carrying out Yahweh's law became, if not less intense, at least more comfortable. Though Moses continued in his obedience and devotion to his God, he was beginning to seem human again.

The first time this thought occurred to her, she ceased her weaving and sat in stunned astonishment. Had she been thinking of her brother as someone more than human? Oh, no, surely not that. He had been born of the same parents as she and Aaron, he had grown up in a court that put great emphasis on human qualities, he had married and fathered two sons. Then what?

But no matter how much she pondered the question, she could not come up with a satisfactory answer. She only knew that during the time of the receiving of the Law and the building of the tabernacle, Moses had walked a road that no other man could possibly have traveled. He was a man who had been touched by God. And I, she thought with satisfaction and pride, am his sister. He depends on me.

One day she glanced up to see Eliezer scampering toward her. "My father's coming," he panted. "When I asked him why, he just said he wanted to talk to you and that I should go play."

Miriam forced herself to frown at the child. If she followed the promptings of her heart, she often thought, the two boys would never be chastised or disciplined. Just the sight of them was enough to make her bones feel like water.

"Then, obey your father," she said sharply, keeping her hands on the cloth in the loom, lest her fingers, of their own accord, reach out to touch Eliezer's hair. "Go and play."

"I'd rather listen," Eliezer confided cheekily, but when his aunt lifted her hand in a threatening gesture, he ran, grinning at her over his shoulder. "It's only because I like to be with you, Dodah," he called.

Miriam lowered her head so that her smile would not show. For this minute, she realized in a rush of warmth, she was totally happy. The child had as much as said he loved her, and Moses was coming to talk to her.

Hastily, she pushed the shuttle between the threads of the loom so that she could stand and prepare herself for her brother's arrival. She smoothed her skirt with careful hands and left the weaving area. She had no desire to talk to Moses with the other women close by, and she was sure that he would feel the same. Not that he talked to her of private or profound things, but still there was an intimacy in their conversation that excluded all others. And she liked it that way.

In a brief time, she saw him coming, walking with all of his old energy, the ends of his head scarf and the skirt of his robe blowing back as he strode along. It was hard to realize, she thought, that he was no longer a young man, and when he saw her waiting for him, his smile blazed in a way that made him look, for one instant at least, almost like a boy. It was easy to overlook the white in his hair and beard, the lines around his eyes, when he walked and smiled as he did now.

"Did Eliezer tell you I wanted to talk to you?" Moses began without a greeting.

Miriam smiled back at him. "He did. I had to send him about his business or he would have stayed to share the conversation."

"I'm never sure," Moses confided, "whether he's a friendly child or simply full of curiosity."

"A little of both," Miriam replied, falling into step with Moses. "But it's hard to reprimand him. He and Gershom are both so dear to my heart that I find it difficult to be as strict as I should be. Since you weren't young when your sons were born, I'm more the age of a grandmother than a mother. Perhaps I'm too fond."

"You've been wonderful," Moses said warmly.

The lavishness of his praise brought heat to her cheeks. "I do the best I can," she said with modesty. "They give me more joy than I can ever give them."

"And there's no reason for that, at least, to change," Moses said.

Something in what he said made her heart pause and then begin to race. What did he mean?

"Of course not," she said, but her words came out breathless, caught in the tumble of her heart.

"It's what I want to talk to you about," Moses said with a quick sideways glance at her. "I have something to tell you, and it's very important that you understand and don't take offense."

"Why should I take offense?" But her quiet question had little to do with the chaos going on within her. It was as though her flesh were already afraid of something her mind did not yet understand.

"Because I know how you love my sons and how they've filled your life since Zipporah died. I don't want you to think that I'm taking them away from you."

She stopped, unable to move or breathe, and stared at her brother. "What do you mean—taking them away from me? You're not leaving?"

"Don't be foolish. How could I leave? These are my people, and my place is beside them until I die."

"Then what? Am I to be sent away?"

Moses tried to laugh, but the sound was hollow. "An even more foolish question. Would the sister of Yahweh's anointed be sent away?" Then his eyes twinkled. "If you were younger, perhaps we might be searching for a husband for you. And if he happened to be one of the nomads in the desert—."

She interrupted him sharply. "This is no time for joking. What are you trying to tell me?"

"No, now." Moses took her arm, and his voice was so gentle that she was filled with even greater alarm.

"What?" she insisted, her arm stiff and resistant beneath her brother's fingers.

Moses glanced at her and dropped his hand. "I have chosen to take another wife," he said in a taut, controlled, colorless voice.

The announcement plunged painfully through Miriam's body like the slash of a knife. This was something she had never even contemplated.

For a minute, she was unable to speak and could only stare blankly at Moses. Then she gasped, "What did you say?"

"I said I have decided to marry again. Yahweh has given his consent because he looks with compassion on his human children and sees their loneliness and need. It would be fitting, he has told me, for me to have more sons."

She stared into Moses' face for a few seconds more, then turned away from him, aware of a bitter taste in her mouth and a heavy weight in her chest. It would be bad enough to lose her brother's confidences and his company, for what man would seek out his sister when he had a new bride in his tent? But it would be worse to lose the children. How would she be given strength to face the day, how could her heart ever be comforted again, if the children were taken from her and put into another woman's tent?

"Why are you so shocked?" Moses asked at last. "Surely it's not uncommon for a man to marry again. Even a man who is no longer young. Why are you so shocked?"

She licked her lips and forced the words past the dryness in her throat. "It's just—well, it's entirely unexpected." She swallowed and then asked, "Have you chosen a particular woman?"

"Yes, I have. Tarbis of Cush."

This time, shock ran through Miriam's body just as lightning sometimes rips a tree. No wonder she had feared and resented Tarbis. She must have known in some blind, instinctive way that the Cushite woman would one day take away the comforts, companionship and delight of Miriam's life.

At first Miriam was aware only of her own grief, of the bitter waves of sorrow that threatened to drown her. She knew that if she made any attempt to speak, her grief would gush out in a torrent of tears.

Moses walked a few steps away, then came back to face her again. His voice was as gentle and persuasive as it had been whenever he had charmed Zipporah out of stubbornness or fear.

"Come, my sister. Can't you rejoice with me? You look as though I had just struck you. Instead, I have told you that you'll be getting a new sister-in-law who will surely love you and be a comfort to you."

The words were finally choked out. "A comfort to me? She'll take my boys."

Moses frowned. "They're my boys, after all. And you admit you are too lenient, too permissive. You'll still have their affection, I'm sure, and be the grandmother you've already said you are. But they need a young mother. They need brothers."

"She's black," Miriam said.

"She's a child of Yahweh," Moses replied in a tone that seemed to warn Miriam not to go too far.

But she had been goaded beyond normal caution. "With all the Israelite women," she cried, "why did you choose a foreigner? What's the matter with you?"

Moses stared at her until Miriam's eyes dropped. She was too upset to say the words of apology that she should have said, and for a few minutes there was only silence between them.

"I had not anticipated such insolence from you," Moses said at last.

"I'm not being insolent," she said. "It was bad enough when Isha married Zarim. I could endure that because—because he had saved our lives and because Isha's only a girl. But you—you are the chosen one of Yahweh."

"I had thought so, too." Moses' voice was caustic. "But it seems I must stand here and be lectured by my sister as though I were a disobedient child."

Stung by his remark, she lifted her eyes again to meet his. "I'm not lecturing you. I'm only questioning your—your wisdom in this."

"I told you Yahweh has given his approval."

All that she longed to say crowded bitterly into her throat. It has nothing to do with Yahweh, she wanted to cry out. You chose Tarbis because she's beautiful, because she has made herself appealing to you with her gentle, feminine ways. You have no right to take the boys away from me and give them to a stranger—just because she's beautiful and pretends to be a faithful follower of Yahweh.

"You think you want to marry her because she's beautiful," she said at last, her voice thick and sullen.

"She's beautiful, it's true," Moses admitted. "Zipporah was beautiful as well. But so were her sisters. I chose Zipporah because she was gentle and good. And now I've chosen Tarbis because she is generous and faithful."

Almost against her will, Miriam remembered how Tarbis had stretched out her hands, filled with gold and jewels, to offer her best to the tabernacle. And she, Miriam, in her pride, had only sat waiting to be given a position of honor.

"But the boys," she repeated. "If she becomes your wife, she'll be a mother to Gershom and Eliezer."

"Of course," Moses said and waited impassively.

I can't stand it, she wanted to cry out. They have become like my own children to me. I have been healed of all my loneliness by their presence in my tent. Oh, please, she wanted to beg. Oh, please, please.

But she would not say the words. If Moses could be so unaware of her pain, so indifferent to her need, then she would not grovel.

"Why did you even come to tell me about it?" she demanded. "Why didn't you just come and take the boys and marry anyone you pleased. It's nothing to me. Nothing!"

"I tell you everything," Moses began patiently. "Why wouldn't I—."

But she would not let him finish. "Well, you don't have to tell me any more," she said, interrupting in a voice that was high and thin and breathless with pain. "You'll have someone else to talk to and you won't need me any more. And as for the boys, take them—take them. I don't even care."

Moses stretched out his hand to comfort her, but she was completely undone by the hurt that filled her. Mindlessly, she struck at his hand and whirled away from him.

"Let me alone," she shrilled. "Just let me alone."

She stumbled away from him and made her way blindly, awkwardly, toward a tumble of rocks that would hide her from sight. Moses made no attempt to follow her, as she had been sure he would not. At last she found a place where she could drop to the ground and weep her bitter tears. Her teeth chattered as she huddled there, and she wrung her hands in desperation.

He has no right, she thought achingly. He has no right to think only of himself. Even if he had to marry again, why couldn't it have been someone nearer his age, someone who looked like us, someone who let me keep the children? Oh, I can't stand it—I can't.

Her thoughts blurred to a stop, and her frenzied weeping gave way to breathless gasping. It took her a long time to realize what was happening to her. The change from grief to anger was so subtle that at first she did not recognize the new emotion that shook her. She had never before been truly angry at either of her brothers. But now, scalding and sudden, anger ran hot through her body, drying her tears and leaving ugly scars of resentment.

= 25 =

The marriage took place with a minimum of ceremony and celebration. Even though Moses was the leader of the people, even though his followers would have welcomed any opportunity to brighten their dreary existence with merriment, still he would not allow any lavish preparations to be made.

"It's only a marriage of convenience," Moses said modestly when Aaron suggested that a celebration be held. "The dancing and singing took place at my first wedding, and at hers, too, I suspect. This is only a marriage that Yahweh has permitted because it's a man's duty to have sons."

Aaron glanced at Miriam and shrugged. Then he turned back to Moses and said, "Well, let it be as you wish, my brother. Do you want an anointing or a sacrifice made?"

Moses nodded. "A sacrifice, of course. A prayer for blessing. It will be enough."

"Perhaps the bride will feel that there should be more," Miriam suggested, but she could not keep the tartness out of her voice.

"The bride will be more than content with whatever I decide. She's happy to get two sons and a husband all at once." Moses kept his voice quiet and expressionless, but Miriam felt the emphasis of the words.

"So you're taking the boys to your tent?" she said stiffly. "Even on the night of the wedding, you're taking them?"

"I'm not a young husband, eager for the wedding bed,"

Moses insisted. "I only want my family together again. I've had little enough time with the boys since we left Midian. It's time they had a man's company. They're too old to be kept with women all the time."

"Tarbis is a woman." But even as she spoke the words, Miriam realized how foolish and petty they sounded.

"She knows that I'll be the one to discipline them," Moses replied. "In her country, boys are turned over to men at a very early age."

"As you wish, my lord," Miriam said coldly and turned away from her brothers.

And so the wedding ceremony took place with very few of the people even aware that it was happening. A thin trickle of sacrificial smoke climbed up from the altar, and Aaron, in his priestly garments, stood in front of the ark and cried out to Yahweh, asking for a blessing to rest upon his brother and the woman from Cush that their marriage might be rewarded with sons.

Miriam watched from a distance, too hurt and angry even to come and greet her new sister-in-law with the traditional embrace and kiss.

Elisheba sought out Miriam after Moses and Tarbis and the two boys had gone to their tent.

"Are you troubled, my sister?" Elisheba asked. "I've never known a woman closer to her brothers than you have always been, and yet you didn't come to share in the prayers."

"I was busy," Miriam said.

Elisheba smiled. "Not so busy as that, surely? But I think I understand. You've been such a loving mother to the boys since Zipporah died, and now they've been taken from you. Even when you and Isha were closest, you never tried to take her away from me."

Miriam stared increduously at her sister-in-law. Elisheba's occasional flashes of perception always surprised Miriam. Yet the words were true. Or mostly true, Miriam thought, resolutely pushing back the memory of the time she had tried to take over the responsibility of finding a husband for Isha.

"I feel as though I have lost my sons surely as the Egyptian women lost their firstborn sons," Miriam confessed. "I never thought this would happen. I never thought he would do this to me."

"Even Zipporah used to say that Moses stopped thinking about human things when he started speaking to his God." Sympathy warmed Elisheba's voice. "I feel so sorry for you. It seems to me that a priestess—and didn't they call you a priestess when you made the song about crossing the sea and when you prophesied the coming of the pillars of fire and smoke?—would have a right to keep the children she wanted."

For a long time, Miriam did not answer. She was afraid to speak for fear she would say too much. Even though she felt a great urge to cry out in affirmation of what Elisheba had said, she knew she must be discreet.

Finally she spoke in a modest tone. "I hesitate to agree with you, my sister, even though your words warm my heart. I can't tell you what a comfort it is to know that someone understands how I feel. But to call myself a priestess, well. . . ."

"But you are." Elisheba was very earnest. "All the people said so. You know how it was. 'Miriam, the priestess,' they called you. 'Miriam, the sister of Aaron.'"

The words burned like a flame in Miriam's heart. Elisheba was right. Yahweh had indeed spoken to the sister of Moses, and perhaps he would speak again, if only she would stop hiding behind this false modesty she had adopted. Moses hadn't slipped into the shadows after Yahweh had spoken to him. Moses had stood boldly in the light of the burning bush and dared to argue with his Lord.

She smiled at Elisheba. "You flatter me, my sister," she murmured. "But you may be right. Perhaps I haven't made myself available enough to Yahweh. Perhaps he would speak to me if I sought him out."

"That's exactly what I told Aaron," Elisheba replied. "Once when he admitted to me that he didn't understand why Yahweh spoke so frequently to Moses and so seldom to the High Priest, I told him he had to demand Yahweh's attention. He was very angry then and told me to mind my tongue, but I still think I'm right."

Miriam felt excitement grow in her. If she and Aaron were to approach Yahweh together, if they were to claim the same attention that Moses received, who knows what would happen? It might be that the Lord God Yahweh would look with favor upon the other children of Jochabed and Amram and grant them his favor and his power.

Her next thought shook her with its intensity. If Yahweh would speak to her, then surely Moses would know that his sister was not to be scorned, not to be taken lightly. Surely he would know then that his sons should be left in her care.

"But even if you're right," Miriam said slowly, "we must not offend Aaron. He was angry, you said?"

"He gets over his anger." Elisheba sounded stubborn. "I look at him in his fine linen robes, I watch my sons walk with pomegranates and bells swinging at every step, and I know that they, too, must be honored by Yahweh. It's just that they don't claim the honor."

The woman's words so exactly mirrored her own thoughts that Miriam felt startled. Could this be a sign?

"Have you mentioned this to Isha?" Miriam asked cautiously.

"Isha! That one!" Elisheba shrugged her heavy shoulders

with disdain. "She's so smitten with her husband and his people that she thinks of nothing else. She was elated when Moses chose Tarbis as his wife. It makes everyone look with favor on her own marriage, you see?"

"Do you think I should be the one to speak with Aaron?" Miriam asked, already planning what she would say.

It was obvious that Elisheba was flattered by Miriam's question. Miriam had always been the one to make decisions. Now their positions were reversed.

"I'll tell him you want to talk to him," Elisheba said. "He listens to me. I may be only his wife, but still he listens to me."

"As do I," Miriam assured her sister-in-law, patting Elisheba's plump arm. "Tell him to meet me by that slope— see? The one that looks as though steps had been carved into it. Tell him to meet me there after he has eaten."

Elisheba smiled with satisfaction. "I'll tell him," she promised. "I'll tell him right away."

"But there's no question about whether or not Yahweh speaks to Moses," Aaron said.

"I never said there was. I never said Yahweh didn't speak to Moses. I only said that perhaps he wants to speak to us, too." Miriam kept her voice reasonable and friendly. There was nothing to be gained in antagonizing Aaron.

"If he wanted to, he could." A note of stubbornness crept into Aaron's voice.

"Of course. And perhaps he does, but we fail to listen."

Aaron stared at his sister. "I'm the high priest," he replied with dignity. "I come into the presence of Yahweh each time I make a sacrifice, each time I use the holy oil, each time I cry out to him in prayer."

"Of course you do, my brother. Haven't I seen the wonderful things you do and heard the marvelous words you say? But still, why does Moses hear the words of the Lord every day? Why do his words come to us only rarely? And well, at least to me, so vaguely? I confess to you, my brother, that when I danced by the sea and when I foretold the coming of the pillars of fire and smoke, I didn't hear plain words or instructions. I only had a feeling."

Her humility seemed to move him as arrogance never could have. At her admission, his face lightened.

"You, too?" he said slowly. "I thought it was only me. Oh, there are times when Yahweh speaks to me as clearly as Elisheba. Though perhaps not so shrilly," he added with a smile. "But there are other times when I feel as though I were groping in smoke and my hands come away empty."

Miriam felt breathless. Even the high priest of Israel felt as she did.

"Do you think Yahweh will continue to speak to Moses even though he has married this foreigner?" Miriam's question was abrupt, unplanned, and sharp with asperity.

Aaron shook his head. "What has she got to do with what is said to Moses?"

"Our God—Yahweh the Mighty, Yahweh the Merciful —has remembered *us,*" Miriam insisted. "Isn't that what Moses has always said? That Yahweh looked down and remembered the children of Israel? But she's a Cushite. Moses has given his sons into the care of a foreigner."

The thought, it seemed, was not a new one to Aaron because there was no surprise on his face. "There are Israelite woman who might have been more suitable," he agreed cautiously.

"For that matter, why did he need anyone?" Miriam cried. "I was raising his sons properly. Isha and Zarim gave them all they needed of young parents. I gave them enough love. And gradually Moses would have found time to play a bigger part in their lives. Why did he need to marry?"

"Oh, come," Aaron said. "Moses is a man. It's true that a man's responsibility is to beget sons. But a man takes pleasure in the begetting. Yahweh created us with appetites and the means for satisfying them. Yahweh took pity on Moses' loneliness."

"And what of my loneliness all these years?" Bitterness shaped the words.

"You're a woman," Aaron said.

There was no answer to that, and Miriam knew it. "Well, regardless of everything else," she insisted, "if Moses had to marry—and at his age, I can't see the need—I still don't think he should have married a Cushite."

"I don't think so either," Aaron admitted. "But it's done now."

"What if he misunderstood Yahweh?" Miriam ventured. "What if, for once, Moses deliberately misunderstood? Tarbis is very beautiful, and what if Moses only wanted her and Yahweh didn't give his permission at all?"

"Watch your tongue," Aaron snapped. "If we begin to doubt what my brother says, then everything we've done since he came from Midian will be a farce."

"I suppose so," Miriam conceded. She was silent a moment and then added, "But I still think it's possible Yahweh would speak directly to us if we begged him to. Aren't we the children of Jochabed and Amram as much as Moses? Wasn't I also reared in the Egyptian court so that I was taught many things most Israelites can never know? Hasn't Yahweh come to you in dreams, my brother? I could be right, couldn't I?"

Aaron looked at her, and she could see compliance dawning in his eyes. "You might be," he said.

"Then, shall we try?" Her voice was eager. "Why don't you put on your linen robe—and I will put my best Egyptian shawl over my head? Not now, but at dawn tomorrow.

We'll meet by the tabernacle and go into the room of the ark. And there we'll cry unto the Lord and tell him that he must speak to us as he speaks to Moses."

"*Tell* him?" Aaron asked.

"I've heard Moses talking to Yahweh," Miriam insisted. "And Moses doesn't cower in a timid way. Moses stands up and argues with him, just as he would argue with you. Maybe you and I have been too humble."

"All men are humble before the God who made them," Aaron replied.

But she was impatient. "I know that! But perhaps the Lord God only speaks clearly to those who expect to hear him."

Aaron's head nodded. "You could be right. I'm willing to try. I've been thinking of it myself, you know. If Moses should die, someone should be prepared to take his place."

"Then I'll meet you at dawn?"

"A little before dawn," Aaron suggested. "Moses comes to the tabernacle at dawn. We should be there before then."

"Yes, of course. An hour before dawn. I'm sure I won't be sleeping, anyway."

Aaron smiled, lifted his hand in farewell, and turned away. Exultant and proud, Miriam made her way to her tent. She had thought that she would spend the night weeping because the little boys were gone. She had anticipated loneliness and anger. Now instead, she was filled with excitement. In the morning, she and Aaron would speak to their God, and possibly, just possibly, Yahweh would answer.

⹀ 26 ⹀

By the time she reached the tabernacle, Miriam's heart was pounding, but whether it was in fear or anticipation, she could not tell. The small lamps that were kept burning constantly shed enough light for her to find her way to where the ark rested on its carved pedestal. Aaron had preceded her, and she felt a great sense of relief when she saw his shadow sway with the movement of the linen walls. The small golden ringing of the bells on the hem of his robe was music to her. Robed in the priestly garments that she had helped to make, Aaron was where he had a right to be. And his acceptance of her made her presence in this place permissible.

"I'm here," she whispered.

"I see you are. Come, stand here in the corner. It's not fitting that a woman should stand so close."

She moved away from the ark and then knelt on the ground. "Will you pray?" she asked nervously. "Will you cry out to the Lord?"

"I'll pray," Aaron answered with dignity. "It's my duty to pray in this place. But I won't cry out. There's no point in waking the entire camp. Be quiet now."

She bent forward until her elbows rested on the ground and then she lowered her face into her hands. A submissive position, surely, she thought. Yahweh will see my submission and know that I am behaving as a woman should.

So Aaron began to pray, and his words rose and fell in the tabernacle, matching the wavering flames in the lamps.

At first, there was only supplication in his voice, and Miriam was tempted to lift her head and try to catch his attention. Doesn't he remember, she thought, that I said we must be —oh, surely not arrogant, but confident.

As though he heard her thoughts, Aaron's words climbed out of a humble chant into a pattern that came close to being a demand.

"We, too, O Yahweh, our Lord, our God, should hear your voice. Not just Moses who is only our brother, after all—but Miriam and I as well."

The sound that swept through the room was like a blast of wind, and the flames bent from their lamps, streaking before it. There were words in the sound, words that beat against Miriam's ears until she felt herself wincing. Such words could not be avoided. They drove themselves into her head where they ached and throbbed.

"Come out!" the Voice commanded. "Come out, you three, to the tent of meeting."

Miriam pressed her hands against her ears and stared up at Aaron. His hands, too, were pressed against his ears, and even in the dim light, she was aware of the pallor of his face.

"Does he mean us?" Miriam whispered. There was no doubt in her mind whose voice it was that poured through the air.

"He means us." Aaron's answer was thready and breathless.

She started to rise, but her knees shook so violently that she was sure she would never be able to get up off the floor. Aaron came to her and held out his hand. Clinging gratefully to it, she struggled to her feet and, cold with terror, followed her brother out of the tabernacle and over to the tent of meeting which Moses had set aside for the assembling of the people when he called them together.

Dawn was edging the sky with a narrow band of pearl

which gradually diffused itself into a dull green. Miriam's thoughts tumbled in chaos. "You three," the Voice had said. But they were only two. Perhaps he hadn't been speaking to them, after all. Perhaps it was only guilt that had driven them out into the morning when they ought still to be praying.

"So you're the other two." Moses was suddenly standing beside them. "I was sure he said 'you three,' but I didn't know the other two would be you."

The ordinary sound of a human voice soothed Miriam's ears, but before she could comfort herself with it, the other Voice was back, battering her head with its awful intensity.

"Aaron," the Voice said. "Miriam. Come here."

Dazed and trembling, Miriam saw a pillar of smoke at the edge of the tent, forming itself into a twisting column that gleamed silver against the paling sky. Aaron approached the pillar and fell on his face in front of it.

"My God, my God!" he cried in a voice of supplication, but Miriam's tongue adhered to the roof of her mouth and her shaking legs would not take her forward.

"Miriam," the Voice said again, and Miriam felt Moses' hand, gentle and strong, under her arm. Leaning shamelessly on her brother's strength, she moved at last to where Aaron had prostrated himself. Wanting only to cover her face and stop up her ears, she sank down beside Aaron and pressed her face against the stoney ground.

"Listen," the Voice said, the words throbbing clearly and distinctly in the very center of Miriam's head. "If there is a prophet among you, I speak to him in dreams. Such, Aaron, has been my way with you. Even you, Miriam, have known a little of what it is to see my vision. But it is not so with my servant Moses."

The Voice grew gentler, though no less intense. "To Moses," the Voice said, "I speak mouth to mouth, and with plain words, not through the dark words of a dream. He is my trusted servant." The Voice suddenly changed with a quick, hard anger. "Were you not then afraid to speak against my servant Moses?"

If she tried to speak, Miriam' thought, her tongue would crumble into dust. Aaron, too, was silent.

"I am very angry," said the Voice. "You will be punished for your wickedness."

Aaron started to weep bitterly, but Miriam felt as though she would never again be able to shed tears as long as she lived. She had turned into dust and dryness, with no moisture left in her body for tears. She looked at her hands, half expecting them to have disintegrated into two heaps of sand. But what she saw was more awful even than what she had imagined. Breathless, terrified, she splayed out her fingers, unable to absorb the horror of what she was seeing.

Her hands were as white as snow, withered, and shriveled. Her hands were leprous.

A sound came from her at last. She had thought a scream would tear itself from her throat, but the noise she made was only a hoarse rasping hiss.

Aaron turned to look at her, and she saw fear in his eyes. "Oh, no," he whispered.

Miriam saw how swiftly his eyes flew to his own hands, and she saw the mingled relief and shame that filled them when he had confirmed the brown, healthy strength of his own trembling fingers. Even in her pain, she could understand his relief.

Aaron turned to his brother. "Oh, my lord," he cried. It was the first time Miriam had ever heard him use that term for his brother. "Oh, my lord, don't let us be punished because we have done foolishly and have sinned. Don't let her be as one dead, with no one to pity her, no one to care for her. Oh, my lord, it's as much my fault as hers."

"No," Miriam managed to croak out. "The major sin is mine. I am the one who was angry."

She had not planned to say the words. They had come out of some deep revulsion. Her spirit, she thought with shame, was as leprous as her body.

"Angry?" Moses said.

She shook her head, unable to explain.

Aaron spoke for her. "She was too fond of your sons, my lord. She had enjoyed being the one you talked to. Your marriage has changed all that."

Moses shook his head sadly. "I never think of the small things. I only know that when Yahweh speaks, nothing else matters. I thought you would come to understand."

Stunned, Miriam saw tears in her brother's eyes. He, whom Yahweh had claimed as his own, was looking at her with pity, not anger. Turning away from them both, Moses hid his face in his hands and wept. Then, prostrating himself on the ground, he cried aloud. "Oh, heal her, my Lord. Heal her, I beseech you."

The pillar of smoke was gone, Miriam realized, and although she was sure, from the look on Moses' face, that Yahweh was speaking to him, she herself could no longer hear the words. And not being able to hear them, she also realized in astonishment, was not a punishment, but a blessing. She remembered the pounding assault of the Lord's voice, and she wondered suddenly how Moses was able to endure it. It was not for everyone, she thought with new humility, to hear the Lord. Oh, why hadn't she been wise enough to know that, before she had tempted Aaron to join her in a sin which had resulted in a living death for herself?

At last, Moses spoke. "The Lord says that you are not to be spared all shame, my sister. He said," and Moses actually smiled as though the words of Yahweh could have humor in them, "that if your earthly father had been angry and had spit in your face, you would be shamed before the whole family. How much more, then, when the punishment has been meted out by your God?''

"And I must remain a leper?" Miriam gasped, staring in new horror at her hands and arms.

"No, only for now." Moses spoke to her as gently as if he had been comforting a child. "Only for seven days. You must remain outside the camp for seven days. Then he will heal you."

"Are you sure?" she begged. "He will truly heal me?"

"He has promised that he will. Do you doubt him?"

And now the tears came, gushing like a spring of water from her eyes. Her body was not wholly dust, not totally turned to ashes. She could weep.

"I do believe," she cried hoarsely. "I believe that Yahweh speaks and that you hear him. Only you, my lord."

"It isn't easy," Moses admitted, "to be the one who hears. I think sometimes the voice of Yahweh has made me deaf to human sounds."

Miriam's tears were washing away all her anger and bitterness and jealousy. And though she was not wholly clean, she was cleaner.

"We have sinned, my brother, against you and against our God," Aaron confessed humbly. "If Yahweh can forgive me, if he will forgive my poor sister, does that mean that you can forgive us, too?"

"Would I ask Yahweh to heal her if I had not already forgiven you?" Moses asked. "You are my brother and my priest. She is my sister and my friend. I love you both. This has been a bad time. We won't talk of it again."

"Not talk of it?" Aaron repeated. "But look at her. Everyone who sees her will know she has leprosy. How can we not talk of it?"

Moses shrugged. "It's true her leprosy will be hard to

explain. But to tell the truth about it would require much courage on your part. And on hers. It's up to you."

Aaron turned to look at Miriam, and instinctively she shrank away from him. "Unclean," she bleated out with the prescribed word of warning.

"Oh, not a true leprosy, surely," Aaron began and moved toward his sister.

"No!" Moses spoke sharply. "Would Yahweh afflict her with something less than the real illness? When she is healed, it will be because the mercy and the might of the Lord, our God, will work a miracle. Till then, stay well back from her."

Miriam, still crouching on the floor, shrank from her brother's words as she had shrunk from the sight of her leprous hands. How could she ever believe that the promised healing would take place? What could possibly comfort her now?

"Pity," she whispered.

Moses put his hand on Aaron's arm to restrain him, and the two men gazed sadly at their sister.

"You know the law," Moses said at last. "Until Yahweh cleanses you, you must live outside the camp. There are other lepers there. They won't welcome you, not at first. It's my understanding that for a few weeks, each new leper must live in a solitary way. And perhaps that is best, because I wouldn't want you to become one of them. But you must go. May Yahweh go with you."

Feebly, feeling very old, and unaware of any sensation in her arms and legs, Miriam struggled to her feet. She ached for a hand to be stretched out in aid and knew that no hand could be offered.

She looked dazedly around the tent of meeting. How short a time ago, she thought, she had knelt here whole and clean. Why hadn't it been enough for her to be well, to be normal? Why had she demanded to hear the voice of the Lord?

She started out of the tent and then turned to Moses. "If I should die before the Lord heals me?" she asked in that rasping voice.

Moses smiled gently. "Lepers do not die so easily."

"But there are wild animals," she protested. "And I'll be alone."

"You will never be alone," Moses said sternly. "Yahweh will walk with you by day and lie down beside you at night."

"But how will I *know?*" she whimpered.

Moses sighed. "In the night watches of Midian," he said, "when I was with the sheep, I saw only stars and heard only the wind, and yet I *knew* Yahweh was there. It has to be that way with you."

He turned to Aaron and spoke sharply. "You, my brother, are a priest, and the Lord surely comes to you. How do you know he's there?"

Aaron hesitated, searching for the words that could make it plain. "I only know. But I can't explain how the knowing comes. All of us believe in our God. How could we eat the manna daily or think about the dividing of the sea and not believe? But to *feel* his presence? That, I think, must come to each person individually." He looked at Miriam. "Open your heart to him, my sister. I promise you, he will come."

Her palsied, white hands came up to cover the face which she knew must also be diseased. None of her brothers' words had given her any peace. She only knew that she must go out into the wilderness alone.

She had walked but a few steps away when Aaron called to her, "May I confess our sin to the people, my sister? Somehow they must understand why you've been banished."

Agony ripped through Miriam. What would Isha think? And Gershom and Eliezer? They had trusted her, perhaps even loved her. But the law which Moses had explained to the people said that every sin must be paid for, and had she not sinned?

"Tell them," she wavered. "Tell them that we sinned and that Yahweh has punished me."

The men were silent as she left the camp. She wondered if they were thinking, as she was, that two had sinned, but only one was being punished. "Help me, help me," she whispered and did not know if even Yahweh would hear her hopeless cry.

☚ 27 ☛

During the days that followed, Miriam sat in a wedge of shade, staring through the shimmering heat toward the camp, straining to hear the normal, ordinary sounds of human habitation. Never, she admitted to herself, had she longed to hear the voice of Yahweh as much as she now longed to hear the voices of her family. But, at first, no one came near, and she had to endure both fear and loneliness.

Each morning, she discovered loaves of bread made from manna and skins of water, but she never saw who brought them. Several times she thought she saw someone approaching, but it always turned out to be a shadow or a wavering heat mirage.

At night, she huddled between two rocks, pulling her robe around her and warming herself against the stones that retained the heat of the sun long after the ground had grown cold. She courted sleep, trying to blot out the agony of her existence with the numbing unconsciousness of sleep. She was used to being cold at night, used to the hardness of the earth beneath her. What she was not accustomed to was the rejection and the loneliness. Until now, she had not known what it was like to be ignored, overlooked, and passed by. Now she knew, and the pain was almost too great for her to bear.

On her fourth day outside the camp, she looked down at the ground to rest her eyes from their endless staring, and a tiny movement caught her attention. A small sand lizard had been startled by her presence into flight and then into frightened immobility. The minute throat pulsed and the lidded eyes stared with blank terror. Such lizards were unclean, not to be touched or eaten, she knew. But there was no revulsion in her. There was no more acceptance for her, she thought with grief, than for this miniature monster. She was almost tempted to put out her hand, to touch something that would not shrink from the loathesomeness of her disease. But the movement of her hand would be enough to send the lizard scuttling in fear. Even to the unclean, she was something to be abhorred. Her loneliness sharpened into despair.

She looked up from the ground to see Gershom and Eliezer sitting on a high rock. They were far enough away from her that there was no danger of even her shadow touching them. Yet they were close enough to be seen and heard. The sight of them was like water to her parched tongue, and she blinked away sudden tears so that she might not miss even a moment of the privilege of looking at them.

"Why are you here?" she asked, hating the rasping sound of her voice, hoping it would not frighten them.

"We missed you," Eliezer said. "It isn't the same without you."

"Tarbis is very nice," Gershom said judiciously, "but it's still not the same."

"I have leprosy," she announced baldly. "You're not to come near me."

They nodded obediently and seemed to measure the distance between them with their eyes. "Our father said we could come this close for a few minutes," Gershom announced.

She felt surprised. "Your father knows?"

Gershom grinned. "He knows everything we do. We can't fool him, Dodah, the way we fooled you."

Eliezer spoke bluntly. "Your face looks funny. As though

you were dead. You aren't dead, are you, Dodah?"

Gershom shoved his brother roughly. "Don't be stupid. How could she talk and be dead?" But he, too, was looking with alarm at her face and hands. "We only came to say hello."

She wanted to cry out in her longing, to beg them to stay so that she could go on looking at them. You needn't come any closer, she wanted to say, I won't even talk to you, only don't go away. The words crowded into her mouth, but somehow she swallowed them. The boys were too young to understand or to feel pity. They had shown great courage and love just in coming to speak to her.

"You shouldn't even have stayed this long," she said hoarsely. "And—and don't come back. It isn't safe for you here." The words ached as they passed through her throat.

"Our father says you'll be well in only a few more days," Gershom said, getting to his feet. "We can stand it for a few days if you can, Dodah."

"I can stand it," she said.

"We're going to be allowed to come to your tent every day," Eliezer shouted. "As soon as you're well, that is. Every day."

"I'll like that," she said, forcing herself to smile, holding back her tears as the boys leaped from their rock and raced toward the camp.

When they were gone, the loneliness was larger, sharper than before. She would have thought that the coming of the children would ease her of her pain. Instead, the pain had been intensified.

On the next day, Isha came. She did not come as close as the boys had, and her agitation was obvious even though she stood far away. This time, Miriam had seen the approaching visitor, and so she was both more and less prepared to talk to her.

"Are you all right?" Isha demanded. After one horrified

glance at Miriam's face, she looked down and concentrated on a fold of her tunic, which she pleated nervously between her fingers. "Are you all right, Dodah?"

"I am as you see me," Miriam grated. "But I'm alive and fed."

"Zarim brings the food and water when it's dark, so that no one will see him. It isn't seemly for a man to do it, but he won't let me since—since I've discovered I am with child."

For a brief instant, Miriam forgot her own condition. "With child?" she cried. "Oh, my dear, my dear—."

The involuntary movement of her hands toward her niece brought her back to herself. "I'll never hold him," she wailed in anguish, rocking herself back and forth. "I'll never hold him."

"The Lord will heal you," Isha insisted, but Miriam saw how stiff the girl held herself, forcing herself to keep from running away. "Only two more days, Dodah."

Two more lifetimes, Miriam wanted to cry out. Two more eternities. And in the meantime . . .

"Only two more days," Miriam agreed. "So go back to the camp, my dear. Don't stay here, not with a child coming. There will be time enough later for us to rejoice."

Freed by her aunt's words, Isha smiled radiantly. "Oh, yes, Dodah. Time enough." She turned, poised to run, then looked over her shoulder. "Go with Yahweh."

"Go with Yahweh," Miriam repeated dutifully and watched her niece flee to a safer place.

Go with Yahweh, the girl had said. Moses and Aaron, too, had expected her to be with Yahweh in this place of rejection and death. How could that be? Would Yahweh come to a sinner, to a leper?

Neither Moses nor Aaron had come, had they? No man would come to seek out a woman afflicted with such a dread disease. The fact that the children had come—and wasn't Isha also a child?—was all the miracle she could hope for.

On the sixth day, Tarbis came. Swiftly, silently, she approached until she stood the prescribed distance away.

"Here," Tarbis said without preamble, without greeting. "I have here clean, new clothes for you to wear when you are healed."

When I am healed, Miriam repeated to herself. Not if, but when, Tarbis had said.

"There are sandals for your feet and a shawl for your head. And here are skins of water for washing." She spoke in a normal, quiet voice that carried clearly, and her eyes looked steadily at Miriam without shock or horror.

"Thank you," Miriam said. "I don't think—I'm no longer sure—I don't know if I will ever be healed."

Tarbis smiled. "My husband says the Lord will heal you. My husband is never wrong."

Miriam said nothing. Her thoughts were not clear enough to put into words. Ever since that moment in the tent of meeting when she had looked down to see her hands withered into whiteness, she had been unable to think clearly. She had been a huddled lump of misery, pain, and fear with no clear, coherent thought. Even the unexpected gift of visitors had not comforted her.

"Do you sleep?" Tarbis demanded. "At night, do you sleep?"

Miriam nodded slowly. She hadn't even considered that, but it was true that at night she slept. After a few minutes of discomfort and despair, she slept each night without waking.

"I've prayed for that," Tarbis said. "I've prayed that at least you would not suffer at night."

"Then you have found favor with Yahweh," Miriam

conceded. "He has heard your prayer."

"And he will hear yours as well," Tarbis promised. "I'm new to your faith, and you, more than most, would know how much I have to learn. But this I know. Yahweh hears us when we cry out to him."

While Miriam stared at her new sister-in-law, unexpected thoughts forced themselves through her numbed and tired mind. That was the important thing, wasn't it? That Yahweh heard his people, not that his people could hear his voice.

"I hate to have to leave you," Tarbis said. "But I have duties at the camp. We are ready to march on, you know, but the people refuse to leave until you are well enough to travel. Do you know, my sister, how much you are loved?"

Miriam shook her head, unable to prevent the tears that wet her cheeks.

"Well, you are. Elisheba loves you, and my new sons love you. My husband loves you. The women who traveled in your care love you. And I—I hope someday you will let me love you, too."

"I'm unworthy," Miriam sobbed.

"You are only frightened and lonely," Tarbis said. "But tonight, if you will trust our God, you won't even be afraid or feel alone. When you're healed, bury the clothes you're wearing. Then come back to the camp, my sister, where we'll be waiting."

She waved and walked away, but she stopped every few minutes to turn and wave again. There was in her none of the eagerness to get away that Isha and the boys had displayed.

Miriam watched Tarbis leave, feeling a new kind of pain. The numbness that had wrapped her for so long was melting away and a sharp awareness was taking its place.

I did nothing to deserve her concern or her prayers, Miriam thought. And I really did nothing to earn the love she says is mine. If I was good to Isha and the boys, it was because they eased my hunger for a child. If I obeyed my brothers, it was because I found joy in doing what they requested. If I was good to the women, it was because I was proud of being their leader. I really did nothing for anyone but myself.

The silent heat shimmered around her. There was no sound except the faint whirring of insects and the sliding scuttle of some small thing crawling through the dirt. Miriam ached with shame, with the stark realization of her failings.

Even if Moses suddenly came from the camp to say I could return, even if he reached out his hand to me, I would not be comforted, Miriam thought. Nothing and no one can comfort me. Not the boys nor Isha nor Elisheba nor even my brothers. I am alone. This, she thought with a feeling of despair, must be how it is to be dead.

If you will trust your God.

Out of the echoing silence, Tarbis's words, scarcely heeded at the time they had been spoken, came over Miriam in a gentle wave.

"But I've surely trusted him," Miriam argued aloud in her rusty voice. She could not bear the silence anymore. "When Moses was a child in the Egyptian court, didn't I tell him about Yahweh? Didn't I continue to believe during all the years of our captivity? Wasn't I the one of the first to believe what Moses said about the burning bush and the staff? Wasn't I the one who sang beside the sea when the waters were divided?"

Her voice creaked in her ears, and her logical questions creaked in her heart. The answer to every question was yes. But Tarbis hadn't asked her to believe. Tarbis knew perfectly well that Miriam believed. Tarbis had asked her to trust.

"As Moses trusts," Miriam said slowly. "As he trusted

when he lay down to sleep that night in Egypt, without fear, sure that the word would come from the pharaoh."

She leaned back and shut her eyes. Could she ever know that kind of trust?

Only submit and the trust will come.

The words did not hammer painfully at her ears, but bloomed gently in her heart. Stunned and frightened, she sat rigidly, without moving. Had she only imagined them?

Only submit and the trust will come. You have been too proud, my child.

Without knowing what she was doing, she reached out as though to touch this presence that spoke within her.

"I'm afraid," she whimpered. "I'm all alone and there's no one to comfort me."

No one? But you have only to call me.

The silence around her was no longer frightening or desolate. The air had turned vibrant and sweet. And suddenly she seemed to feel a touch as if by the hands of all those she had loved—her parents, the princess, Jehu, her brothers, her nieces and nephews—and none of them afraid of her, leprous as she was.

But they *would* be afraid, she thought. No person would deliberately touch a leper. And yet I feel I am being touched.

"Forgive me," she wept, pressing her face to the ground, knowing at last whose touch she felt. "Forgive me, my Lord and my God."

Weep no more. Only trust in me.

So was this what Moses had known all this time—this tender, compassionate presence in his life? If so, then no wonder he could bear all that he had borne.

"Only stay with me tonight," she begged. "Just for tonight, keep me unafraid."

There was no answer. She didn't need one. She wrapped

her shawl around her body and turned onto her side to sleep. She was not alone, nor would she ever be alone again. Her family might leave her or die, but Yahweh, mighty be his name, was always near—if she only reached out to him in humility and trust.

On the morning of the seventh day, Miriam awoke early, still filled with the peace that had come to her the night before. Her eyes went first to the sky with its promise of dawn and the first words she spoke were words of praise.

"My Lord and my God, hear me. You are great and wonderful, and I would never have known how much I needed you if I hadn't been banished from the camp. Keep me humble, O my Lord. Keep me obedient to you."

There were no answering words, but she had not expected any. The Lord had already spoken to her enough.

She looked from the sky to the distant silhouette of the camp. A surge of affection filled her for all those who slept in their rough tents. When she was well again, she would show them how much she loved them. When she was well again. . . .

Now she was looking at her hands, staring at them while her heart pounded in awe and joy. Her hands were no longer white, the skin no longer dried and taut and dead. Her hands were brown and healthy again, the skin softly wrinkled. Her arms were clean and normal. Her face had lost its rough scaliness. She had been healed.

For a long time, she knelt, gazing up into the sky. She was unable to shape into words the gratitude she was feeling. But Yahweh knew, she was sure, what joy and peace filled her heart.

She took off her old clothes, and gave thanks for the sight of her own healthy skin. Then she dug a shallow depression, buried the old clothes, and heaped stones upon the little grave. She scooped up handfuls of sand and scrubbed her body until it tingled. Only then did she realize that there was no food left for her in the usual place—only the skins of water that Tarbis had brought the day before. Carefully, trying not to waste it, she poured the water over herself, rejoicing in the cool, fresh feel of it. Finally, she went to where Tarbis had left the new clothes. She slipped the shift over her head, knotted the rope around her waist, and flung the shawl over her head. She was ready to start back to the camp.

Even if no one greets me, she thought gratefully, I won't grieve as I once would have. I don't need them as I did before. I love them, and I hope they will love me. But Yahweh is my comfort now. Understanding came to her. No wonder Moses sometimes lost sight of us, she thought. He must know Yahweh in a manner I can't even comprehend.

The closer she got to the tents, the more hesitant her steps became. Would they still think of her as a leper? She heard someone call to her.

"Here. Come here." It was Aaron. He stood between the camp and the wilderness, and the early sun glinted on his fine linen robe and on the pomegranates and bells that ran around the hem. "Let me anoint you with holy oil, that you may be declared clean."

His fingers, glistening with the oil, touched her gently. His eyes were shining. "Welcome back, my sister," he said.

Not trusting her voice, she only smiled. And when she turned away from Aaron, she saw Moses.

"Yahweh has healed you," he announced, but the emotion of his voice contradicted the baldness of the words.

"Yahweh has healed me," she agreed. "He has healed my body and he has healed my heart."

Moses smiled and stretched out his hand. "Then come,

my sister," he said warmly. "There's much to be done."

Manna to be gathered, she thought, so that the people would be fed. Thread to be spun, so that there would be decent, soft cloth to wrap Isha's baby in when it's born. Water to be drawn and carried, so that the people would not go thirsty. Human tasks to meet human needs.

"Yes," she said, "I know. There's much to be done."

Absurdly happy, she walked, as was proper, slightly behind her brother as they made their way toward the tent where her family was waiting.